OUR
LITTLE
Secret

Q.B. TYLER

Copyright © 2024 by Q.B. Tyler

All rights reserved.

No part of this publication may be reproduced, distributed, or transmitted in any form or by any means, including photocopying, recording, or other electronic or mechanical methods, without the prior written permission of the publisher, except in the case of brief quotations embodied in critical reviews and certain other noncommercial uses permitted by copyright law.

This is a work of fiction. Names, characters, businesses, places, events, and incidents are either the products of the author's imagination and used in a fictitious manner. Any resemblance to actual persons, living or dead, or actual events is purely coincidental.

Content Editing: Kristen Portillo- Your Editing Lounge
Interior Formatting: Stacey Blake- Champagne Book Design
Cover Design: Emily Witting Designs
Cover Image Photographer: Ren Saliba

"Life is messy. That's how we're made."
—Meredith Grey

OUR
LITTLE
Secret

Prologue

Marissa

May 2018

"I'LL HAVE WHAT SHE'S HAVING."

I'm standing at the bar, having just ordered myself and the maid of honor another shot of tequila to go with the bottle of champagne we are about to pop open when I hear his voice from next to me.

Smooth. Deep. Sexy. Rich.

It's almost eleven, which means if I recall correctly the wedding reception is almost over and whoever is still standing will be heading to the hotel bar for the after-party. *But honestly, I'm not totally sure about where we are in the itinerary; I've been riding a decent buzz ever since the wedding party took pictures.*

I turn my gaze toward the voice and lock eyes with one of the groomsmen. *Most importantly, the best-looking groomsmen of them all.* He looked like one of the Hemsworth brothers but with darker hair. Not the one that was married to Miley, the older one, and if I were more sober, I'd be able to remember his name or the name of this particular groomsman for that matter. There were eight bridesmaids and eight groomsmen and last night at the rehearsal dinner was the first time I'd met most of them. So, while I don't remember his name, I do recall thinking that he may be the most gorgeous man I've ever seen in my life. Blue eyes, dark brown hair with traces of a lighter brown that is styled perfectly, and a light layer of stubble across his jaw. He's lost his tuxedo jacket, his bow-tie is slung around his neck, and the top few buttons of his white button-down are undone revealing a bit of chest hair.

He is walking sex and the smirk pulling at his lips tells me he knows it.

I raise an eyebrow at him as the bartender pours a shot for him and he leans against the bar, propping one elbow up on the top as he stares at me with a cocky smile that I know all too well. He has a highball glass of whiskey in his hand and I try to inconspicuously search his left hand for a ring. I'm fairly certain, my eyes give me away. He raises his hand, downing the rest of his drink before setting his glass on the shiny mahogany counter.

No ring.

"You going to the after party?"

I hear the subtext in his question loud and clear. I am twenty-one and this is already the third wedding I've been in this year. I don't know what is in the water that all of my friends wanted to spend their twenty-first birthdays getting drunk '*for the first time*' at their own weddings, but this is my third friend to walk down the aisle and if the third time is really a charm, I'll be sneaking out of a groomsmen's bed tomorrow morning.

I grab the two shots and give him my best flirty smile. "Maybe," I say, but I don't wait for his response before I start towards the wedding party table where the bride—my friend Alexis who had been my college roommate for the past four years—is sitting in her new husband's lap feeding him cake in a way I wish I didn't have to witness.

"Can you guys please get a room?" I ask as I sit down with the two shots of tequila. I pan the table searching for the maid of honor, her older sister Meredith. "Where's your sister?"

"We have a room." Alexis flicks her ash blonde tresses over her shoulder. It had long since fallen out of the braid that had been intricately woven with flowers.

"Then go to it." I blink at her and she rolls her eyes before letting out a giggle as Owen, the guy she just married, squeezes her tighter against him and presses his lips to her neck. I'll admit they are cute as hell, even though it was a whirlwind romance, a quick courtship, and an even quicker engagement that her parents begged her to prolong. Being cute as hell aside, there is a thirteen-year age difference between them and Owen was just getting out of an almost decade-long relationship when they met.

It was a little under two years ago when we were out at a bar letting loose after just finishing our finals one semester. I still remember it vividly, her dancing with another guy, and Owen marching up to them and asking if he could buy her a drink like the other guy holding onto her hips didn't exist.

Big dick energy if I ever saw it.

Alexis, who hadn't believed in casual sex or one-night stands, went home with Owen that night and they've been inseparable ever since.

"I think Meredith went to bed," Alexis says in response to my question and I want to curse her for doing an Irish goodbye without me when we'd been together all night.

"Guess you'll just have to settle for taking this with me." I didn't realize that the hot groomsman had followed me but when I turn to look at him, he's giving me that same cocky smile revealing his perfect teeth as he holds his shot in his hand.

"Chris!" I hear Owen's voice shout and when I turn towards

him, I'm shocked not to see his lips attached to some part of Alexis. "You met Marissa?" he asks, pointing at me.

His eyes trail down my body so seductively that it causes a tightening between my legs. He cocks his head to the side as one side of his mouth ticks upward in the sexiest crooked grin. "I'm trying to."

Owen, who I swear is the poster boy for golden retriever energy beams at us. "Marissa, meet Chris, my oldest friend in the world. Chris, this is Lex's roommate."

"Former roommate!" Alexis cheers and I roll my eyes, an annoying reminder that in a month's time, I'll have very different roommates known as Mom and Dad.

"So, you're old too, huh?" I quip, realizing that if this is Owen's oldest friend, then he's also thirteen years older than me.

"I like to think I'm still young at heart." He clinks his small glass with mine just before we take our shots. The burn feels like nothing more than a tingle after how many of these I've had tonight. "You want to dance?" I turn towards the dance floor that is slowly clearing out but the band is playing a cover of "I Say a Little Prayer." I start to protest when I feel his hand in mine, tugging me towards the dance floor. "Come on."

I hear Alexis let out a cheer as we make it to the almost empty dance floor save for some of Owen's drunk relatives. Chris spins me around the second we hit the shiny wood flooring and I let him lead me around the space.

"You're a good dancer," I tell him after a few minutes of silence and he smiles.

"Comes with age, and a lot of weddings." He winks as he pulls me a little closer, touching the bare skin of my lower back due to the backless bridesmaid dress. The band continues into another song and we don't stop moving, our bodies moving in perfect synchronization like we've been practicing for months. "I've been trying to talk to you all night." He's at least half a foot taller than me and I'm not short but I still have to tilt my head up to meet his gaze and his eyes twinkle under the low lighting in the tent. "You were the most gorgeous woman in the room tonight. Hell, you're the most gorgeous woman I've seen in any room."

A smile pulls at my lips that I couldn't hide if you paid me. "You must say that to all the bridesmaids from all those weddings you've been to." I chuckle.

"No," he says in a lower register than his normal voice. "Just you." He spins me again, and I'm so glad he's leading because my ability to keep myself balanced is lowering faster than my inhibitions.

"Well, what was stopping you?" I ask. "From talking to me?"

"Honestly? Thought you'd think I was too old for you."

"You definitely are." I raise an eyebrow at him.

He chuckles and narrows his eyes slightly, still keeping me gently pressed against him. "Something tells me that doesn't bother you."

The music starts to slow and I vaguely hear the sound of the singer of the band say something about a final song and where to go for the after-party.

"So, where'd you land on going to the bar?" he asks and the effects of that last shot hit me just in time for the words to leave my lips before I have a chance to think.

"Or we could have a different kind of after-party?" I look up at him. "I'm sharing a room though."

"Good thing I'm not," he says as he drags his hand across my back so slowly, I feel it between my legs.

We barely utter a goodbye to Owen and Alexis before we're in the elevator, his lips on mine as we ascend to his room on the twelfth floor.

"Tell me you have condoms," I whisper between kisses.

"Sure do," he says low in my ear as he grabs my hips and

pushes himself against me. His lips are so fucking soft which is such a sexy contrast to the stubble on his jaw. His lips are on my neck, and I feel his tongue and his teeth on my flesh. My body hums in anticipation of feeling it on the rest of my body.

"Plural." I reiterate because I already know I'm going to want more than one round.

"Oh, someone's greedy." I gasp when he bites down on my neck. "I like it." He pulls me out of the elevator as soon as it dings but we barely make it a step before I'm pressed up against the closest wall, his lips back on mine as his hands slide up my body and cup my breasts. "You have the best fucking tits. I've been trying to keep from staring at them since last night at the rehearsal dinner."

I've always had bigger breasts. I rarely hide them and my bridesmaid dress is a halter style that definitely showcases my C-cups well. He drops his head, dragging his tongue up the valley between them, and I feel like if I don't get this dress off of me in the next thirty seconds I might combust. I'm drunk off both the liquor and this gorgeous older man that is pressing what feels like a very big dick into my stomach and I want to feel it *everywhere.*

"Your room." I moan and then I feel my legs moving fast and I realize we are literally *running* to his room. When he swipes his card over the reader, the door slams open so hard it bangs against the wall and rattles the mirror against it. I briefly worry it's going to fall before I'm lifted into his arms and my worries fade away as he walks me through what looks like a suite and into his bedroom.

He sets me on my feet gently, wrapping his arms around me and sliding up to my neck to undo the bow tied at my nape. His eyes don't leave mine as he undoes it slowly and not with the urgency he'd just had, like he wants to savor this moment of getting me naked. "I'm going to remember this night for fucking ever," he says as the dress moves slowly down my body. "The night I went after what I wanted and got it: the most gorgeous woman I've ever seen in my life." My black dress lands in a pile on the floor leaving me in nothing but a lace thong. "Fuuuuck." His eyes drag over my breasts and his hands immediately go to his dick, palming it, and I reach for his belt, sliding it off of him.

He toes off his shoes and sends his slacks down his muscular legs before pointing to the bed. "Get on the bed." I do as he says, propping myself up on my elbows as he undoes his shirt leaving him in nothing but his briefs. He has a smattering of chest hair over his *two, four, six, eight!* Pack; I count with my eyes.

"Wow." I thought I only said that in my head but apparently, I said it out loud because he chuckles and kneels on the bed.

"You're the only *wow* in this room." He glides his hands up my legs and then drags two fingers over the waistband of my panties. I reach down to remove my heels when he halts my hand. "Leave them on. I want to feel them on my back while I eat your pussy." He grips the crotch of my panties and moves them to the side exposing me to him. I'm already obscenely wet, having spent the better part of the last thirty minutes building to this moment. "I knew it'd be gorgeous, just like the rest of you." He licks his lips and I feel like my heart could hammer out of my chest from lust.

I raise my hips upwards, desperate for his mouth or his fingers or anything that will cause friction against my clit. "Please touch me," I beg just as he lowers a hand and rubs a circle around my clit and I resist the urge to come at the minor touch.

"You're wound tight as fuck, aren't you?" He leans down, his mouth just hovering above me. "I'll give you this one to take the edge off but then I need you to wait for me." He winks before he takes one obscene lick through my sex, swirling his tongue around my clit in a tortuously slow circle eliciting the most feral groan from him that rattles through me.

"Oh my god." I moan, dropping my hands to his hair as my orgasm already dangles just out of reach.

"Say my name when you come," he tells me. "I want to hear it fall from those pretty lips while I have my mouth on you."

"Oh fuck!" My entire body is fucking vibrating at this point and my pussy is tingling to the point of pain. His beard rubs so deliciously against me just as he lets his lips suction around my clit. He lifts my thighs, sending them over his shoulders and I remember what he said about my heels. I press them gently into his muscular back, and it's as if something inside of him snaps at the feeling because I hear the sound of my underwear ripping and when I look down, his piercing blue eyes are already on me, watching me hungrily. This wasn't my first time with a guy's mouth between my legs but I've never locked eyes with someone while they did it. It feels so erotic to have someone staring at you while they lick your most intimate area.

He speeds up his strokes, his eyes still on me as he drags his tongue along my clit over and over and... "Fuck, I'm going to come," I whimper as the feeling sucks me under.

I feel the bed moving and I notice his hips grinding against the bed almost and in time with his licks. "I feel like I could come just from the taste of your cunt alone."

"Oh god!" I cry out in response just as he suctions his lips around my clit and drags his teeth over the sensitive bundle of nerves gently.

"My name," I manage to hear him grunt, just as I go over the edge.

"Chris!" I scream just as my eyes flutter shut and I fall to my back, the feeling of euphoria spreading through every inch of my body, into my bones and my brain and my heart and my soul, and I have a brief moment where I wonder if this is the man I'll do this with for the rest of my life.

Holy shit. That was the best orgasm I've ever had.

When my eyes flutter open, he's hovering over me with a smile on his face. "I've never seen anyone come like that."

My body is still humming, making me wonder if I'm having one of those orgasms that go on for longer than a few seconds. "What...what did I do?" I ask, wondering what made me so different.

"It was just so...enthralling. I couldn't take my eyes off of you." He traps his bottom lip between his teeth as he traces my face with hooded eyes.

This man radiates sex.

His covered dick slides across my pussy and bumps against my clit in the process and I whimper, still feeling overstimulated from my climax. I grab his biceps as I try to anchor myself. "You're so sensitive."

"Not usually like this." I moan, feeling myself build just from that minor brush of him against me. He leans back on his heels and stares down at me. He lifts one of my legs, sliding one shoe off before the other, and tosses them off the bed. "I don't usually come that easily."

He presses his lips to my ankle before he lets his mouth glide up my legs tortuously slow. "Well, that was only the first. We have a long night ahead." He smirks as he pulls his briefs off revealing the biggest dick I've ever seen in my life pointing straight up with precum pooling at the tip.

"Oh my god." I bite my bottom lip, my eyes wide as he gets off the bed and grabs a box of condoms out of his open suitcase in the corner.

"Don't worry gorgeous, as wet as you are right now, I'll slide right in." I swallow nervously, my eyes still not blinking when I feel his hand under my chin and lifting it gently. "Should I eat you out again? Make your hot little pussy wetter for me?" He presses a gentle kiss to my lips, sliding his tongue through them and rubbing against mine. His sinful words mixed with the taste of my pussy on his tongue sends a tingle through me and I shiver against his lips.

"No..." I whisper. "You haven't come yet."

"So?" he asks. "This isn't tit for tat. I'll make you come a hundred times before I let you touch me if you're not ready. Besides, the scent of your cunt drives me fucking wild."

Jesus Christ.

"You have a filthy mouth."

"You already know that." His tongue darts out to lick his bottom lip, reminding me of where it's just been.

My eyes trace his lips before moving to his eyes, my heart hammering in my chest not only out of lust but out of something else I'm not sober enough to pinpoint.

"Fuck me," I breathe out and I can hear the desperation in my voice. I reach my hand out, rubbing a French manicured fingernail over the tip of his cock and collecting his cum on my finger before sliding it through my lips. "And then I'll put my mouth on this."

"Fuck. I'm going to blow before I even get inside of you."

"I want to ride you," I tell him as I push him onto his back and straddle his hips.

"Fuck yes, let me get a condom on, babe," he says and the familiarity of the pet name mixed with the fact that we are definitely not familiar with each other makes my pussy throb.

"One sec. I just want…to feel it for a second." I don't make a move to touch him as I wait for him to agree to the idea of fooling around without a condom.

"Fuck yes. Rub my dick against your pretty clit." He lets out a shaky breath before he nods. "But do not let me inside your cunt because I won't be able to pull out," he grits out.

I move myself closer to his cock, grabbing it in my hand as a groan leaves his lips followed by a hiss when I squeeze it gently. I move up and then down slowly, letting the underside of his shaft slide through my slit.

Both of his hands find his face and he lets out a chuckle. "Christ, that feels good. Do it again." He scrubs one along his jaw as he looks down at where we are touching.

I notice that cum is starting to pool at the tip and I move slightly to rub my tongue over the head to collect the drops that are forming. His eyes widen and a boyish grin pulls at his lips. "You want my dick in your mouth?"

I nod. "After you fuck me."

"Fuck." He groans. "Where have you been all my life?"

I cock my head to the side with a smirk on my lips. "You want me to answer that?" I quip, referencing our vast age differences before swiping my tongue along the tip again.

"Oh, fuck you." He chuckles before I get back on my knees and grab his dick. I let the tip circle my clit and begin to rub myself against it like it's my vibrator. *Except this one is connected to a person that I kind of want to take home with me and try out in my bed.*

I feel myself building and my eyes flutter closed as I rock my hips back and forth over the tip of his cock letting him drag through my sex.

"Marissa…" I hear his shaky voice, breaking me through the haze of my looming orgasm and when I look down, I see he has a condom in his hand. "Put it the fuck on so I can get inside you." His eyes are hooded and I can tell he's gritting his teeth. I feel him pulsing in my hand and I rip the condom open before sliding it slowly down his length. I barely get it to the bottom before he has both arms on my biceps and he's holding me up over him. "Get on my dick right now."

I waste no time sheathing myself on him, pushing myself all the way down until my mound hits the base of his dick. "Oh fuck," I whimper just as a feral growl leaves his mouth.

He looks down at where we are conjoined, where his dark pubic hair presses against my bare cunt, and his eyes shoot up to mine like he's shocked at what he's seeing. "I didn't think it was possible for your pussy to get any prettier, but I love seeing it stuffed with my cock." Both of his hands find my hips. "You ready to move?"

And I don't know what it is about those specific words but they turn me on even more. "Fuck yes." I moan as I drop my palms to his chest for leverage as I begin riding him. I bounce myself on him, squeezing his cock all the way up and slamming myself down.

"Fuck." He moans. "Your pussy was made for my dick, wasn't it? Look how well you take me." He grits out. "And you were worried." One hand moves from my hip to my breast, palming it before rolling the nipple between his fingers. He licks his lips and then he's sitting up, still inside of me as he sucks my breast into his mouth. He holds me in place to stop me from moving almost like he's worried it'll remove my nipple from his mouth. I feel his teeth bite down gently and I whimper when he soothes the sting with his tongue. He moves to the other and I clench my pussy around his dick alerting him that I want to move. "Okay okay," he chuckles as he looks up at me. "You're fucking incredible you know that?"

I push him onto his back again and start riding him again, my next orgasm already dancing beneath my skin. "Chris, I think I'm going to come again."

"Are you? Fuck, grind that clit against me. It's fucking hot, I know it is."

I rotate my hips slowly, dragging my clit against the base of his dick. "Yessss." I moan.

"I love how fucking responsive you are."

"It helps that your dick is perfect." I moan again as electricity pulses through me before moving down to congregate between my legs.

"I can tell you're close. Fucking get there, Marissa. Do it now," he grits out. "And when you go over, you better take me with you," he commands. "I want to come while your pussy is squeezing my dick."

"Oh shit."

He grabs my ass, squeezing it hard. "You ever had a dick here?"

I haven't and the thought of him putting his dick in my ass both terrifies me and turns me on and the gruffness of his voice sends me over the edge. "OH FUCK!" I scream as I continue fucking him through my orgasm just as I hear my name and then I feel him expand inside of me.

"Oh, fuck fuck fuuuuuck." He groans and before I even have a chance to come down, he's flipped us so I'm on my back and his lips are on mine kissing me like he's trying to climb inside of me.

I feel his dick softening and then he slides out but his tongue is still ravaging my mouth. His hands move under my back pulling me harder against him and it forces me to wrap my legs around his back and lock my ankles. My wet sex drags against his torso and there's something so hot about his abs rubbing against my clit that I let out another moan. "I'm not fucking done with you," he says as he pulls away from my mouth finally. He's breathing hard so I wonder if he only pulled away to take a breath.

"That was…" I blink up at him as I struggle to put into words just how amazing that was.

"Yeah." There isn't a smile on his face like I know there is on mine. He almost looks worried and it would worry me if I didn't feel his fingertips grazing up and down my sides and his lips at my shoulder. "Fucking perfect." A sleepy smile finds my face as the high of two orgasms and all the alcohol I've had starts to catch up with me. I feel my eyes getting heavy when I hear his voice pushing through my half-conscious state. "Don't fall asleep," he whispers in my ear. "I don't want this night to end." I feel his hands in my hair, gently pulling out the pins that had kept half of it up.

"I'm not," I whisper as I cuddle into his chest, feeling his warmth against me as he wraps his arms around me. I want to tell him that we could have more nights. That I'll give him my number in the morning and we can repeat this again, but I fall into a deeper sleep before I can open my mouth again.

The next morning when I wake up to an empty room, with his suitcase gone and a note on the nightstand without so much as a phone number or a way to contact him, I feel my heart sink into my stomach with humiliation.

Thank you for last night. Definitely won't forget it.
I got a late check out so leave whenever you're ready.
Order room service.
-C

It wasn't exactly a blow-off but I could read between the lines. This was a one-time thing. I swallow past the knot in my throat because even if this was just a one-night stand, I wasn't even warranted a goodbye? Have a nice day? Have a nice life?

I go through the motions of getting dressed, grabbing my shredded underwear, and pulling on my dress from last night. With shoes in hand, I prepare for this cliched walk of shame.

I thought there was something between us. A spark? Was I that stupid?

Yes, my subconscious snarks. You knew the guy a whole day before you fucked him. Did you think he was going to have a ring ready for you in the morning?

No? But maybe morning sex and hungover breakfast?
Ugh.

I chastise myself with every step closer to my room for letting my drunk and delusional brain think this would be more than a one-time thing. That it wasn't only the best sex I'd ever had but that we had a connection.

I roll my eyes, pushing him out of my thoughts, and decide not to obsess about it. More importantly, I vow to absolutely not talk to Alexis about it. Clearly, he didn't want anyone to know and Alexis would have a million questions and probably berate Owen for it in defense of me. I don't need to bring anyone else into this humiliating situation.

I hold my key card over my door and let out a sigh of relief when I see Meredith is still passed out cold and will be none the wiser that I hadn't slept here.

I can just forget about it.

It never happened and I'll never see him again.

Little did I know that in three months' time, I'd learn that the best sex of my life was with a married man.

Chapter ONE

CHRIS

Three Months Later

"Beck, come on, one more drink?" I ask my best friend Wes Beckham as he gets up from the bar stool after draining the contents of his beer. I can practically hear the pleading in my voice.

"I have to be in early tomorrow." He looks at me from over the top of his glasses giving me a look that isn't exactly scolding but direct enough to tell me he thinks I should follow suit. "As do you."

"We've had like two beers, come on. You act like I want to get hammered."

"You're avoiding going home." He crosses his arms over his chest.

"Obviously." I drag my hand through my hair. "Holly is getting worse," I say, rubbing my fingers over my temples as I think about the woman I'm married to. "I even suggested counseling again and she still will not go for it."

Beck drops to his seat with a sigh and holds up a finger towards the bartender signaling another beer. "Why?"

"Something about it not being anyone's business but ours what goes on in our marriage."

Beck's face forms a frown as he pinches the bridge of his nose. "Okay, but…it's a counselor and you guys have been having trouble for a few years now."

I snort. "Tell that to her."

I've been married for almost six years. I would say only the first two years were good but even that feels like a stretch. It was like after we got married and settled into our new life, something changed and I've been holding onto hope ever since that she'd revert to the woman I fell in love with. The woman who was sweet and charming. Fun and independent. A woman who actually cared about me and not just my bank account.

But it's been six years and I'm beginning to think all of that pre-marital bliss had been smoke and mirrors.

Holly and I met on my first weekend here in Philly almost eight years ago. I'd moved here somewhat on a whim because Wes Beckham, my mentor and one of my best friends, decided to start a company and he wanted me to be his CFO. I had just finished grad school and was dreading the thought of going to work in the shadow of my grandfather so I jumped at the opportunity to go off on my own and make something of myself that wasn't bordering on nepotism.

The weekend I moved here, we'd gone out and I met Holly that first night. Beautiful. Flirtatious. Fun. I hadn't laughed that much in ages and maybe it was the high of the move and the excitement of Wes' business plan but I'd gotten her number that night and spent the next several weeks pursuing her. Looking back, I realize how enamored I was with the idea of having it all. The career and the relationship. I loved the idea of her.

We did all the steps. Dated for a year. Moved in together. I proposed. We got married. It was all so easy. *And then, it wasn't.*

It was as if a switch flipped overnight. She quit her job, which was fine. *Beckham Securities* was off the ground at this point and was starting to thrive so I was technically able to support us on my income alone. I'll admit it bothered me that she hadn't even talked to me about it before she did it though. I was literally the last person to know and that wasn't until weeks later.

When I asked her what she was planning to do, she said it was in preparation for us having a baby. *Another thing we hadn't talked about.* We'd only been married about two months at that time and I was working nonstop. I definitely wanted children, but I wanted to get to more stable ground financially and for us to have a little more time as a newly married couple before we had children. She agreed quickly and then proceeded to take vacations every month. Shopping trips every other day. The most expensive dinners. Long weekends with her friends at spas on our dime because *'we could afford it.'*

When I confronted her about a month where she spent almost fifty thousand dollars on our credit card, she lost it. Called me every name in the book before storming out and staying with her best friend for three days. We'd only been married about five months at that point and I was already beginning to wonder if I'd made a mistake. We were doing well, but not well enough for me to afford that kind of credit card bill every month in addition to everything else I was paying for.

When the money started flowing more easily, I thought things would get better. I knew there was a mounting problem in our marriage, but I was hoping I could sweep it under the rug for the time being. Then I realized there were even bigger problems. Holly had this condescending nature that really got under my skin and it bothered me the way she talked to literally everyone. Specifically, anyone that worked for me. It was like she got off on letting everyone know that she believed she was better than them.

It was a constant battle between us. I was so miserable and fed up over it that one night after one too many drinks I went home with someone else.

I felt like shit.

I held it in for a week before the guilt started to eat me alive and I confessed everything. She blinked at me like she was unfazed before shrugging and saying, "It's whatever." I was shocked. *She didn't care? She wasn't angry?* And then she looked me up and down and said with a patronizing pat to my cheek, "You shouldn't want me to be angry. I didn't sign a prenuptial agreement so if I'm angry enough to want a divorce, I get half of everything."

Her words were like a punch in the gut.

She couldn't be fucking serious.

"Did…did you ever love me?" I'd asked her, my words getting caught in my throat. It seemed I'd not only climbed into bed with the devil, but I'd slid a ring on her finger tying us together and creating my own personal hell.

"I do love you, Chris. You're successful and brilliant and we are going to create such a legacy."

"You love my money."

"Your ambition," she'd corrected as she turned back to her phone without another look at me.

I went out that night and fucked someone else.

That was almost two years ago and for a while, it was the only thing that kept me sane. It felt like one of the few things in my life I had any control over. I wasn't proud of it, but I felt like I was drowning.

Until three months ago.

Until my childhood best friend's wedding when I slept with the most gorgeous woman I'd ever met, had the best sex of my life, and then snuck out before the sun rose because I'd woken up to approximately twenty texts from Holly and I felt like an asshole.

Not for cheating on Holly again, but for dragging Marissa into my dysfunctional life without her knowing.

So, I left like a coward instead of telling her the truth. At least if she hated me, she wouldn't be tempted to contact me. I didn't even know her last name and as much as I wanted to, I didn't probe Owen for any details on the bridesmaid that I couldn't stop thinking about. I didn't even tell him what I did. *Mostly because I knew it would lead to a lecture about it being time to leave Holly.* And I'd hoped she wouldn't try to find me because I was in no place to offer her anything even if I wanted to.

A part of me wasn't even sure I did want to. Yes, the sex was amazing and she was gorgeous and incredible, but I hardly knew her. Not to mention I'd been fooled and burned by a woman once already and I'd become skeptical of everyone's motives.

I reach my hand into my slacks pocket and pull out one of the hair pins she'd had in her hair that night. She'd had three, all silver and made to look like a tree branch with crystals as the leaves. I'd taken one, hoping she wouldn't notice or would just assume she lost it, but I wanted a memory of what had become the best night of my life. I've been carrying it in my pocket every day for the past three months.

I drag my thumb over the stones again and feel Beck's gaze. When I look up he's staring down at my hands. "Still thinking about the girl from the wedding?" he asks, having heard the story the first time I pulled it out of my pocket. *And then at least once a week since.*

"I'm never *not* thinking about her," I confess. Sometimes, I even let myself think about a life where I get out of this mess with Holly and Marissa forgives me for disappearing into the night. *Morning, whatever.*

"Maybe you should try to reach out."

"And say what? Want to be my mistress?"

He winces in response. "The truth? But I mean…maybe this is the time to get a divorce."

I groan, putting a hand over my eyes. "And give Holly almost four hundred million dollars? Maybe more? Fuck, I should have done this years ago." I feel sick for the umpteenth time thinking about the fact that I could have been done with this hundreds of millions of dollars ago before *Beckham Securities* really took off.

"I won't say I told you so," Beck says…because he definitely had, multiple times. "Look, what's the alternative? Being miserable for the rest of your life? Chris, we'll make more money. Take it from me, you will feel so much better once you leave the wrong partner." I nod, thinking about Beck's ex-fiancée, Hannah. She and Holly were like two peas in a pod. So similar that it was almost comical and yet the irony that they didn't like each other somehow still made perfect sense. "I go home to peace and quiet and can do whatever I want."

"And you don't even appreciate it. You could literally fuck anyone and you haven't since you and Hannah broke up."

He shrugs and stares down into his beer like the answer is in the amber liquid. "I'm tired of the casual sex thing. I want something real. Just because I didn't want to marry Hannah doesn't mean I don't ever want to get married. I just want the right woman."

Normally, I'd rag on him a little bit about his hopeless romantic nature, but the truth is I haven't slept with anyone else in three months. Not since Marissa. I haven't been able to stop thinking about her long enough to even entertain another woman.

My wife included.

Holly and I rarely have sex, and now we even sleep in separate bedrooms, but there were a few times here and there where she'd initiate it and I'd go with it for the sake of keeping the peace. She hadn't in months though, and for that I was grateful.

I don't think I fell in love with Marissa after one night of drunken sex, but I'd be lying if I didn't admit that I felt something and I'm sure she did too.

Maybe it wouldn't hurt to at least find out her last name. I could stalk her on Instagram or LinkedIn because as I've been thoroughly informed by Alexis, "*People don't use Facebook anymore, Grandpa.*"

Beck and I stay at the bar for a bit longer, both of us

commiserating over how lacking our love lives are, and for the hundredth time, I'm reminded that all the money in the world really can't buy happiness.

There's a knock on my office door and then my assistant, Christine, is pushing through the door with a cup of coffee and a stack of pink post-it notes in her other hand. "Mr. Holt, I have your coffee and some messages," she says as she pushes her glasses up the bridge of her nose. "Also, Mr. Beckham asked if you can handle the onboarding orientation for the new hires."

I groan, thinking about the six new members of the sales team that are starting today. The last thing I feel like doing right now is talking to a bunch of twenty-one-year-olds fresh out of college who are far too chipper and eager to impress. I'm not in the mood to be *on* right now and that's exactly what I have to do. Get them excited to work for us. Tell them that they made the right decision coming to work at *Beckham Securities* and that this is a great place to work, healthy work-life balance, my door is always open, *blah blah blah*. It's true, but I'm in a foul mood.

Holly and I got into it over the same old bullshit last night and I jerked off in the shower thinking about Marissa for the millionth time before going to bed annoyed and horny.

I'd woken up annoyed and horny.

"Where is Beck?" I ask her, because he better have a good excuse as to why he's pushing this off on me. He may be my boss technically, but I can still tell him to fuck off when necessary.

"He got called into a meeting with the Seattle team."

I look at my watch and snort at the fact that it's three hours earlier than it is here. "At seven a.m.?" I ask. "He's full of shit." Christine sighs and gives me a look that says *don't shoot the messenger*. "He just doesn't want to deal with it either."

"Okay, well they need someone in ten minutes." She shrugs as if to say *you two work it out.*

Ten minutes later, I'm walking towards the conference room when a familiar smell hits me. It's feminine but not too floral or fruity and somehow has the power to make me hard because I feel myself thickening in my pants. I turn around, looking for the source of the scent and trying to recall why I recognize it. When I see nothing and no one out of the norm, I ignore it and open the door to the conference room. As Dana and the rest of the Human Resources team go through their PowerPoint slides, I stand and watch in the back of the room, leaning against the wall with my arms crossed as I take in the six new members of our team. Their backs are all to me and it's not lost on me that the scent from the hallway is even stronger in here which means someone is wearing that perfume.

I've slept with women that have worked for us before but it always got messy, and even though someone in this room has the power to make my dick hard with just a whiff, I am not interested.

Though I'll admit, no one has made me this hard since Marissa.

Maybe I'm getting over her.

"Oh, and here he is." Dana points towards me. "This is our CFO, Christopher Holt. You will all be reporting directly to him."

Their heads turn as I make my way towards the front. "Hello everyone, welcome to—" I stop short when I get to the front of the room and have dragged my eyes over all six people seated at the conference table.

One very familiar person sits in the front, her legs crossed and her eyes wide, almost scared, as she meets my gaze. Those dark brown eyes that stared up at me while I was on top of her, that looked down at me while she rode me and while I ate her pussy.

God, she had the sweetest cunt.

Her hair is a little longer, more wavy than curly with one side pushed behind her ear, but she has the same high cheekbones and a full pout that is painted bright red. Warm brown skin that looks darker than I remember, like she'd spent the whole summer being kissed by the sun and I grit my teeth at the memory of running my lips all over her skin. *Christ, she's even more gorgeous than I remember her.* I reluctantly pull my gaze away from her so it's not obvious that I'm blatantly staring but not before I sweep my gaze over her bare toned legs that I can still feel wrapped around my waist.

My mouth goes dry and I feel like someone has knocked the wind out of me. I don't know how much time has gone by but I think I recover quickly as I give them my very accelerated introductory spiel wanting to get the hell out of this room to collect my thoughts. "I'll be conducting meetings with each of you today after onboarding," I add as an afterthought wanting, *no needing*, a moment alone with her.

"Today?" Dana holds up her folder in front of our faces to give us a second of privacy and looks at me. "One on one's this soon?" she whispers.

I nod before turning back to the six individuals all giving me varying looks of trepidation. "Very informal. I just want to get to know each of you." I hold my hand out for the folder in Dana's hand. She hands it to me and I open it doing a brief scan of the names.

Marissa Collins.

I snap the folder closed. "Great. Alphabetical order please."

Chapter TWO

Marissa

OH, MY FUCKING GOD! I'M PACING THE LENGTH OF the bathroom trying to stop myself from having a panic attack.

Deep breaths. In and out.

I know I only have a small window before someone comes to check on me but I'm hoping that maybe if I pass out, they'll just send me to the emergency room and I won't have to have this meeting with the guy I hooked up with three months ago. "Oh my god," I say out loud just as I press the contact for my older sister for the third time in the span of a minute. When she sends me to voicemail, *again,* I leave her a panicked message.

"Heaven forbid I need you for something! This is a nine-one-one EMERGENCY!" I say before letting out a sigh. "Not life-threatening, just maybe the worst thing that could ever happen to me short of that." My older sister is five years older than me and a litigator so there's a good chance she's in court today, but HELLO, *my life is going up in flames!* "If I don't answer when you call me back it's because I'm in meetings. I'll talk to you later. Love you." I squeeze my eyes together hoping that when I open them, I'll be transported somewhere else.

While they're closed, I wrack my brain trying to remember if I ever heard his last name at the wedding reception but I come up empty.

I open my eyes to stare at myself in the mirror. "You did nothing wrong. He did. He should be pacing his office. Why are you worried?"

It's not necessarily that I'm worried, it's more embarrassment that I have to face him.

I stare at my reflection, happy that I'd gone with the midlength black business dress that cinches my waist and tastefully highlights my curves. Coupled with my favorite black heels, I'll admit I look good and am happy with my choice of outfit for the first time he's seeing me in three months. I touch up my lipstick and add a few more coats of mascara before tucking a few strands behind my ear.

"Let's get this over with," I whisper to myself as I push my way out of the bathroom. I make it to the lobby and allow someone to walk me to his office.

"He's expecting you. Go right in!" A red-haired woman, who I assume is his assistant, sits several feet in front of his office door and gives me a sweet smile. I don't go in right away and I hear her speak again. "He's very sweet. Much nicer than the CEO." She whispers the last part like it's a secret as she comes around her desk and points at the office at the end of the hallway. "Mr. Beckham? Kind of a bear. Mr. Holt is all bark and no bite and sometimes his bark is more like a yap." She giggles as she pushes her glasses up on her nose. "I'm Christine." She's shorter than me and her red hair is such a gorgeous color I can't help but wonder if it's natural with green eyes and freckles that dot her cheeks.

"Marissa."

"Honestly, the worst thing about Mr. Holt is Mrs. Holt," she says and my neck snaps to her so hard I swear I hear something crack.

"What?"

"Mrs. Holt? His wife. God, she's the worst. I keep hoping he'll leave her but…I guess six years is a long time."

Oh. My. God.

"Six…years?" I stammer. *No. No. No!*

"Yep," she says casually, like she hasn't just detonated a bomb five seconds before I'm supposed to walk into a war zone. I feel like I can't breathe and I'm wondering if all of this is worth it. What if I just walk out of here and never come back? *Okay, I suppose that's job abandonment, but maybe Chris, or* Mr. Holt *would understand.* Now that we can add infidelity to the list of infractions, I'm sure he's even less excited about me being here.

I'm contemplating this when the door opens and I'm face to face with the guy who I told myself to forget about but have thought about nonstop for three months.

I'd been hurt. Spent three months rationalizing the fact that he disappeared and never tried to contact me.

But now I know the truth.

He's MARRIED?

Oh, I am pissed.

"Miss Collins, please come in." He says, extending his arm into his office and I enter, wanting to scream but realizing that may be the fastest way to get fired.

He closes the door behind me and when I turn around, he gives me a look that probably matches the look on my face. Despite the anger building inside me, I can't deny how good he looks in his gray suit. Maybe Armani? Or Tom Ford? Zegna? It looks expensive. His hair is a little wilder than it was at the wedding, some of it falling a bit over those gorgeous blue eyes that I can see vividly in my dreams.

"What are you doing here?" he says, his words hard but low

and my mouth drops open because why the hell is he asking *me* that?

"Excuse me?" I cross my hands over my chest and watch as his eyes zip to the movement before moving back up to meet my gaze. I narrow my eyes at him as if to say *don't even think about it.*

"Did you ask Alexis where to find me?" he asks as he breezes by me and leans up against his desk, his brows furrowed and his entire posture tense and combative.

"No? I was just as surprised to see you here. And for the record if I had told Alexis about that night, which I absolutely did not, don't you think she would have told me that you were *married?!*" I snap, raising an eyebrow at him. "Surely would have saved me the shock of learning about it from your assistant twenty seconds ago."

His face falls and he lets his head drop before letting out a sigh that makes it seem like his whole body is exhausted. One of those sighs you let out when you feel like you've got the entire weight of the world on your shoulders and you just want a reprieve from all of it.

"I'm sorry," he says still staring at the ground, like he can't even meet my eyes.

I narrow my eyes at him. "You have a lot of things to be sorry for; you're going to need to be more specific."

"Everything." He finally looks up at me. "I shouldn't have… that night."

I swallow and take a deep breath in and out through my nose, doing my best to quell my anger. "You weren't wearing a ring."

"I took it off."

I scoff and shake my head, disgusted. "So, you went out with the intention to cheat?"

"You don't get it."

My lips form a straight tight line. "I surely do not." My tone is clipped.

Anger flashes across his face. "You don't have the right to judge me."

"You stuck your dick inside of me without telling me you had a wife at home and then left me in your hotel room without so much as a goodbye, I have a fuck ton of rights," I retort. *He has got to be joking.*

"I left a note," he says, like that makes everything better.

"Which was honestly worse than not saying anything." I swallow, fighting the tears because I refuse to spend any more time being upset about him. "That was the shittiest thing anyone has ever done to me."

He narrows his eyes in sadness. "I'm so sorry. Holly started calling—"

"Ahhh." I put a hand up, my blood starting to boil upon hearing his wife's name. "Please do not try to explain, it will only make it worse."

"My marriage isn't…" He lets out a breath. "We aren't happy."

"Sounds like bull. You're a rich guy who cheats on his wife. That really lacks originality, Chris. And based on the way you treated me, I'm going to assume it wasn't the first time."

"You don't know shit about it," he snaps. His blue eyes are cold and his tone is angry.

"And who's fault is that?" I snap back.

He sighs and the look of anger is replaced with contrition before he moves around his desk to sit in his chair. "You don't understand. I hated leaving you like that." He leans back in his chair and stares at me. "I wanted you that morning. Wanted to take you to breakfast. Lunch. Dinner. Hell, hide away with you in the Hamptons for the week."

"You're married, Chris. You were going to do all that before, what? Going back to your wife? Did you think I would just be okay with you being married? Maybe you're used to women like that, but it's not me."

"No." He pauses before he speaks again. "I know, and that's

why I left because I knew I'd want more with you and I didn't have more to give."

His words hit me hard causing conflicting feelings to arise. On one hand, I finally feel the validation that I've wanted for months. That I wasn't the only one that felt something. That there was something there. On the other hand, I'm angry that he put us in this situation when there's nothing either of us can do about it.

Neither of us say anything for a few moments before I speak up. "If what you're saying is true about not being happy…is divorce not an option?"

He doesn't respond right away and he rubs his forehead like maybe he's going over his answer before he says it. "It'll cost me a lot." He looks at his computer. "Like *a lot*."

"Oh," I whisper. I'd recently seen while I was researching this job that Wes Beckham, the CEO of the company had just hit Forbes' youngest billionaires list. I assume as CFO of the company, Christopher Holt must definitely be dancing around the high hundreds of millions. I think about my student loans and credit card debt and briefly wish I could be the kind of woman who could date a married man for a few months. Forty thousand dollars seems insurmountable at times for me, but to a man like Chris, it's probably nothing. "Are you going to fire me?"

"What?" He shakes his head as if my suggestion was the most ludicrous part of this conversation. "No, no of course not."

"I just mean…is it okay for me to work here given our history?" I don't know what answer I'm hoping for. Part of me hopes he'll say no. That it would be too hard to be around me and that he'd write me a stellar recommendation to go literally anywhere else, but the other part of me wants this job. I've done my research and this company is just new enough and already wildly successful that getting in early is a very smart decision. It's like getting in on a start-up that is on the verge of really exploding.

"What happened between us was before you worked here. It's okay. It's no one's business."

"Okay," I shake my head. "I won't tell anyone, of course."

"Probably best." He gives me a sad smile. "Beck knows."

"Beck?" I ask, wondering who he means.

"Wes. The CEO. He's been my best friend since college. He knows I slept with someone at Owen's wedding. Not specifically you, of course."

"Oh," I repeat.

He leans forward and twiddles a pen between his fingers. "Yeah, I kind of haven't stopped thinking about you so, yeah he knows."

I blink several times trying to keep the tears at bay again because none of this matters. It doesn't matter that he felt something or that I did or that he can't stop thinking about me.

He's married and that's it.

"Well, I appreciate the opportunity," I say. "And ummm, I'll send in the next person."

"Marissa," he calls as I turn towards the door and when I turn back to face him, he's moving towards me. He grabs my hand and rubs his thumb over my knuckles gently. "Please don't hate me."

"This would be easier if I did," I whisper.

"Fuck, I am *so* sorry." My older sister Autumn sits across from me drinking a cosmopolitan as we eat our favorite sushi from the restaurant near her apartment she shares with her fiancé. I just finished going through the details of my day from hell and I feel like I've just been to war. Autumn knows all the gritty details from my night with Chris. I had broken down and told her after several glasses of wine, even though I'd contemplated not telling her at all because she has only ever slept with one guy and she's currently got his ring on her finger.

"Oh, did I mention my boss also yelled at me?"

She gasps as she holds her drink an inch from her mouth

giving me her signature older sister, *I will kill someone for you* look, followed by *I will find a way to sue him too.* "Wait. He yelled at you too?"

"Oh no. Not him. His boss. The CEO. Wes Beckham? Kind of a dick. A few people warned me and they were *not* kidding." I rub my head in memory of crying in the bathroom after he yelled at me for emailing him the wrong sales report.

On my first day!

I have thick skin so the tears didn't come just because of him, but the day as a whole was awful.

"I can't believe he's married. I say this with all the love in my heart, but I swear I would not survive the dating scene. I don't know how you do it." Autumn shakes her head with a shudder.

"Thanks," I mutter followed by my fakest smile.

"Listen, I've offered several times to hook you up with Eric's friends," she says, referencing her fiancé.

"I'm good," I say, not because I don't like Eric. I do. He would do literally anything in the world for my sister, which he proved when he turned down going to Stanford Law School—his number one choice of school—because my sister got into Yale which was her number one choice.

Yes, they're both lawyers and both fucking insufferable at times.

Eric is okay, but the company he keeps? Fucking awful.

It makes me want to keep one eye on Eric at all times because don't assholes usually travel in packs?

"Fine, but let me know if you change your mind?" She points her chopsticks at me. "I know you're still young, and maybe not thinking about marriage but your mid-twenties will sneak up on you before you know it!"

"Okay, and?"

"And don't you want to be married by thirty?" she asks, her eyes wide. We look almost identical except her hair is lighter and straighter with bangs and her eyes are a lighter brown. But we are the same height and build and bone structure; people oftentimes think we're twins.

"I'm twenty-one, Autumn," I reply, sardonically.

"Just sayin.'" She shrugs before taking a long sip of her drink.

"You're twenty-six and you're not married."

"And mom does not let me forget it." She groans. "I am trying to spare you the drama. I even have it easier because I've been with Eric for forever, but if I'd been single? Jesus, I can hear her now."

I'm the youngest of three with an older brother, Shane, who's a neurosurgeon married to a psychologist with two children. Then my lawyer sister is engaged to another lawyer. And then there's me: single, still living at home, and working in sales. *In a family of overachievers, care to play which of these things is not like the other?*

"Then again," she adds, "you are the favorite. Mom and Dad don't put half as much pressure on you."

Here we go.

According to both Shane and Autumn, I have somehow become the favorite because I have the least amount of pressure on me about anything. I got to pursue whatever I wanted whereas they were only given the choices my parents approved of. My sister wanted to be an art major in undergrad before my parents swiftly nixed that and my brother wanted to study philosophy before my parents told him, *"We think the fuck not."*

I'll give my parents that one because what exactly does someone do with a philosophy degree?

I wince at her words. "I don't think that's the flex you think it is. It means they don't expect me to amount to anything." I tuck some hair behind my ear and try to ignore the gnawing feeling in my gut that my parents think I'm a lost cause.

"No, it means they expect you to amount to whatever you want and in your own time," she corrects. "But that's the beauty of being the baby of the family."

I feel the prickle of annoyance in my nose and scrunch it. "You act like they coddle me."

"You're the only one still on their credit cards."

"I've been out of college for three months!"

"You're also the only one that got a car at sixteen," she combats and I already know she's got a list of these arguments waiting.

"Dad had just become the chairman at his company! Also, he had just finished helping Shane with med school and you with your first year of law school. You and Shane ran Mom and Dad way more bills than I ever did. They already told me they'd help but weren't paying off my student loans."

"Probably because you live at home." She takes a healthy sip of her drink. "But here's another one, you're the only one who got to study in Paris for the summer in high school." I purse my lips together because, okay I'll give her that. Autumn begged our parents to let her go and they told her no. "Face it, you're the favorite. Also, it means they're living with you when the time comes."

I snort. "Good one. Dad is going to live with Shane and Mom will go anywhere Dad goes."

"Fair point," she says with a giggle. "So, what's going to happen with you two?" she says changing the subject.

"With who?"

She furrows her brows and blinks her eyes at me several times in confusion. "You and your hot boss, obviously."

I shift nervously on the barstool, not wanting to get into this. "How do you know he's hot?"

"One I know the kind of man that turns your head, Marissa Lee, and two, I googled."

I sigh. "What do you mean 'what is going to happen?' He's married. That's it. Case closed."

"You think he'll leave her?"

I snort. "Do men ever leave their wives?"

"Sometimes." She shrugs.

"Something tells me the door has closed on him leaving her based on what he said."

"Or maybe he hasn't had the right incentive." She reaches across the table to tap my nose and gives me a dramatic wink.

"I don't want to be any man's incentive to leave his wife."

"So, if he leaves her, you won't give him a chance?"

"We are talking about something that isn't even close to happening! I don't want to even think like it's an option. Besides, I still don't like how he handled everything."

"Hmm you're being a wee bit holier than thou and it's so unlike you." She scrunches her nose. "It's weird."

"He's married, Autumn! Since when are you not a rules girl? You literally went to school for a career that makes people adhere to them."

"Laws yes, but not rules of the heart." She puts a hand over her chest.

"Oh, you're drunk." I snort as I pick up my phone to text my future brother-in-law. "I'm texting Eric."

"No!" She puts her hand over my phone to stop me. "Listen, I've never seen you talk about anyone the way you talked about Chris."

"It was great sex. That's all."

"You liked him."

"I liked his dick," I correct

"*And* him," she retorts.

I cross my arms over my chest and let out a bored sigh. "Okay fine, so what if I did?"

"Oh my gosh, it's like *Scandal*! You guys are like Fitz and Olivia!"

"Okay, first of all, don't start." I groan, thinking about my sister's obsession with that show. "Secondly, they were toxic as hell."

She shrugs. "You still rooted for them."

"I mean, yeah, of course. That was the point. It's also fiction. I would not survive one day as Olivia Pope."

Her eyes widen as she points at me. "And it totally fits! You said his wife was awful."

"I said *he* said that. But what else was he going to say? 'Sorry but I'm madly in love with her, that night was just a lapse in judgment?'" I scoff before taking a sip of my drink.

She sighs and picks up another piece of sushi before swirling it around her soy sauce. "Fine, you're right." She looks at her drink. "And I think you're right, these were stronger than I thought."

I shake my head at her, knowing that she's going to be complaining about her hangover tomorrow when my phone lights up next to me. I stare at it skeptically when I see it's a number I don't recognize.

Definitely not answering that, I think because whatever random number that could be calling me at seven-thirty on a Monday night is someone I don't want to talk to. It stops ringing and I don't see a voicemail notification so I assume it's a spam call. No more than a few moments later, my phone lights up with a text message from the same number.

> **Unknown Number: Hey, it's Chris.**

My mouth drops open and while I'd normally tell my sister, she's clearly in another world right now and would probably suggest sending him nudes. I drop my phone into my lap and type out a reply.

> **Me: Hey, I'm getting dinner with my sister. Did you need something?**

I'm pretty sure he's not calling me regarding anything work related, but I'm going to play dumb for the sake of self-preservation. I do, however, save his number in the meantime.

> **Chris: How is that?**

Small talk? Is he serious?

> **Me: It's fine.**

> **Chris: You tell her about how awful your first day was?**

I narrow my eyes at my screen because I know he's not making light of this clusterfuck.

> **Me: She's aware that I've slept with my boss, yes.**

> **Chris: I feel like shit, you know.**

> **Me: Well, that makes two of us.**

> **Chris: You shouldn't. You didn't know.**

Like that matters! I realize I haven't said anything in a minute and when I look up, I see Autumn on her phone grinning like a woman in love. I look back down just in time to see another message come through.

> **Chris: Can I see you? Outside of work?**

> **Me: You cannot be serious.**

> **Chris: Just have dinner with me. Please.**

"I'm going to the bathroom. I'll be right back," I tell my sister as I get up from the table. I'm barely around the corner before I have the phone to my ear.

"Hey," he answers on the first ring. "I know you're at dinner. I'm sorry—"

"Are you kidding me?"

"No."

"You're married."

"I know."

"And you're asking me out on a date?"

"Yes."

"Chris, can't you see how fucked up this is?"

"Yes," he says sadly and I'll admit I'm impressed that he doesn't say anything else. He doesn't make an excuse. I guess he's got nothing left to do but own it at this point.

"Tell me what makes her so terrible."

He sighs. "Can I tell you over dinner?"

"Aren't you worried about getting caught?"

"We'll go somewhere outside of the city. There are fraternization rules in place, yes, but no one—"

"I meant caught by your *wife*, Chris." I frown, realizing that he cares more about our company finding out about our affair than the woman he's cheating on. I can't ignore the judgment coursing through me over that thought.

"Oh…no. She doesn't care."

I frown and narrow my eyes as I try to figure out what the hell he means by that. "Do you have an open marriage?" Because if that's the case, I still don't want to get involved, but then maybe I can stop feeling like I fucked this poor clueless woman's husband.

"Not exactly."

"You're talking in circles."

"She doesn't care that I sleep with other women."

Other women. Plural. Love that.

"So, there's multiple of us. Just what every woman wants to hear," I reply with all of the sarcasm I can muster in an attempt to mask the underlying hurt.

"As much as it pleases me that I've struck a jealous nerve, I don't want to piss you off any more and I know I'm on thin ice," he says and I'm pissed at myself for reacting to that. "I haven't slept with anyone since I slept with you."

"You mean anyone other than your wife?" I ask weakly, not sure how either answer will make me feel.

"No. I haven't slept with anyone at all since I slept with you. Holly included."

I groan as I put a hand over my eyes. "Please stop saying her name. I am trying not to picture her as a person with feelings and emotions and someone who will get hurt."

He snorts. "Trust me, she does not have feelings."

I lean against the wall in the hallway next to the restrooms. "Answer me. Why did you marry this awful woman? Because I'm having a hard time understanding why you married her in the first place if she's so terrible. And what even makes her so terrible? It makes me feel like you'd say anything. For all I know, she's as sweet as Mother Theresa and you just have a wandering dick."

"That's not it and if you just let me take you to dinner, I'll explain everything." I can hear the begging in his voice.

"Or you could just explain it now."

"Aren't you at dinner with your sister?"

"I can call you when I get home."

He lets out a sigh, "I also want to take you to dinner as an apology. For…that morning."

"It's fine, I'm over it." *Hardly.*

"I'm not," he says simply. "Please. One dinner. I'll expense it if it makes you feel better and we can say it was a business dinner."

I chew nervously on my thumbnail, careful not to ruin my manicure but needing something to distract me momentarily. "Chris…"

"Please."

"What do you think dinner is going to accomplish? Sleeping with me again?"

"No." He pauses. "Well, maybe," he answers honestly, and I'll admit I kind of respect that.

"That's not happening," I say a little harder than I intend to and I'm not sure if it's for his benefit or my own.

"Let me live in my delusion." He chuckles and I bite my lip

to stop the giggle bubbling in my throat. "I respect your boundaries, and I would never do anything you didn't want."

I shake my head even though I know he can't see me. "I'm not worried about that." I never thought for a second, he would force or coerce me to do anything. I'm not worried about him using his power as my boss against me.

"What are you worried about?"

"You charming my dress off again." *Since we are being honest.*

"What if I promise to be a perfect gentleman?" he asks. "Unless of course, you ask me not to."

I scrunch my eyes together. *This is a really bad idea.* "One dinner."

"Yes," he says, like a prayer. "Yes. When?" he asks immediately, like he doesn't want to let me off the phone until I give him a day.

"Maybe Friday?"

"That's too far away."

I need time to get myself together.

"How about tomorrow?" he asks and as much as I want to say yes, I refuse to make it that easy. *Make him sweat.*

"I can't tomorrow," I say, already making a mental note of what reason I can't in case it comes up.

"You really going to torture me until Friday?"

I let out a breath. "Thursday, final offer."

"Okay. Yes. Thursday is great." I can hear the relief in his voice.

"Just dinner and we are only talking," I reiterate.

"Of course."

"I want the truth, Chris. No bullshit."

"None, I promise," he says immediately.

"Okay." I nod, suddenly feeling awkward and unsure how to end the conversation. *Or if I even want to.* "I'll see you tomorrow."

"Tomorrow. Enjoy the rest of your dinner with your sister."

"Thank you. Have a good night." I end the call and make my way into the restaurant to see my sister staring in my direction.

"I was about to come looking for you. Everything okay?"

"Yeah." I nod. I don't want to tell her about dinner with Chris because I know she'll want to talk about it and I'm not even sure how I feel about it yet.

I try to tell myself that it's just a harmless dinner but I hear the unspoken lie loud and clear.

Chapter THREE

CHRIS

I CAN'T EVEN HIDE THE SMILE ON MY FACE AS I TOSS MY phone to the side. *She said yes.* I mean I know I didn't make it easy for her to say no but I half expected her to tell me to fuck off. I stretch my feet out, propping them up on the coffee table in my home office which has become my only place of solitude. There have been weekends when I haven't left this space at all because I didn't want to be bothered. Not only is it my office, where I come to work but there is also a full bar in the corner complete with a refrigerator, sink, and microwave. A flat-screen television is mounted on the wall with a couch and two loungers set in front of it. A pool table is in the corner and there is a full ensuite bathroom nestled in the other corner. I never use the term '*man cave*' exactly, but it is one place Holly rarely bothers me.

Speaking of Holly, is she even home?

I hadn't gotten the alert that anyone had opened the door or the garage since I got home, so it's possible that she's out. I would call her to check on her but that usually causes an argument I am not in the mood for. I think about calling Beck to see if he wants to stop by but it's getting late, and I know he's got a lot to do before he travels to Miami in a few days. I mindlessly flip through the channels, trying to find something to watch but my mind is elsewhere. I am so fucking restless and I've been like this for months. I make my way out of my office, turning off some lights and leaving some on for Holly when she gets home before I decide a workout will relieve some of this tension. I run a few miles on the treadmill and lift for a while before I realize what it is I'm feeling. I'm anxious.

I'm anxious over dinner with Marissa. Nervous excitement pumps through me that the spark between us is fueled by more than just sex. I towel off after spending an hour trying to rid myself of this tension before making my way towards the bedroom where I sleep alone and into my personal bathroom.

The thought of Marissa sharing this bed with me pops into my head reminding me that she's the last person I've shared a bed with. She'd fallen asleep in my arms after she'd sworn she wasn't going to and I chuckled as she snuggled up against me, pushing her face into my chest and nuzzling against it. I'd watched her sleep for I don't know how long, watching the cute little faces she made in her sleep before pressing a gentle kiss to her lips and falling asleep with her in my arms. I turn my head towards the king bed and a mental image of her crawling across it, *naked*, flashes through my mind, and my dick throbs at the visual my brain is concocting.

I head towards the bathroom, discarding my sweaty clothes and tossing them into my laundry basket before turning on the water and preparing to fuck my fist *yet again* at the memory of her.

I step into my walk-in shower with my hand already wrapped around my dick. I pull it once as I picture her coming up behind me, her arms wrapped around my middle as she presses her breasts to my back and drags her lips along my shoulder.

"You know, if you keep doing this and thinking about me it's the only thing that's going to be able to get you off." She moves to stand in front of me and gives me a sassy smile.

"It already is," I think as I picture her hand wrapped around my dick.

"You're torturing yourself."

"I know."

"Why?"

"Fuck, Marissa, give me your mouth baby."

"You don't even know what my mouth feels like."

"We should change that."

"Hmmmm." She taps her chin. "I don't know."

"Am I really arguing with you in my fucking fantasy?"

"Yep, and you're still hard." She giggles. "Do you think I'll give in on Thursday?"

"I don't know." I pull harder on my dick, trying to chase my climax but all of the questions and uncertainties are preventing me from getting there.

"I know you're hoping I do, but what are you going to do if I don't? You certainly can't do this forever." She's looking down at where I'm starting to jack my dick faster.

"Babe. I don't know. I just fucking want you."

Her fingertips move up my chest before they're on my face and when I open my eyes, I can see her face clear as day giving me a solemn look. "I want you too but you're not mine to have."

I don't even know how to respond to that in a fantasy because she's right.

"Maybe you need to figure out what you want and what exactly is possible for you and me before you take me out." She cocks her head to the side and gives me that sexy smile that I've thought about no less than twice an hour since the first time I laid eyes on her.

"You're right."

"I know," she sasses before she lowers herself to her knees in front of me.

"Oh fuuuuuck." I groan as I think about her lips wrapped

around my dick. I jack myself harder, rubbing myself from root to tip.

"It's a shame you didn't get to come down my throat before." She flutters those long eyelashes at me. "You can do it now."

"Fuck yes, let me."

She swipes her tongue across the tip sexily like she did briefly that night and it's an image that plays through my mind on a loop. I want to see her do it again and again and fucking again, preferably right before she sucks me between those pink lips.

"If I ever get you in a bed again, I'm not letting you out until we do everything."

She strokes her tongue up the underside of my shaft. "Everything?" Her eyes are wide and unblinking before a wicked smirk finds her lips. "Sounds like you want to put your dick in my ass."

"Fuuuuuck." I groan, my balls tighten, and my release shoots out of me. My eyes slam shut and I slap one hand against the shower wall for balance as I come all over the floor wishing like fuck it was going inside Marissa Collins' mouth.

The week goes by as quickly as I hoped. I hardly see Marissa because she's busy doing new hire work, and with Beck out of town, I have more on my plate than usual. We have a few casual texting conversations during the evenings but other than that we barely speak.

It's finally Thursday night and I'm meeting Marissa at a restaurant forty minutes away where I've already reserved a private room for us to be alone. She insisted on driving herself there, but I already have a car on standby to take her home and also someone to drive her car should she have too much to drink. I'm standing outside of the restaurant, waiting for her when she appears from around the corner, and I swear my heart almost stops. A few strands of her dark hair are pinned back again, reminiscent of that first night we were together allowing me to see all of her face. She's wearing a sleeveless mid-length black dress with a slit that goes up to mid-thigh exposing her smooth toned legs. The dress looks like it's painted on her, with a hint of cleavage and shows off her delicious curves that I'm desperate to kiss again. She somehow manages to look both classy and sexy, and the smile on her burgundy-painted lips when she approaches me, lets me know that I am not doing a good job of hiding what I think of her dress.

"Just dinner?" I ask her and she scrunches her nose as she looks down.

"What? It's a nice restaurant," she says innocently.

"That is not a *it's a nice restaurant* dress. It's an *I want to torment a man* dress, and you know it." She looks a little guilty and I wrap an arm around her waist squeezing her gently. "I like it. I welcome the torment. You look…stunning." I want to run down a list of synonyms because one word doesn't seem like enough to describe her.

Inside, I've barely uttered my last name to the hostess before we are being escorted back to our room. The restaurant is massive with tiny lights hanging from the ceiling and the sounds of live jazz bouncing off the walls. We walk down a long dark hallway with only candlelit lanterns lining the walls, my hand resting against Marissa's back as I follow her. We pass three doors before the hostess pushes one of them open and gives us a smile. "Mr. Holt, Miss Collins, here is your private room. Someone will be with you shortly. I'm Anna, please let me know if there's anything I can do for you while you're dining with us," she says with a polite smile as she ushers us inside.

I hear a tiny gasp next to me and I take that to mean Marissa likes the room. I asked for this one specifically because it is the biggest and has the best view. The room has only one table at its center; a rich mahogany one, clearly meant for ten to twelve people. The carpet is the color of rich burgundy with traces of gold illuminated by the chandelier hanging from the ceiling. There's one entire wall of windows and one is open letting the September air move into the space. It is still on the warmer side of the month where the nights are comfortable until closer to midnight when the air finally ticks below seventy degrees.

I am pleased that the restaurant followed my instructions as I note the three dozen red roses in crystal vases placed on the table and the small card in front of them with Marissa's name on it. She picks it up as I move towards the small bar cart in the corner to pop the bottle of champagne that's chilling in a bucket of ice.

"Thank you for dinner. This is already the best night I've had in months," she reads aloud what I had them write on the card. "These are beautiful," she says just as I pop the cork and begin pouring both of us a glass of champagne. I move towards her and hold one out for her.

"Believe me when I say this, they do not hold a candle to you."

She takes one of the flutes before sipping the champagne. "You're really pulling out all the stops, huh? I thought you said you were going to be a perfect gentleman." She raises an eyebrow at me and purses her lips.

My dick throbs. I resist the urge to groan at the fact that now even her sassy attitude is a turn-on. "I am."

"No, you're being romantic." Her eyes dart around the massive room. "A private room with roses and champagne?"

"All seem like gentlemanly behaviors." I reach for one of her hands and spin her around slowly. "Besides, you're wearing a dress that calls to my very ungentlemanly side."

She slides her hand out of mine and gives me a mild scolding look. "You promised."

"But you wore this to tempt me." I let my eyes rove slowly down her body and then back up even slower, in a way that there is zero mistake as to what I'm thinking. She doesn't say anything, so I take a step closer to her and I'm pleased when she doesn't retreat. "You want to know what I think?" I'm standing as close as

I can without touching her. "I think you want me to break. You want me to push us towards something you can't admit you want." She swallows nervously and I'm pretty sure she's not breathing. "Breathe," I whisper and she shakes her head like she doesn't trust herself to inhale or exhale while standing this close to me. I look down and from where I'm standing, I get the best view of the tops of her breasts.

I finally take a step back allowing her to take a breath.

"This hardly seems fair."

"Did you think I was going to be?" I raise an eyebrow at her and a scowl crosses her gorgeous face before she sits down at the table and I take a seat diagonal from her. "What do you want to know?"

"Everything."

"Everything, huh? Can you be more specific?" I take a long sip of my champagne, already wishing I had something stronger for this conversation.

She looks away from me for a moment and closes her eyes before taking a deep breath and turning back to me. "Why doesn't she care that you sleep with other women?" I don't say anything and the silence must be unnerving to her because she continues. "I would care. I couldn't…be with someone who I had to share with other people. Explain to me how she can?"

"She doesn't love me." I shrug simply because it took quite a long time and more time than I care to admit with my therapist to come to that conclusion.

"I don't believe that. Who wouldn't love you?" Her mouth drops open. "I mean, if they knew you well enough to marry you." I don't even stop the smile from crossing my lips at her slip. "Ugh," she scoffs though I see a hint of a smile pulling at her lips. "Don't be annoying."

"Right." I smile, knowing that I'll be riding the high of her essentially calling me lovable for weeks. "She loves the money."

She'd been leaning forward but now she sits back, resting

against the back of the chair like she wasn't expecting my answer. "Oh."

"I met her…before *Beckham Securities* was even a thing." I stare off into space. "When Wes and I were just two kids with a dream." I chuckle before turning to look at her. "There isn't a prenuptial agreement."

"I see," she whispers.

"One night after a particularly bad argument, I stormed out and went to a bar and slept with a woman. I felt so guilty, I confessed and she basically told me she wasn't going to leave me and if she ever did, she was taking half of everything." My lips form a straight line. "That was three years, and in the spirit of being transparent, several hundred million dollars ago."

"So, you're just going to stay with her forever?"

I sigh at the question that Beck has asked me several times and my mother has asked me even more. I have two older sisters, both of whom are married with kids, but my mother wants more grandchildren and she knows I won't be having any with Holly at this point. I stand up and walk towards the window pushing my hands into my pockets. "I think that was the plan." I turn around and I see her looking at me like a child who just learned that Santa Claus isn't real. Like the idea of living in a loveless marriage for the rest of my life is unfathomable and the saddest thing she's ever heard.

"Forever?"

"I was waiting to hit a breaking point I guess."

"Wow."

"I think I hit it," I tell her and she tilts her head to the side in question. "About three months ago." I move back towards the table and take a seat, dragging it closer to her so I can grab her hand. "I know it's not right of me to ask you for a chance, but I have to ask you. If I wasn't married, would I have one? Or was that night just…was it just sex for you?"

At that moment, the door opens and a tall slender woman

with shiny dark hair walks in. "Mr. Holt, how lovely for you to be joining us this evening. Have you had a chance to look at our wine or cocktail selections?" I notice immediately that she's only acknowledged me. I'm also aware that her top button is undone and her chestnut hair flows around her shoulders when I know they are required to keep it up and out of their face. *I assume this is all for my benefit then.*

I flit my eyes towards Marissa and she meets my eyes with an amused expression.

"I'll have a Macallan eighteen neat." I reach for Marissa's hand and drag my thumb across her knuckles before dragging them across my lips. "Babe?"

She looks at where our hands are joined and she meets my gaze as I continue kissing each of her knuckles before shooting her a wink. "Manhattan, please," she says, her eyes still on mine. I don't know how long we stare at each other when I hear the faint sound of the door closing. "Babe?" she asks and I see the playful glint in her eye that makes me think she liked the show I put on for the woman who may or may not be interested in me.

"I didn't want her to think I was available." My hand is still wrapped around hers and I hope she doesn't make a move to pull out of my grasp.

"Well, you're not available," she says, looking disappointed.

"I am for *you.*"

"Not…exactly." She sighs. "Fine, your wife doesn't care. *I* do. I can't share the man I'm seeing. I don't work like that."

"You would not be sharing me…I don't…we don't…"

"It's so much more than just sex, Chris." She stands up effectively removing her hand and I already miss the feeling of it wrapped in mine. "Don't act like you don't understand what I'm talking about."

"I do. Marissa, sit down please."

She crosses her arms and takes a step back. "This is not a good idea. Getting sucked into this with you." She presses a finger to the corner of her eye and scrunches her nose and I hate that it looks like she's about to cry. "I'm just going to get hurt."

I'm out of my seat instantly and have her in my arms. "I wouldn't hurt you."

"You don't have any plans to leave her. I don't see how you could avoid hurting me because what happens? I just become your mistress…forever?" She scrunches her nose. "I don't like that word."

I rest a finger under her chin and tilt it up gently to look at me. "You'd be more than that. You'd be everything. I'd take care of you."

She scoffs, pulling away and taking a step back. "I don't need to be taken care of, Chris, and you say I'd be more…but until what? Someone better comes along?"

"Not possible."

"What happens when I want to get married or have a baby?" She opens her hands when I don't respond. "Right. No answer to that?" She shakes her head and lets her eyes flutter shut. "Yeah, it's better that we just stop this now before either of us gets in too deep."

"Too late," I murmur.

"We had drunken sex once, three months ago. I think you will be fine getting over me."

"That hasn't worked out well so far." Her brown eyes are shining with unshed tears but she blinks them away before any can fall. "Tell me you didn't feel anything."

"What?"

"You heard me. This is my second time asking. When we slept together, was it just sex for you?"

"It doesn't matter, Chris."

"The hell it doesn't."

"It doesn't matter what I want or what I feel because you're married! You are not an option for me!" Her voice rises slightly before she takes a deep breath and puts a hand over her eyes.

"What if I leave her?" The words are out of my mouth before

I can stop them and she drops her hand and stares at me with wide nervous eyes.

"I...I don't want you to leave her for me."

"Who else would I be leaving her for?"

"You," she says. "If you leave her for me, you go through what sounds like would be a very expensive and difficult and tedious divorce proceeding and then say things between us don't work out? I don't want you to resent me for blowing up your life and then I'm not even there when the dust settles."

"I'd hope you'd stick around and be there."

"I'm not saying I wouldn't but we hardly know each other, Chris. It's possible that our night of amazing sex won't translate to an amazing relationship."

I move towards her and I'm relieved that she doesn't move away before I can wrap her in my arms. "We could get to know each other." The door opens and in walks a different server and it's not lost on me that it's a man this time. He sets our drinks on the table before giving us both a curt nod and he leaves without another word. "How about we not label or define anything?" I suggest. "We just...get to know each other?"

"You're married," she whispers and sighs like she's tired of saying it. She sits down and takes a sip of her drink before turning back to me. "When did things start to go south?" she asks and I'm taking it as a good sign that she didn't flat-out tell me no.

"Two years in was when it got really bad but I can remember things as early as two months into our marriage."

"Does she want kids?"

I shake my head because even if she wanted them, she was not getting them from me. "Her and I having kids is off the table."

"Do you want kids?"

"Yeah." I nod. "With the right woman." I'm well aware that she's twenty-one and I'm thirty-four so she's probably not thinking about them tomorrow but she mentioned them earlier.

"You don't sleep with her?"

"We don't even sleep in the same bedroom," I tell her. "I sleep in a different room and more often than not in my office."

"If you...had a girlfriend...any girlfriend. Not. Me. Specifically," she says, annunciating each word. "Would you even be able to stay the night with her?

A smile spreads across my face at the thought of falling asleep with her in my arms again. "Any night she wanted me to."

"Well, I live at home with my parents, so it's a moot point."

"We could change that."

"What?"

"We could go look for an apartment for you."

"Chris, be serious. I'm not getting an apartment just for you to have a place to screw your girlfriend."

The harshness of her words slides over me and I wish it didn't sound so ugly. "No, but if it will make you happier and allow this potential boyfriend," *not necessarily me but I hope to God it would be,* "to stay the night..." I trail off and she starts to protest but I hold a hand up. "I get that maybe that's too much too fast. For now, maybe this woman and I would just go to my penthouse in the city." I don't suggest the idea of her staying there on a semi-permanent basis, but I wouldn't hate the idea of it.

She narrows her eyes at me. "So, what is that, like...a fuckpad?" she says, looking thoroughly unamused by the thought.

"I do not call it that." I wince.

"But you take women there."

"I have," I tell her honestly. "I'm not denying that I have a past, or that I'm married, or that I haven't always treated women the way they deserve." She asked for no bullshit and something tells me that Marissa will only respond to explicit honesty. "I'm telling you that you've been on my mind nonstop for three months. I haven't so much as looked at another woman because you're all I can think about. I know I fucked up by just leaving you that morning, but believe it or not, I was just trying to do the right thing. I was trying to avoid all of this because I know it's messy and I'm complicated, but now you've walked back into my life and I really don't want to let you go a second time."

She doesn't say anything and I wonder if she's just letting what I said sink in. Her eyes dart around the room, before landing on the thirty-six long-stemmed roses sitting on the table before turning her gaze back to me. "I really hope you're not lying to me." Her voice is sad and I wonder if it's just this situation in particular or if there's something in her past that may make her unable to trust me.

I reach for her hand again and give it a gentle squeeze. "I'm sorry that I've given you a reason to think that I would."

She bites her bottom lip and takes another sip of her drink. "I'm not saying yes."

"Okay."

"Or no." Hope flares in my veins and I nod with a smile on my lips. "Have you ever done this?" I shake my head because while I've had casual sex it never went further.

"I'd say this is the first date I've been on that wasn't with her in almost a decade."

She nods towards the flowers. "Three dozen roses is a little overkill."

I detect a hint of flirtation in her voice. "I wanted to make a good impression."

"I see that." She picks up the card again, dragging her fingers over the edges of it before sliding it into her purse.

"How'd I do?"

"I'm not sure yet," she says before she shrugs. "But the night is still young."

Chapter FOUR

Marissa

I HAVEN'T BEEN ON A TON OF FIRST DATES IN MY LIFE. I have only ever dated one guy seriously and we were together for my first three years of college. Since then, I wouldn't necessarily say I've dated so much as I've met guys for a drink or at a party and then waited to see where the night took us. But of all the dates I've been on, Chris shot all of them out of the water. From one date, I could see he only knew how to do things one way and that was 'the best.'

We are standing in front of the restaurant when a black BMW with tinted windows slows to a stop in front of us.

"I have a car to take you home."

"I drove here," I tell him, blinking at him several times.

"And you had a Manhattan and a glass of champagne."

I sigh. "Right. You have seen how much I can drink though. You can't possibly think those two drinks over the span of four hours could possibly affect my ability to drive home."

"Humor me. I know you won't let me take you home, but at least let me make sure you get home safely."

"What about my car?"

"It'll be there shortly after you."

"Chris—"

He slides his hands into his pockets and I make yet another mental note of how good he looks. *He really knew how to wear the hell out of a suit.* "Don't give me a hard time, alright? You said you wanted a gentleman. This is me on my best behavior."

"What if I wanted to see you *not* on your best behavior?" I tease and though his eyes darken and drag down my body, he shakes his head and opens the back door of the car. I'll admit I'm impressed by his restraint.

After our conversation, he surprisingly kept things pretty PG at dinner. He held my hand a few times and there was one brush of his knuckles down my face that had me almost melting into a puddle, but he didn't push for more. If I'd had another drink, I may have but I'd put boundaries in place and he respected them.

And dammit, if that didn't make me want him more.

He shakes his head slowly, with a smug grin on his face like he's enjoying this. "You said only dinner."

"Fine." I move to stand in front of the open door and a part of me hopes he'll attempt to kiss me.

"I'll see you tomorrow."

"Right. Yes." I nod but don't get in the car. *Smooth, Marissa.*

He looks towards the backseat and then back at me. "Is there…something else?" he asks with a knowing smirk and I hate that I'm being so obvious.

"Nope," I say before I tap his nose gently. "Thanks for dinner."

"Pleasure was all mine," he says as I slide in and he closes the door behind me. He taps the window gently with one knuckle and when I roll it down, he leans down so we're at eye level. "So, when can I see you again?"

I look at the driver and a part of me wonders if he knows

that Chris is married and that I am most definitely not his wife. I wonder if he's the loyal driver who knows where all the bodies are buried. I turn back to Chris and flash him my most flirty smile, just as I send the window back up. "Tomorrow at work, obviously," I say just before it hits the top.

I've only been home about twenty minutes when my phone lights up with a message.

> **Chris: Thank you for tonight. Did you make it home?**

You know I did. I giggle to myself thinking about the fact that his driver probably had strict instructions to let him know the second I was through my door. My car arrived a few minutes later.

> **Me: You don't know the answer to that?**

> **Chris: You give me a lot of shit, you know that?**

> **Me: Yep, and I'm not sorry.**

> **Chris: Good. It makes my dick hard.**

I gasp and almost drop my phone because *did I read that correctly*? I pick up my phone and scan the word again and I don't miss the way my nipples tingle at the salacious words.

> **Chris: I only promised to be a gentleman at dinner. Now, that dinner is over, I can tell you that I wanted to fuck you all over every inch of that private room.**

> **Me: Is that why you requested one?**

> **Chris: No. I requested one because I wanted privacy for the**

conversation we were going to have. I wanted you to be free to yell at me if you wanted to.

Me: What a shame I didn't capitalize.

Chris: You will have plenty of chances to yell at me.

Me: You sound awfully sure of yourself.

Chris: Says the woman that was begging me to kiss her with her eyes before she left.

Me: I was not!

Chris: You definitely were and it took everything out of me not to climb into that car with you and kiss you for the entire drive to your house.

Me: I may have let you.

Chris: Now you tell me this

I drop my phone on my bed and head into the bathroom and when I return to my room, I see I have a missed call from Chris. I go to call him back when I see the bubbles indicating that he's typing and I decide to wait and see what he's going to say.

Chris: I don't know if you fell asleep, but what are the chances that you'll go out with me again on Saturday?

I press the number to call him and he answers after only two rings. "Want to take me out again, huh?" I'm sure he can hear the smile in my voice but at the moment, I don't care. I haven't even taken my makeup off from the date we'd just been on and he's calling to take me out again. *Gotta love a man that's consistent.*

"Yes."

"What did you have in mind?"

I half expect him to say something along the lines of a repeat of Alexis and Owen's wedding. "Well, I was thinking we'd go to New York."

"On Saturday?" *I love New York. It's one of my favorite cities and I love being so close to it.* Growing up only an hour train ride away, we spent more weekends than not discovering all the places to go. Even when it was probably way too dangerous to go with just a handful of your other barely legal friends.

"Actually, I was thinking we would leave tomorrow night."

"Uh huh. Is that so?"

He chuckles. "I'll get you your own room at the hotel."

"I see and when would we come back?"

"Sunday."

"So, you want the whole weekend? Not *just* a date on Saturday," I correct.

"We could leave Saturday night if you want, it might just be late after the show."

"Show?"

"Yes, I was thinking we could see a show if you wanted. *Beckham Securities* has a box and we can see pretty much anything we want. We just have to let them know a few days in advance if we won't be using it, but we typically use them." He laughs. "If no one in the office wants to use the box, we offer it to clients."

I remember them mentioning taking future and existing clients to shows but I hadn't realized they had tickets all the time. "Okay, what show is it?"

"Have you seen *Hamilton* yet?"

My eyes widen and my mouth drops open in shock. "Are you kidding me?! No, I haven't seen it. Tickets have been sold out for what…a year!?"

He chuckles. "So, I'll take that as a yes to another date then."

I would have said yes to a picnic in Central Park but HAMILTON!?

"Yes definitely, sounds great," I tell him as I practically jump off my bed and run to my walk-in closet to try to decide what to wear.

"So, you're okay with leaving tomorrow night? We can leave Saturday if you prefer."

"And what's the plan for tomorrow?"

"Well, I was thinking we could have dinner."

I drag a hanger across the rack nixing dress after dress. "Okay, what time should I be ready?"

"Can I pick you up?"

I think about how vague I can be when I tell my parents I'm going to New York for the weekend without having to lie to them. I hate lying to them, probably because I've never really had to. But I really don't want a bunch of questions if they figure out I'm crossing state lines to spend the weekend with a man that they've never heard me speak of. "I suppose," I say. "Just…don't get out of the car."

"You embarrassed of me or something?" he jokes.

"I would prefer not to explain who the gorgeous older man is that's picking me up for a weekend in another state if you don't mind?"

"Would your parents have a problem with my age?"

"No. They'll have a problem with your marital status though."

"Fair."

"My parents are…" I squint my eyes because my parents are very hard to explain. Very smart, opinionated, a little judgmental, and it takes a while for them to warm up to you. But when they do, they're loyal as hell and they'll go to war for you like you are family. "They'll just have a lot of questions and my mom will want to have you over for dinner and know all about your family and…"

"I can come over for dinner. It's been a while since anyone's cooked for me."

WHAT? "I am not ready for that."

"I'm kidding. I get it. I won't get out of the car."

"Okay, what time?"

"How's six? It will give us time to get to the city and get settled before dinner."

"Are we taking the train?"

"No, I want as much time alone with you as possible. I'm going to drive."

Fuck. I mouth thinking about being in an enclosed space with Chris for almost two hours. I squeeze my eyes shut and send up a silent prayer that the ride won't end up feeling like foreplay.

At least, he'll have to focus on the road.

"Where are you going, young lady?" My mother peeks her head out of her office as I roll my carry-on suitcase towards the door. She pushes her glasses down on her nose and gives me a look similar to the ones she'd give me as a teenager when I was off to get into trouble. "Overnight it seems?"

"Yeah, it's a work thing." I nod, knowing that the fewer details I give the better. I'll admit, Shane and Autumn were right in some ways. I definitely have always gotten away with more. In my early teens, I could sleep over at any of my friend's houses without a ton of pushback. I had a later curfew and I rarely got grounded for breaking it. *Which I did often.*

By the time I was eighteen, my parents were ready to be empty nesters and spent most of that year traveling around Europe then Africa and then Asia. I threw *so* many parties that year. Even now, my parents treat me like I'm just a third roommate who just happens to not pay any bills and have made zero comments about me needing to move anytime soon. Shane and Autumn had three months to get their lives together before they were pushed out the door.

Maybe I am the favorite?

"On a weekend?" She crosses her arms as if to say *yeah right*. "Don't lie to me."

"It's for team building. All the new hires were invited. We are even going to see *Hamilton*."

Her mouth drops open and she puts a hand over her chest. "You're kiddin'! Your Dad and I saw it in its first run. Fabulous." She claps. "I thought tickets were sold out?"

"*Beckham Securities* has a box."

"Okay, fancy!" She pushes her glasses into her hair before making her way towards me. "What are you wearing?"

"No clue." I sigh. "There's like four different dresses in here. I guess, I just have to see what everyone's wearing." *Or whichever one makes Chris lose his mind.*

She nods in understanding before running her fingers through my hair. "What about your hair?"

"What about it?" I run my fingers through the curls and hold a few strands under my nose. "I just washed it today."

"Oh, that's why." She nods before she scrunches her nose. "You know your hair always looks better on day two."

"Thanks." Sarcasm drips from my voice as I follow her to the kitchen.

"You have time to eat before you go?"

"Oh, I'm going to eat in New York. There's a dinner!" I say. *At least, I haven't had to lie too much.*

"Okay. Well, when will you be back? Sunday?"

"Yep." I grab a bottle of water from the fridge. "I'm getting picked up in about twenty minutes," I say as nonchalantly as possible so that maybe she'll think it's just an Uber.

"Okay, well make good choices. Have fun. Be careful. Take pictures. Let us know when you get there, please. Are you taking the train?" she says all in one breath.

"No…we're driving."

"Driving." She scrunches her nose again. "Why?"

Fuck, I should have said the train. "They just thought it would be fun."

She narrows her eyes. "Driving…into the city…on a Friday night…? Who in the world thought *that* would be fun?"

"Mom, it'll be fine."

"It just seems silly when the train is an option and you can have a drink." My parents have become the life of the party in their older age and have the mindset of nineteen-year-olds where every activity requires a pregame.

"Again, I'm going for work and I'm new. I'm not planning to be hammered the whole weekend."

She shrugs. "Well, your father and I are going bowling. Did you know on Friday nights it's Cosmic Bowling!?"

"Yes, mother, I know."

"Ah, it feels like my youth. Bowling and cheap pitchers of beer."

"Mom, you don't even drink beer." I chuckle.

"I know," she scrunches her nose. "Maybe I'll just bring a bottle of Pinot Grige with me. Oh! Can I borrow your green *Gucci* bag since it's neon? I feel like it will go with the vibe I'm going for." She swings her hips from side to side and I roll my eyes before letting out a chuckle.

"To go get drunk with teenagers at Cosmic Bowling?" I blink at her before I relent because to be fair, she did buy it for me. "Sure, let me go get it." I chuckle as I head up the stairs.

I'm just grabbing it from my closet when I hear my mother. "Whose Maserati is this outside? If your father bought one, I'll kill him! He was supposed to take me when he went to look at them!"

My heart plummets as I look at the watch on my wrist. FUCK! I almost stumble over my feet as I hear the front door open and then steps retreating. *No no no no no!*

"Mom, wait!" I say as I fly down the two flights of stairs to the main floor just in time to see my mother approach the car not in our driveway but sitting in front of our house.

"God, I know you are not really on my side about the whole married man thing, but PLEASE, cut me some slack," I whisper as I cross my fingers and look up. I drop the bag on the credenza in the foyer before grabbing my suitcase and purse and begin rolling it out the front door towards my mother who is already walking around the car to the driver's side.

"Fuuuuck me," I mutter under my breath. "Mom!"

The door opens and I watch as Chris steps out looking like pure sex. Dressed casually in jeans and a Henley with sunglasses in front of his gorgeous eyes, he towers over my mother's tiny frame. I watch as she lowers her glasses and sizes him up slowly before she turns her head even slower to look at me over her frames with a raised eyebrow.

I give her my best smile like everything's normal and nothing out of the ordinary about an older man that looks like *that* picking me up. I point behind me towards our house. "I left the bag for you."

"Hello there," Chris says as he holds a hand out. "It's so nice to meet you, I'm Chris. You must be Marissa's older sister." He flashes that grin at her and twenty-one years of knowing Kimberly Holt shows me that my mother is already on board.

My mother giggles in that way she does when she's flattered. "Oh, you're trouble." She points at him before she shakes his hand. "Marissa's mother."

"Impossible," he retorts and I roll my eyes, even if I'm slightly impressed at how quickly he's winning my mother over.

"Yes, well I was ten when I had her," she says as she waves him off and she makes her way back towards me. He follows behind her and grabs my suitcase from me, smiling at me like he knows he's probably in trouble for this but it was all worth it.

"Chris works at *Beckham Securities* also," I say because I don't want my mother to think I lied right to her face.

She looks me up and down once before leaning in to kiss me on my cheek. "Mmmhmmm. Well, you two kids have fun," she whispers in my ear. "Wear the shortest dress."

"Mom!" I whisper.

"Phew, if I was just a few years younger."

"I'll be sure to tell your husband that." I roll my eyes at her.

"Snitch," she says back to me before she waves at Chris who's standing in front of the passenger's side open door. "Take care of my child, please!"

"Yes ma'am." He nods and I watch her scurry back into the house. I wouldn't be surprised if she was on the phone with my aunt before Chris is even back in the car.

I'm still rubbing my forehead when he's back in the car and I slowly turn my gaze towards him and stare through narrowed slits.

"What did you want me to do!?" He laughs.

"Park down the block!?"

"And what? Have you walk? No, Marissa." He snorts and I note we aren't moving.

"Can we go? Before my mom starts running your plates and figures out your whole life story? As is, she's probably already running a background check."

He props his elbow on the console between us and pulls his sunglasses off so I can see those blue eyes. "Can I have a kiss first?"

I blink away from him because I think if I stare into them too long, they could convince me to do anything. "No."

"I can sit here all day, you know."

I cross my arms and shoot him a look, half annoyed and half amused. "You really want the first time we kiss again to be out of manipulation?"

"Ah, so you admit there will be another kiss?" I scowl but I can feel the smile trying to force its way through. He shifts the car out of park and pulls away from the house. "That's enough for now." He makes it to the end of our street and I let out a sigh of relief because at least my dad wasn't home.

We're an hour into the ride when we hit the first bit of traffic. We'd been listening to music for the most part, the silence comfortable and sensual as the sounds of a pretty decent playlist plays through his speakers.

Al Green, Adele, Bruno Mars, The Beatles, Stevie Wonder.

And he's got taste in music.

He turns down the music as the red brake lights get closer. "So, is your mom a cop?"

"Huh?" I ask.

"You said she'd be running my plates. Is she a cop?"

"Oh. No. She's a retired college professor."

"Very cool. What subject?"

"Sociology. She was a social worker but she stopped after she had my older brother and decided to teach a few years after she had me." I pause. "But my dad's a retired judge. So, yeah, she has access." I laugh.

He whistles. "Intense."

"Yes. I'm glad he wasn't home. You may want to drop me off around the corner on Sunday unless they're out somewhere."

He nods, though something tells me he's not in agreement with doing that. "Your mom seems fun."

"The life of the party."

"I like that. My mom is far from that." He laughs.

"What's she like?"

"Quiet. Very quiet. She didn't used to be but…losing my Dad hit her hard."

"Oh." I frown, thinking about losing one of my parents. "I'm really sorry. How long has it been?"

He narrows his eyes like he's trying to count. "Maybe thirteen years now?" He whistles again. "Damn, doesn't seem like it's been that long. I was a junior in college, so yeah, that's about right."

Younger than I am now. I frown, my heart breaking for him

because I couldn't imagine not having either of my parents. "You were so young. I'm sorry." My frown deepens. "Has she not remarried?"

"Nope." He shakes his head. "I think she might be seeing someone now though. I don't know the details; I only know that there's been a new guy sniffing around. She still lives in Michigan where I'm from and I think my sisters are keeping me out of the loop on purpose because they don't want me to come to town and scare him off."

"Would you?" I ask, tilting my head to the side. "Scare him off?"

"No, but I don't want some asshole taking advantage of my mother."

I eye him curiously. "And your sisters wouldn't make sure that doesn't happen?"

"Not the same way I would," he says. "My sisters are...too sweet. They have no bite to them."

"Ah." I giggle, thinking about Chris' assistant saying that he also had no bite.

"I know I'm supposedly the nice one at the office, especially compared to Beck, but that's work. I can be ruthless when it comes to my family. I guess it came with being the only man once my dad died." I nod, though a nagging feeling flashes through me, reminding me that he has another family. "Or anyone I care about," he adds and when I turn to look at him, I can sense his gaze on me.

I'm glad I'm wearing a maxi dress under a denim jacket because goosebumps arise everywhere. The last of the sun is starting to set so he pulls his sunglasses off.

"Are your sisters younger? Older?" I ask, not trying to go down the road of unpacking what he meant or if he was implying that he cares about me.

"One older, one younger. I know you have an older sister, but is that all?"

"An older brother also," I tell him.

"Fuck, and you're the baby. I'm screwed." He chuckles as he changes lanes with ease and I hate how fucking hot he looks maneuvering this very sexy car through the traffic. "Tell me about your brother. How can I win him over?"

"Why? It's not like you're going to meet him."

"Why wouldn't I?"

"Chris…this is all very cute in an *'I'm probably going to hell for this'* kind of way, but I'm not about to drag my family into… whatever this is."

"I mean eventually I'll have to meet them?"

"How do you figure?"

"I don't see you as someone who wouldn't want your family at your wedding."

"Who said I was marrying you?!" I squeal probably about three octaves too high.

He shoots me a wolfish grin before he runs his eyes over me so sexily that I look down to make sure I'm not accidentally flashing him or something. "Me."

My eyes move back to his and I blink at him several times in confusion. "You're married."

"So, you're not okay with being someone's second wife? That could be a problem."

My stomach twists with nerves and excitement and confusion and I wish I was not in the small confines of his car because I want to text Autumn right the fuck now.

"You're insane," I say finally, before turning my head to look out the window.

His hand on mine, and his thumb rubbing over my knuckles drags my attention to where they are connected. "I know I'm complicated and asking a lot of you, but give me time to be worthy of you, please."

I grit my teeth, wanting to say something smart, but go for honesty instead. "I'm here, aren't I?" *Okay, that was smart.*

He chuckles and then my fingers are being brushed across his mouth. "Yes, thank you."

We pull up to *The Plaza* Hotel and while I assumed we'd be staying somewhere nice, I was not expecting one of the most expensive hotels in the city. He pulls into the valet spot and someone is already opening my door before the car is fully in park. "Mr. Holt." I hear from behind me and there's a man in front of me, handing me a glass of champagne.

"Miss." The young man says with a boyish smile. "Welcome."

"Thank you," I say as I lift the flute from the tray with a nervous smile.

Chris comes around the car, two people following behind him with our luggage. "You ready?" He pulls the other flute off the tray as he nods at the guy and shakes his hand more than likely giving him money. He guides me up the stairs and through the revolving door before we make it into the massive lobby which is exactly what I pictured and still I'm in awe. It screams wealth and glamor and prestige, and while I grew up very comfortably, this is another lifestyle entirely.

He guides me towards the elevator and I eye him curiously. "We don't have to check in?"

"They gave me the keys at the valet." He hands me my own keycard. "Should I drop you off at your room first?"

"You…got me my own room?"

"I said I would."

"I know but…" I trail off just as the doors open and he guides me in with his hand on my back.

As soon as we are inside, flashes of the last time we were in an elevator together come rushing back and I can tell a noticeable difference in my breathing. "But what?" I hear next to me and when I turn my face, he is standing very close to me, looking down at me with a smirk on his full lips, and I wonder if he's thinking the same thing I am.

"I guess I figured you'd tell me there was some kind of mix up and they only had one room for us." I roll my eyes and he chuckles as the elevator dings on one of the penthouse floors.

"With the kind of money *Beckham Securities* spends here, they know better than to come to me with a mix-up."

I'm grateful he's behind me and doesn't catch the flush of lust that heats my face in response. *Why is that so hot?*

He leads me towards a door. "Here you are."

"Where…are…you?" I ask, not sure I even want to know the answer. I'm trying to sound nonchalant but I wonder if I come off *very* chalant.

He nods one door down. "Want to see my room too?"

You know you're going to sleep with him again. If you weren't, what exactly was the point of yesterday's wax?

Okay yes, but make him work for it.

Harder than he already has?

Yes.

I shake my head as I press my key against the reader. "Just curious."

He follows me inside but keeps a respectable distance and I'm shocked to see my bag already inside. "How…?" I point at my luggage in shock because how did it get here so fast?

"Magic," Chris says as he holds his hands out, wiggling his fingers. "We are cutting it a little close for dinner. I'm going to push the reservations unless you think you can be ready in thirty minutes?"

Uh. NO?

"Yes…umm…I can be," I say weakly, not even believing the words as they leave my lips.

"I'll push them." He chuckles before he heads towards the door. "I meant to tell you earlier. You look beautiful." He smiles and then he's out the door.

Chapter FIVE

CHRIS

I CAN'T EVEN HIDE THE GRIN WHEN THE DOOR CLICKS behind me.

Okay, this is going well.

I'll admit, I thought I'd shot everything to hell when I pulled up to her house and her mom practically skipped outside, probably assuming I was someone else. Marissa knew I was coming and I was only a few minutes early, and I figured no one was home or she would have actually pushed for me to meet her around the corner. *But even that went well.*

I walk into my room and reach for my weekender that's sitting in the foyer along with my laptop case. Unfortunately, I do have to do some work tomorrow, but I have the perfect thing for her to do during the day. I pull up my messages for the first time since I picked her up and see one from Beck.

> **Beck:** Who are you going to New York with?

> **Me:** None of your business

> **Beck:** Interesting since you're using the company box tomorrow and the suites we use. Sounds like it's very much my business.

I mentally give him the finger before I press a button to call him. "Alright fucker, it's someone I'm seeing."

"Well, I knew you weren't taking your mother. Who is it?"

"Just a woman. I've known her for a while."

"Okay. Vague but okay. Frankly, I'm surprised. I figured you were still stuck on the woman from Owen's wedding."

I clear my throat. "Yeah…" I trail off and I hear a laugh on the other end.

"I knew you'd break down and call Owen. Okay, wow. So, you're pulling out all the stops then. Let me guess, taking her shopping tomorrow?"

"No." *Yes.*

"Dinner at The Landry?"

"No." *Also, yes.*

"So, yes to both. Should I let our lawyer know you'll be reaching out to draw up papers soon?"

"Jesus, Beck. It's still early."

"And if you broke down and figured out who she was because you finally realized obsessing over her for the rest of your life was not healthy, it means you are finally ready to start the process of divorcing Holly." He sighs. "I think you should have gotten your ducks in a row first, but at least we are moving in the right direction. Where does Holly think you are?"

"New York."

"With me?" he asks.

I grab the garment bag that's already hanging in my closet and unzip it, pulling out the jacket and pants I'm planning to wear tonight. "I don't know, maybe."

"Do you even bother hiding it?"

"Why would I? She doesn't care."

"God, this girl has her work cut out for her. She's probably already noticed you have money. Just make sure she's not Holly 2.0, okay? Make sure she's with you for you."

"Yeah," I say. I've been so enamored with her for months that I hadn't thought about the fact that she's just learning who I am in the past week. She may have been into me before but now she knows about all the things that come with being with me. "Fuck," I mutter. "I shouldn't have done all of this so soon."

"No. Man, I didn't say that. If she's into you, I'm saying it doesn't matter either way. And women do love to be spoiled, just keep your eyes open better this time, yeah? You know how to spot someone only interested in you for your money much better now."

"Right." I let out a breath as a call comes through and I groan.

What the fuck. I sometimes go days without talking to her and she's calling thirty minutes after me checking into a hotel.

"I have a call. Let me call you back."

"No need. Have fun. Call me if you need something."

"Thanks, Beck." I hang up and switch to the other line, already walking towards the bar knowing I'll need a drink after this conversation.

"What's up?" I ask.

"Where are you?" Her voice already grates on my nerves but it feels even more annoying than usual.

"I told you I was going to New York for the weekend. What do you need, Holly?"

"Oh right," she answers flatly. "Well, the realtor for the house in Aspen called."

Called her instead of me? I pull the phone away from my ear as I scroll through my call log to see if she'd tried to call me first. "Why didn't she call me?"

"I don't know. You're busy?"

"Okay…well, what did she say?"

"That the house we originally wanted is for sale."

Four years ago, when I was much more invested in our marriage and we were looking at houses to buy in Aspen, the one we both fell in love with wasn't available. Nobody was living in it, but the owners weren't interested in selling. The owner's wife had just died and he was feeling a sentimental attachment to it. I guess now he's moving on and wouldn't mind being attached to the eighteen million dollars he wants for it.

"The house we have is fine."

"But it's not the house we wanted."

"Holly, we haven't been to Aspen in years." *At least not together.*

"I go all the time."

"And there's nothing wrong with the house we have." If I'm about to start the process of getting out of my marriage, I'm not about to start a completely different process of selling and buying a new house.

"I know. I'm saying we should get this one too."

"What the hell do we need two houses in Aspen for?" *She's insane.* "I'm not paying two mortgages on two multi-million dollar houses in Aspen." We also had a house in the Hamptons that I absolutely hate. It's tacky and way too big. All I wanted was a small beach house and somehow ended up with a monstrosity that has appeared in House and Garden. *Twice.*

I rub my temples thinking about the headache of how we are going to go about splitting up those properties when the time comes.

"I really think we should."

I drop two ice cubes into the glass and open the bottle of Scotch from the minibar. "No."

She huffs. "Stop being a dick."

"Because I don't want to blow almost twenty million dollars on a house we don't need? We have a house, Holly." And I'm beginning to think she is the one who reached out to our realtor and not the other way around.

"Ugh!" She scoffs. "When will you be home?"

"Sunday."

"Fine. Enjoy your whore." She hangs up without another word. I down the drink in one swallow, hoping it can stop the anger from bubbling up inside me. My phone begins to vibrate and without looking I groan because *what now?*

When I look down and see Marissa's name across the screen, I feel like the entire weight of the world has been lifted and I'm already smiling when I answer. "Miss me?"

"Oh shit," she says. "I did not mean to call you." I can't tell if she's messing with me or not so I go with it.

"Oh, no worries. I'll let you go."

"Wait!" she says with a huff. "You're no fun. Do you think you can help me with something?"

"Name it."

"Can you come to my room?"

I'm moving towards the door before the sentence is fully out of her mouth. I knock on her door and notice she's ended our call before she opens the door. My heart immediately takes off as I take her in, my eyes dragging over her barely clothed body. "I'm just not sure what to wear." She winces. I notice she's already done her makeup and her hair looks curlier than it did earlier, dusting the tops of her shoulders every time she moves.

"Hopefully more than that," I say as I follow her into the room. I do my best to adjust my dick when she turns around and I notice the string between her cheeks. She's only wearing a bra that's basically sheer and matching underwear that look like they're being held together by strings. Now that we are in a better light, I can almost make out her bare slit behind the sheer fabric. "If you're putting on a fashion show, mind if I make a drink?" I ask her as I make my way to the bar and pour a larger drink than I did earlier before sitting on the couch in front of the king-sized bed I wanted to be in with her. *Now.*

She pulls on a red dress first. Tight. Short. Highlighting her tits and her gorgeous legs. *I wanted to rip it off of her with my teeth.* I spin my index finger in a circle indicating I wanted her to turn around. She does and god, even her ass is perfect. I'd yet to meet a woman I couldn't decide what part of her I loved best. Usually, it was obvious. Breasts, ass, legs, smile, eyes. With Marissa, I really can't tell and they all seem to come second to her sense of humor.

"Are you staring at my ass?" she says, and when I look up her eyes are narrowed and laced with humor.

"It was staring at me first," I say before I take another sip. "I like it, what else?" She picks another dress off the bed and holds it up. It's a jade green, longer and backless. "Let's see it then." She pulls the red dress off, and when she bends over with her back to me, I let my head drop to the back of the couch because there's a good chance, we are not making it to dinner if she keeps this up.

"Okay." She moves her hips from side to side. "What about this one?"

It fits her like a glove and makes her look like some kind of mermaid goddess. "You're gorgeous in everything." I rub my mouth. "I think I like the red one better though."

She smiles. "Okay, last one." She pulls on a champagne-colored dress that has tiny straps and is a little looser than the red but just as short and has flecks of gold that highlight her warm brown skin.

"That one," I tell her as I stand up, not wanting to wait another second to have my hands on her. I wrap my arms around her and let my hands slide down to cup her round ass. "You have fun tormenting me?"

"I just needed a third opinion." She lets her fingers trail up my chest to wrap around my neck.

"I wasn't the second?"

"No, I talked to my sister."

"What did she say?"

"The gold."

"She know you're here with me?"

"Yes, news travels fast in the Collins family. My mom called her." She pulls out of my grasp to reach for a pair of shoes. "She obviously didn't tell my mom anything, but she suspected it was you and she called to confirm." She pulls on her shoes and holds her arms out. "Okay, I'm ready."

"I am not." I chuckle, looking down at myself. "You want to come watch me change? I don't have multiple outfits for you to choose from but I'll still make it worth your while."

She takes a drink from her champagne just as she drags her eyes all over me before sliding her hand into mine and letting me pull her towards my room.

We move through the suite and she follows me into the bedroom, immediately sitting down on my bed and I shake my head. "Absolutely not. Sit somewhere else."

She frowns and looks around herself like she's trying to appear confused. "Why?"

"You know why." I hold my hand out for her to take. "Literally anywhere else. I'm still hard from your little fashion show and the visual of you on a bed is not helping."

She looks up at me, shooing my hand away, and stares directly at my groin. "I want to see."

I shake my head, taking a step back wondering how I'm supposed to survive the whole night if she's already teasing me like this. I pull my Henley off over my head and watch as her pupils dilate. I'm glad I've worked out an extra time every day since she's walked back into my life because it's obvious, she likes what she sees.

"Did you just…flex?" She giggles and I guess I had absently. Heat crosses my face over getting caught trying to show off for her but when I look into her eyes, she's still staring at my body with her lip trapped between her teeth.

"Stop biting your lip, Marissa," I tell her. She immediately lets it go just as I slide my slacks down. I groan when I watch her tongue dart out to lick her bottom lip. "No licking them either," I grunt and she puts a hand over her mouth, hiding her smile. I move towards her and stand in front of her leaning down to put one hand on the bed on each side of her. "I was very helpful in helping you choose and did my best not to react, you know. Despite the fact that all I could think about was moving those see-through panties to the side and running my tongue through your slit to see if you taste the same as I remember." I notice her breathing has changed and her eyes are looking at my lips. "Do you want me to kiss you?"

"I don't like being asked questions the other person already knows the answer to."

"You have a smartass little mouth, Marissa Collins."

"You like it."

"I fucking love it." I pull away from her and I can tell she's about to protest. "We are running late and if I put my mouth on you in any way, we aren't making it to dinner and you need to eat."

"This fancy hotel doesn't have room service?"

I laugh, my dick screaming at me to say fuck the reservations and go with her plan. "After all the trouble I went through to pick out a dress?" I ask her as I slide on the white shirt.

I don't miss the groan that leaves her lips. "Christopher."

"Oh, my government name?" I point at her. "Alright, well Ethan is my middle name, when you're ready to break that out."

"Cute." She purses her lips. "Mine is Lee."

"I know," I tell her with a wink.

"How?"

"You do remember you work for me, right?" She glares at me and I laugh at her trying to appear affronted. "Damn near memorized your entire file. You really speak fluent French?"

"When called upon, yes."

I side-eye her, wondering if that was just a bald-faced lie, and in reality, she doesn't know more than *bonjour* and *au revoir*. "What does that mean?"

"It means, if you dropped me in Paris, I could eat and figure out how to get home and go shopping, but don't ask me to conjugate shit."

I let out a laugh as I pull my pants up. "You been?"

"To Paris? Yes, in high school. I studied there for a summer."

"Have you been since?"

"Once. I studied abroad in Belgium in college and we went to Paris one of the weekends."

My mind is already working in overdrive about how fast I can get us there. *Aren't I supposed to be making sure she likes me for me and not planning a trip to one of the world's most romantic cities?*

"Have you been?" she asks.

"Many times," I tell her. "We are actually opening an office there."

"Oh, maybe I should go work there." She looks at her nails like it isn't a big deal.

"Maybe not," I reply flatly.

She looks away from her nails and I see the amusement in her eyes. "Why?"

"Because I'm not doing a long-distance relationship and Beck would lose his shit without me here. You ready?" I say, not giving her a chance to refute that she and I are in a relationship.

As much pull as I have, everyone who dines at The Landry does, so demanding a private room the day before we were set to arrive was next to impossible. We are still in a more secluded area but it's not the private room I'd hoped for that would have made it acceptable for Marissa to sit in my lap.

"You're staring," she says just as she takes a sip of her champagne.

"You're gorgeous," I respond without missing a beat.

She doesn't say anything but I watch the goosebumps pop

up all over her skin and I love how much I affect her. "Can I ask you something?"

"Anything."

"How come you didn't try to contact me after?" I'll admit that's not what I thought she was going to ask. "I mean even just to explain that you weren't available." She blinks at me. "You kind of made me feel like shit. Like I'd done something wrong or… wasn't good."

"Trust me, that wasn't it," I tell her immediately. "You were perfect. I'd never had a night like that." I rub my mouth, dragging a finger over my bottom lip. "I jack off thinking about it daily."

She gasps. "Daily?"

"Sometimes multiple times in one day." I reach across the table and grab her hand. "I'm sorry, I did that."

She nods but then raises her eyebrows as if to say, *Well?*

"You freaked me out a little. How you felt. How *we* felt. It was the first time it had ever been like that for me."

"Me too."

"I'd never slept with anyone that made me question what the fuck I was doing still married." I pause, wanting to clarify. "Make no mistake, I question it daily, but no woman had ever made me think I was missing anything by not being single." I sigh. "I didn't know how to tell you that."

"So, you just ghosted me?" I go to protest when she holds a hand out. "If you say 'I left a note,' I swear to god…"

"Well, I did," I murmur. "And I saw the room service bill, so I know you saw it."

"I should have ordered more."

I chuckle. "Yeah, you should have." She doesn't say anything else so I continue. "It's going to take some time," I tell her. "To… get out. I'm just asking that you be patient and have some faith in me. I'm not going to fuck you over."

"Isn't that what all men tell their mistresses?"

I know the comment is meant to be a dig even if it's the truth.

"Alright, I let the first one slide. Don't call yourself that. What happened to not liking that word?"

"I can not like it and still know that's what I am." Sadness mars her features and I hate that I've contributed to putting it there.

"You're not."

She cocks a head to the side and raises her eyebrows. "Oh?"

"Fine, if we are going by Webster's dictionary definition fine. But I'd like to think of you as the woman I'm preparing to walk through hell for."

She purses her lips. "Maybe I'm overstepping, but...is it really all about the money? I mean, I don't have any experience with your level of wealth but even if I weren't in the picture making you question all your life choices, would it really be worth it? Stay with her and be miserable in favor of a higher bank balance?" I hate how she makes it sound like it should be easy. That I shouldn't want to live a life of misery in favor of more money. "Sorry, I didn't mean it like that. I know you work really hard—"

"You're right." I can't stop my heart from pounding at the thought that her views on money are unbelievably different than Holly's. I give her a sad smile. "Damn, I wish I'd waited for you."

Chapter SIX

Marissa

"Y OU WANT TO GO UPSTAIRS? THERE'S A HEATED rooftop bar. Or if there's something else you'd like to do, tell me." Chris gets up from the table and holds his hand out for me.

When I reach for it, he pulls me to my feet and into his arms, and I love how good it feels to be pressed up against him. He runs his hands down my back, gently stopping just shy of my ass and I'd give anything to feel his hands there right now, but he moves them back up and laces our fingers. "Upstairs is fine, but I don't really party that much."

"Just at weddings." He winks and I shake my head as we walk away from the table.

We are making our way through the restaurant when a thought hits me. "Wait…did we pay?"

"You think I'm making you dine and ditch on our second

date? That's more like third or fourth date activities, don't you think?"

I smack his arm, "I'm not saying that, I just thought maybe you forgot or…" I wince, realizing he probably already handled it without me seeing.

"They have my card on file. They just send me the receipt at the end of the night," he informs me as we enter the elevator.

We still haven't kissed again and I can feel the hum between my legs getting stronger with every elevator ride. When we exit the elevator, the rooftop is empty save for one table in the corner with another couple.

"There's no one up here? Seems like it would be busier?" I ask as I look around, confused.

"It's only open to VIPs on Fridays," he says. "You need a special code to access it."

"Oh." I nod. "Why only VIPs?"

"Gives people privacy. Sometimes celebrities come up here. They don't like you taking pictures or using your phone at all really."

He guides me to an area that's blocked off by larger plants and lights and it feels like we are completely alone. There are two chairs and a small loveseat and he shocks me by sitting in one of the chairs instead of the couch. My eyes dart between the options before I take a couple of steps to stand in front of him. He raises an eyebrow at me before he spreads his legs slightly and I slide onto his lap.

"I was hoping you'd choose this seat."

"It's just preventative," I tell him. "In case, I get cold and need your body heat."

"Oh well, I could just give you my jacket." He leans up slightly and starts to slide it off. "Or if there's another way I can warm you up"—he's moved us so my legs are draped over his lap putting us at eye level. He leans closer so our lips are almost touching—"you'll have to tell me."

Movement in my periphery pulls my eyes from his in time to see a man setting down two glasses of champagne and a tray of chocolate-covered strawberries before disappearing. "Did we order that?"

"They just bring it by. Do you want something else?"

I look at the table in front of us and turn back to him. "Maybe something else."

"Oh? Tell me what it is. Whatever you want." My eyes drop to his lips and then back up to his eyes before scanning over his jaw, nose, and cheekbones and then returning to stare into his piercing blue eyes.

"Touch me." I bite my bottom lip for emphasis and I feel his dick twitch beneath me. "Reach your hand between my legs and touch me."

He leans away from me, resting his back against the chair, and scratches his jaw. "Are you wet?" I nod. "Since when?"

I open my mouth, not sure of what to say before I go for the sexiest answer I can think of. "Since you picked me up from my house."

He winces and shakes his head before sucking his teeth. "Well, I've been walking around permanently erect since you showed up in my office on Monday, so I think I win."

"I didn't realize we were competing but okay, what do you want?" I am more than aware I didn't give him a blowjob that night, so I already know that's probably high on his list of priorities this weekend. Fine by me. I regretted not sucking that perfect dick in my mouth every night for weeks.

"I want another taste."

Fuck yes, me too. His mouth was insane and I liked that he seemed obsessed with putting it on my cunt. "Okay." I nod. "Should we go?"

He shakes his head before he lifts me up, holding me in his arms, before sitting me where he was seated in the chair allowing him to kneel in front of me. "Here!?" I whisper-shout and he chuckles.

He raises an eyebrow before he parts my legs gently. "No one is going to see anything even if they happen to come around, but they won't. They've already brought us our drinks."

"Chris, you can't be serious."

"We're talking about my tongue in your cunt, trust me I am very serious." My eyes dart around, and no one is even within our line of sight but still! "Listen if someone were to walk by, all they would see is my head between your legs."

"Uhh ya, kind of the point?"

"I'm saying, they wouldn't see any part of you." He shrugs as he drags his hands up my thighs. "Tell me I can."

I let out a shaky breath, shocked that I'm even considering this as I let my eyes once again scan the perimeter of the essentially empty rooftop. "Be fast."

He gives me a deadpan look. "I'll be down here all night if you let me."

He reaches his hand fully under my dress and skims a digit slowly down my pussy, pressing it slightly into the seam through my panties. "Has anyone been here since I was?"

"Would it matter if someone had been?"

He swallows, like he's thinking about it before he shakes his head. "No."

I think about toying with him, trying to make him jealous at the thought that someone had touched me, but ultimately, I go with the truth. "No. You're the last man that's been there." I shake my head.

His nostrils flare and he pushes my panties inside of me a little harder, rubbing his finger over my clit. "Why?"

"Why what?"

"You're twenty-one and gorgeous and funny as hell. Smart. A ballbuster. Guys must be banging down your door to get to you."

His eyes meet mine and I squirm under the intensity of his

gaze and his finger on my clit. "I don't tell guys where I live," I say simply although I know there's a lot of meaning behind my words given that he's already been to my house.

He grits his teeth before he moves up my body and stares into my eyes. "I hope you know I'm not letting you go. So, get good and comfortable with having me around because I'm not going anywhere."

His words are like a shock to my entire system and my heart flutters in my chest like it's trying to jump out of it and into his hands. I lean forward slightly, pressing my lips to his gently. I just want to seal what he said with a kiss. A kiss that I hope tells him I'm on board with the idea of being stuck with him for a while or maybe even forever, but he deepens it, sliding his tongue into my mouth and removing his hand from between my legs to cup my face. I don't know how long we kiss, me in the chair and him on his knees in front of me as our mouths reconnect for the first time in months, but I know that I have never felt happier than I do at this moment.

When he finally pulls back, he sucks my bottom lip into his mouth and a smile tugs at his lips as he slides my dress up revealing the apex of my thighs to him. He leans closer and there's no way that anyone passing by could see anything. He pushes my panties to the side, reminiscent of the first time he did this and a cocky grin finds his face. He's still staring at my bare wet pussy when he asks, "Did you get waxed for this trip?"

"Maybe." I squirm under his lustful gaze. His eyes meet mine and I roll my eyes. "Don't give me a hard time for being prepared! Did you bring condoms?"

"Obviously," he says, "but I hope you won't make us use them." I've never gone bare with anyone. Even us fooling around without one briefly that night was something I'd never done before. "You can think about it; you don't have to make a decision now. And if you prefer that I put one on, I don't care. I want you, however you'll take me."

I think I believe him. I don't think this will be the last time we have this conversation, but at this moment, I don't think he'll pressure me about it.

"I...I'm on birth control."

A smile pulls at his lips as his mouth descends down my body and between my legs. He pulls me closer to the edge of the chair, lifting my legs slightly before his mouth presses against my pussy in a hot open-mouthed kiss. His tongue darts out instantly sliding through the lips of my sex and swirling it around before it touches my clit lightly like he's not sure he wants to touch it yet. I let out a whimper and then a sigh when he moves to my opening, sawing in and out of me so slowly.

Better than I remembered, I think. I'm wound the fuck up and fairly certain I'm already close to coming when I hear the clink of his belt.

Oh my god, is he going to try and fuck me here?! The thought arouses and excites and terrifies me, and I guess we can add this to the ever-growing list of things I'm doing with Christopher Holt that I've never done. I expect him to move off my cunt, but he continues, lapping at my clit like I'm a cone of ice cream and he doesn't want to waste a drop. He holds one hand in front of my face. "Spit."

I gasp out of lust and shock because I feel pretty wet already but I do as he says and I watch as he pulls away from my pussy for a second to spit in it also before he's back to fucking me with his mouth. Instantly, his breathing gets heavier and I can feel it against my wet flesh. "What...are...you doing?" I manage between rapid breaths.

"Eating your pussy gets my dick so hard. It's never been like this with anyone but you."

"Are you...oh god!" I moan when he flicks my clit with the tip of his tongue. "Masturbating?"

"Yes, and I'm going to fucking come."

"Because of...the way I taste?"

"And feel." He grunts. "Softest fucking pussy." The crassness of his words washes over me. He slows his strokes and I feel myself nearing the edge. I drop both of my hands to the back of his head, keeping him where I want him as I rock my hips against his mouth. *Fuck I want him. Bad.*

"Chris, oh my god."

"Good girl. You remembered." He sucks my clit into his mouth and I fucking *lose* it. At the peak of my orgasm, I remember where we are and slap a hand over my mouth to muffle the sounds of me going over the edge. I hear a low groan somewhere in the distance and I hope that means that Chris has come too.

I drop my eyes to him just as he plants a final kiss to my cunt causing me to tremble, and when he pulls away a string of his spit and my cum connects his mouth to me before it breaks.

I grab his slick jaw, rubbing my thumb across his bottom lip, smearing my wetness into his skin. "You look good on your knees in front of me." I lean forward and run my tongue across his lips. "But I'll bet I look better."

Chapter

SEVEN

CHRIS

THE RIDE BACK TO THE HOTEL MAY JUST BE THE hottest ten minutes of my life. The second I slide into the backseat, Marissa is in my lap straddling me and grinding her still very wet pussy against me. I'd gone to the restroom before we left the rooftop to clean up the mess I'd made in my briefs as best as I could, but I have a feeling I might come again before we even get back to the hotel with the way she's moving up and down on me.

"Fuuuuck, babe, you're going to make me come."

"Hold it. I want the next time in my mouth." She seals her dirty words with a kiss, licking her way back into my mouth as she humps against me.

"You're killin' me." I groan against her lips as my hands fall to her hips, keeping her steady and pressed against me. I jerk upwards just as she grinds down and I am very grateful that I had the oversight to request a car with a partition. "You're acting like you want me to fuck you back here." I flick my tongue along her jaw and grip her hips tighter.

Her hands are on my belt in an instant. "Yes yes yes, fuck me here." The begging in her voice is sexy as hell and makes me want to give her whatever she wants.

"Here?"

She nods against my mouth and I smile, wondering if my eating her pussy on the rooftop was her foray into sex in public settings. Maybe I unlocked a side she didn't know she had and I'm happy to explore it with her.

"Unzip me and take it out," I say through shaky breaths because I feel like my dick might explode already from the friction and I'd like to thrust more than once before I come.

She does it without a second thought and holds me in her hands before lining herself up and hovering over me. I grip her panties, sliding my fingers over the crotch area, and push them to the side before she slides down.

"Oh my god." The backseat is dark, but enough for me to make out how her eyes flutter closed the second I'm seated inside of her. "Fuck," she whispers. "My god, I forgot how big your dick is."

I try to move her up but she grabs my hands to stop me. Her eyes dart up to meet mine and they're so big and gorgeous, highlighted by long eyelashes that I find myself lost in until she squeezes her silky cunt around me. She doesn't move, I'm just buried inside of her while she squeezes herself around me and just feeling her fit snugly around my dick as she squeezes her inner walls is enough to make me ready to come.

Her lips move to my neck, dragging her teeth over my pulse point followed by her tongue. "I can't wait to get you upstairs." I pull her from my neck so I can look at her. "We have a lot of fucking making up to do from the past three months." Her pussy flutters around me and I press my lips to hers just as a moan escapes her. "You just going to torture me?" My voice comes out sputtered like she's got her hand wrapped around my throat the same way her cunt is strangling my cock.

She clenches again *and again and again*. She spins her hips in a circle as she throws her head back and I can tell she's getting closer based on her movements but I know we're also getting close to the hotel and I want her to come before we get there. "You need some help?"

She tilts her head back up to meet my eyes and nods slowly, that delicious bottom lip that I've become obsessed with biting caught between her teeth in a way that makes me want to come. I make a show of dragging two fingers across my tongue slowly, *not because she's not already wet but to let her know what she's in for* before I drop my fingers to her clit and begin to massage her in a circle. "Now we're almost to the hotel. I need you to come the fuck all over my dick before we get there," I tell her.

Our lips are merely an inch apart so the very quiet, "*Oh god,*" she whispers seems ten times louder and I'm reminded of how much I affect her. I'm reminded of how amazing that night felt three months ago and how I can't believe my luck that the universe brought us together a second time.

"Give it to me," I tell her just when I feel her clenches get harder and more frantic around me and then she pushes her face into my shoulder and moans low into my shoulder as she climaxes around my dick.

"Oh my god, I'm coming," she whispers against my skin as she squirms on top of me.

Fuck me.

She pulls back as I feel us slowing down and when I turn to the right, I see the lights of the hotel in front of us. "Should I have him go around again?" My tongue darts out to run across her lips and she shakes her head, pulling off of me slowly, and when I look down, my dick is shiny and wet and she's looking at it with equal fascination.

"You're looking at it like you want it in your mouth," I tell her as I zip myself back into my pants and she sits next to me just in time for us to slow to a stop. We are out of the car quickly and moving fast through the lobby, both of us ready to get back to my room, and I'm just about to press her into the wall and kiss her senseless when an older couple follows us into the elevator.

They are probably in their mid to late sixties, dressed like they just got back from a night out. The woman gives us a knowing smile as we begin to ascend and she looks at our hands laced together.

"There was a time or two we couldn't wait either," she says with a wink. "You kids enjoy your night." She laughs with her husband right behind her who nods on his way out.

We still have a few floors before ours and I take the time to press my lips to hers. "Every time we got on an elevator today, I wanted to do this," I whisper between frenzied kisses.

"Me too."

The elevator dings and we make our way down the hall. "My room or yours?" she asks and I yank her towards mine.

"Ours," I tell her as I push her gently against the door. "Now, before we go in, I have to ask you something."

"Okay?" There's a twinkle in her eye like she already knows my question is going to serve as some sort of foreplay.

"Do you want me nice or nasty first?"

She raises an eyebrow at me and takes the key from my hand. "Didn't I tell you I don't like when people ask me questions they already know the answer to?"

I dig my teeth into my bottom lip. "When we get inside, I want you to strip and then get on your fucking knees."

She spins around and swipes the card, pushing through the door, and barely makes it a step before she kicks her shoes off and reaches for the bottom of the dress to pull it over her head.

"Slowly," I tell her as I pull off my jacket and begin unbuttoning my shirt. I watch her through hooded eyes. "Do you want a drink?"

She shakes her head as she unsnaps her bra letting those gorgeous tits that I haven't seen tonight yet spring free. I lick my lips remembering what they felt like in my mouth. How her nipples felt between my teeth and against my tongue. That pretty dusty rose color that I fucking see in my dreams. I turn down the lights, letting the ones from the city skyline illuminate the room before I make my way to where she's standing in the middle of the living space. I watch with anticipation sizzling in my veins as she slowly peels her underwear away from her wet cunt.

I put my drink to my lips and take a long sip just as she gets on her knees in front of me. "Take it out," I tell her as I let my shirt fall to the floor. Her hands go to my belt instantly, unbuckling it and sending my slacks and briefs down my legs in the span of a second leaving me completely naked. She looks at my dick, still glistening from her pussy being wrapped around it, and then up at me. "Stick out your tongue." I see a flash of embarrassment cross her face and I grip her jaw. "Don't make me tell you again."

The look quickly fades and is replaced with lust as she sticks her tongue out. I grip my dick and guide it towards her mouth. "Do you know how many times I've had this fantasy? How many times I've regretted not letting you suck me off three months ago?" I groan the second the underside of my shaft slides across that velvety pink muscle. "Fuck, and now you're here." I cup her face. "Do you know how much I want you?" She doesn't say anything but nods once. "Good girl. Never forget it." I move my hips, slowly sliding my dick into her mouth. "Now, suck me off until I come in your slutty little mouth."

Excitement flashes in her eyes and she wraps her lips around my length, pushing herself all the way down my length. "FUCK!" I grit out as I look down. "You don't have a gag reflex?" I ask her and she shakes her head.

At that exact moment, she swallows, pushing me a little further down her throat and I gasp. "Oh fuck, your mouth is so fucking good." She's starting to suck me harder, moving up and back faster, and just when I feel myself nearing the edge, she pulls me out of her mouth and drags her tongue down my shaft, swirling the tip of her tongue over one of my balls. *Fuck fuck fuck.* "Suck them into your mouth, pretty girl. Do it."

"Mmmm." She moans just as she wraps her lips around one like it's the best thing she's ever had in her mouth before doing the same to the other, all while using one of her hands to jack me off.

"Back on my dick," I groan after a few seconds, needing the friction of her warm mouth to push me over the edge. "You're a man's wet dream, you know that? On your knees, mouthful of my cock." She suctions me harder at that, like the thought of being a turn-on makes her hot. She sucks harder and I feel the familiar tingle in my balls as I prepare to come. "Fuck, I'm going to come." I grit out. "Don't swallow it all, I want to see it on your tongue."

I see the excitement in her eyes and it spurs me on, fucking ecstatic that she's as nasty as I am. I put a hand on both sides of her face and pump a few times before going over the edge as I fuck her face in time with her sucks. "Fuck, Marissa. Right there, babe. Right fucking there," I say through gritted teeth as my cock expands. I shoot my cum into her mouth and she sucks me through it. Some of my cum slide past her lips from how much there is but she keeps the majority of it in even as she lets me fall out of her mouth, and I watch as she swallows slowly. Then with the sexiest look on her face, she opens her mouth.

The cum sitting on her tongue is enough to make it hard again. "Fuck, you're gorgeous," I whisper as I down the rest of my drink and let the glass drop to the carpeted floor with a dull thud. "Swallow."

She does and then looks up at me with a smile on her face. "Did I do a good job?"

Okay, someone has a praise kink. Got it.

"You did a great fucking job, beautiful," I tell her and she beams up at me, her eyes sparkling while a smile pulls at her still-shiny lips. I toe off my shoes, pants, and briefs before I pull her to her feet and then pull her behind me toward the bedroom. "On the bed." She does as she's told as I drag a mirror from the corner of the room directly in front of the bed. "Have you ever watched yourself come?"

"I don't think so."

"You're missing out." I get on the bed behind her and pull her between my spread legs. She's sitting almost on my dick and she squirms as it rubs against her ass. "Spread them." The room is lit enough that she can watch us in the mirror and she does as she's told before finding my gaze in the reflection. I spread her open with one hand making her look at herself on display for us both before pressing my other fingers to her clit.

"Look at that pretty pussy." I press my lips to her cheek. I rub her clit in circles and I can already tell she's building. "How do you make yourself come? Your fingers or a vibrator or maybe a little teddy bear you don't tell anyone about?"

She whimpers when I slide a hand up her torso to pinch one of her delectable nipples. "Vibrator…fingers…"

"Do you think about me?"

"Fuck." She moans and lets her head fall back against my shoulder. I lay a smack directly on her clit and she cries out. "Yes!"

"Eyes on us." She lifts her head and I can see the lust all over her pretty face.

"What do you think about?"

"Your…mouth…" She pants. "Your dick…all of you." I have two fingers on her, rubbing her clit in fast circles. "When you rubbed your dick on my clit. Oh g-god. Right fucking there."

"Yeah? You going to come all over my fingers? You're so wet; your clit is pulsing against them."

"Fuck." Our gazes lock in the mirror before both of our eyes drop to where my fingers are touching her.

"Oh yes, that's next," I murmur low in her ear as I lick a line up her neck.

"I want…"

"Tell me, gorgeous. Tell me what you want."

I apply more pressure and her breathing becomes more erratic. "To sit on your—ah! Face!"

"Oh fuck yes. You better make that sweet little pussy come all over it." Her hands drop to my thighs and she digs her nails in slightly as she moves her hips in time with my fingers. I feel the pierce of her nails straight to my dick and it throbs in response.

I slide two of my fingers inside of her all while still keeping a thumb on her clit and when I crook one upward to rub a spot just beyond her opening, she detonates. "Oh, fuck right there! Oh my god, yes, I'm coming!" Her eyes flutter shut and though she tries to keep her eyes open she lets her head fall back as she rides out the high. I, on the other hand, watch very closely as her pussy quivers and contracts around my hand.

God, she is fucking perfect.

No more than a second after she's come down from her high, she's turned around catching me somewhat off guard. "I need more. I want to come all over this again," she says with her hands moving up and down my dick.

"Get on your knees, ass up." She doesn't waste any time and soon I'm lined up behind her, pushing my dick inside of her bare again. It's fucking intense and I can already feel myself slipping under the haze of raw sex. "Can I come inside?" I ask through shaky breaths as I grip her hips tighter, pulling and pushing her harder onto my dick.

"Fuck," she chokes out.

"Marissa, answer me," I say through gritted teeth and she moans again, but when she doesn't respond, I lay a smack to her ass causing her to squeal.

"Yes, fuck!"

"Answer me next time," I grit out and almost want to laugh when she holds her middle finger up.

She lowers herself even more arching her back and her pussy practically strangles my cock with how tight it is. I feel a hand on my balls, massaging them and pulling gently and I don't think I've ever been with a woman that was so eager to pay them attention. "You like my balls?"

"I love them," she moans, "but I love everything about your body."

"You do, huh?"

"It's perfect." She purrs and my dick hardens further inside her in response to her praise.

Her hands move away from my balls but I can feel them on her every time I thrust. "Are you rubbing your clit?"

"Yes," she moans.

"You have a greedy little pussy, huh? How many orgasms does it take to feel satisfied?"

"Ah!" She gasps as I begin fucking her harder, my pelvis banging against her ass and I feel her pussy tightening around me.

"Oh, you're close, aren't you? Your hot cunt is probably dripping down my dick."

"Chris, oh my god! I'm going to come again."

"Yes, fucking *please*. Get there." I groan when I feel her begin to spasm around me and it triggers my own. "God dammit, Marissa. Fuuuuuck." I hear her screaming my name beneath me but I'm momentarily over-sensitized and my body is tuning everything out by my sudden orgasm. My heart feels like it could beat out of my chest as well as my dick with the pounding I feel between my legs. When everything begins to refocus, I'm still inside of Marissa and she's still pulsing around me. I pull out of her slowly and I see my orgasm slowly start to leak out of her pussy. I rub her gently, pushing my cum back inside of her and she whimpers when I tickle her clit.

In an instant, I push her to her back and climb between her legs, letting them wrap around me. "That was incredible." I press my lips to hers gently.

"Yeah, it was," she whispers and I can tell her mind is somewhere else.

"What is it?" I rub my nose against hers and she still doesn't say anything. "Talk to me. What's wrong?"

"Nothing…" I give her a look that I hope tells her that I'm not buying whatever she's selling, and she sighs. "Well…it's just the last time we had really great sex in a hotel room, you left before I woke up, so I'm just feeling a little vulnerable after the orgasm that history might be repeating itself."

I nod in understanding and although I know what I want to say, I also know that it won't be enough until she wakes up tomorrow and sees for herself. "I promise, it's not going to."

Chapter

EIGHT

Marissa

LIPS GHOSTING ACROSS MY CHEEK ROUSE ME FROM A delicious, sex-induced slumber and I wonder what time it is since I still feel a little delirious. I'm not exactly what someone would call a morning person, and somewhere in the back of my mind, I remember it's the weekend and I do not need to be up for work. I put a hand over my face, shooing away whatever is touching me when I hear a chuckle and then a kiss on my forehead and then my lips.

Well, there are worse wake-up calls.

I open one eye, squinting through it as I take in the hazy vision in front of me: Chris *shirtless*. I pry open the other eye because if I had to be awake, I at least want to fully appreciate the visual of this gorgeous man's naked torso.

"What?" I chuckle with a hint of annoyance.

"Good morning to you too, dear. Sleep well?" He pulls a mug to his lips and takes a sip.

"Better if it were noon. What time is it?"

"Seven-thirty."

"A.m.?" I groan and pull the covers up over my head. "Why? We went to bed like two hours ago." Unlike the first time we had sex three months ago, Chris and I had sex multiple times in multiple different positions last night. We'd talked in between, ordered late-night crepes at two in the morning, and fell asleep just as the night started to trickle into the morning.

"I have to take a call." He sighs and I lower the covers to see the disappointment all over his face. "I'll be in the living room, but I didn't want you waking up without me again." Even though I'm not even fully awake yet, my body hears the sentiment loud and clear and my heart skips a beat. He nods toward the other side of the room and I follow his gaze to see a table with what seems to be an impressive spread of food. "I ordered breakfast. Everything that needs to stay warm is still in the warmer if you're not hungry yet, but I wasn't sure what you liked, so I got a bit of everything."

I sit up a little to see the table before turning back to the man who may have woken me up but who did it half-naked and with food. *At least, he did it with style.*

"I like French toast," I tell him. "So you don't have to order the whole menu next time."

"So, there will be a next time?" He smiles before he leans down and presses his lips gently to mine.

I had put on a very short and sexy silk two-piece pajama set for bed—*that yes, I bought specifically for this trip*—but it barely covered much so when I sit up, I'm practically exposed.

"God you're fucking hot." He chuckles as he takes another sip from the mug in his hand. I hold my hand out, wanting his coffee, and he hands it to me. I take a sip without even looking at it and as soon as it hits my tongue my instant reflex is to spit it out. I hold it in my mouth and make a face before looking down at the damn near white coffee.

He chuckles and gives me a look. "You okay?"

I reluctantly swallow and hand him back his mug. "What is this?!"

"Coffee?"

"This is…cream…with sugar? I detect no coffee. The color of this coffee looks more like you than me!" I let out a sigh.

"I like my coffee sweet."

"You drink scotch straight. That nasty Macallan shit and you drink *this* in the morning?" I scrunch my nose, hating the taste it left behind.

"You're being dramatic. This coffee is brown by the way." He rolls his eyes as he points to the mug.

"It needs to be darker than me," I tell him pointing to my hand and let out a sigh.

"Fine, how do you take your coffee?"

"Black. Like how God intended."

He snorts in response. "Ah, so you're a coffee snob. Noted."

"Hey, I enjoy a good latte every now and then or a cutesy little drink with a four-dollar splash of almond milk from a coffee shop but for the most part, I just want it black. And it shocks me that you like this. God, do you drink frappuccinos too?" I get out of the bed and he lands a slap on my ass.

"I love a frappuccino." I scrunch my nose because if I'm going to drink a frappuccino, I might as well get a milkshake. I move towards the table and take in the food. *He really did order the whole menu.* I'll admit, I'm more tired than hungry, but he pulls something out of the warmer and I smell the cinnamon before I see it. He pulls off the top and I nod vigorously as I reach my hands out suddenly starving.

I mean I guess I did work out for multiple hours last night.

I sit on the ottoman and he sits next to me, drinking his horrible coffee. "So, are we doing anything before we see *Hamilton*?" I say as I cut into my French toast.

"So…I actually have two more meetings this afternoon that I couldn't move." He winces. "I'm sorry."

"Oh, it's okay."

"It's not okay. When I envisioned today, no part had me working."

"What did you envision?" I ask before pushing a piece through the river of syrup on my plate and taking a bite. "Holy crap, this is good." I cut another piece and hold it out for him. "Try it." He wraps his lips around the fork, pulling the bread off slowly, his eyes not leaving mine, and I don't know how he makes eating French toast look sexy as hell but I avert my eyes before I suggest finding another use for the syrup in front of us.

"That is good. I'm normally more of a waffles guy, but that is great," he says as if he doesn't realize how much that simple act has affected me. "And to answer your question, I was thinking we could just walk around Central Park, maybe go to the Met or MOMA. But based on when my meetings are, that may be tough. I do have another idea though."

He gets up and grabs something from his pants and when he sits back down, he hands me a credit card. I just stare at it, confused. I'd never seen a black one up close before. "What's this for?"

He shoots me a smile, excited like he just came up with the best idea anyone had ever heard. "Figured you could go shopping."

"For what?"

He chuckles. "Whatever you want."

I blink at him, suddenly realizing what he wants me to do. "Yeaaaah, I don't think so."

He frowns, confused. "Why?"

"Because…this just feels…cliché. The married man spoiling his…" I give him a look and point to myself, to avoid saying the word he doesn't want to hear. "To keep her from leaving and-or happy. It's a little insulting."

"I…didn't mean to. I just thought…you'd want to?" He sighs and drops his card on the table and I hope I haven't offended him, but this is just not what I want. "It's just what…" He trails off. "I've never had a woman say no to that. I'm not doing this to keep you from leaving. I want to do this."

"And I'm not saying you can't. But maybe...get to know me and find out what I like so you can buy it yourself? It'll mean more to me coming from you anyway and not just things I picked out on your credit card."

His eyes narrow but I see a hint of a smile tugging at his lips. "You're...different."

"Don't get me wrong, it's a lovely gesture and I appreciate it, but this is still all very new and...I'm just not very comfortable with that." I take another bite of the French toast that is easily one of the best I've ever had. "You've already spoiled me plenty." I bite my bottom lip. "There's a lot of things I like about you, Chris, and I don't even think your money cracks the top ten."

The one thing I love about a luxurious hotel is the bathroom. The bathtub and shower situation are usually unbelievable and I am ecstatic about taking a bath in what some would call a small swimming pool. Almost an hour after breakfast, I'm sitting in the bathtub, a mountain of bubbles as high as my neck as I read on my Kindle when Chris walks in.

"What are you reading?" he asks and I give him a smirk before putting it to sleep and setting it down on the ledge.

"Wouldn't you like to know?"

"Sounds like something spicy." He says as he raises his eyebrows up and down a few times.

"Maybe," I tell him with a wicked grin.

"What kind of smut do you like?"

"All kinds. I do not discriminate." I giggle because really, I don't. I have a password on my Kindle for a reason. I'm not ashamed but I'd rather my mother not know what I'm reading if she picks it up to be nosy. *And she absolutely would.*

"Anything you want to act out?"

I can't even stop the smile from breaking out across my face. "What?"

"Isn't that a perk of having a boyfriend? Make him do all kinds of shit you read in your spicy books?"

I think my brain momentarily short-circuits hearing the word boyfriend. *Okay, I know he's made multiple points about us being long term but it all felt so abstract. Hearing the term boyfriend feels real and final and...legitimate.*

Could I really be a girlfriend to a man that also has a wife?

"Okay, first of all, boyfriend?"

"What would you prefer to call me?" He pulls his shirt off and my pussy reacts as my brain is already convinced that he's getting in the tub with me.

"I guess I...hadn't really thought about it."

He slides his sweats down his legs revealing his bare dick and my mouth waters for a taste of him. "Can I join you?"

"You wait until you're naked to ask? What if I didn't want a bath time companion?"

"I thought I'd lead with an offer you couldn't refuse." He looks down at his dick.

"What if I peed in here?" I joke.

"You didn't."

"You don't know that," I say with a shrug.

"I'll take my chances," he says without another word as he climbs in and takes a seat in front of me.

"So, you think of me as your girlfriend, is that what you're saying?"

"Yep." He runs his hands up my legs and slowly massages my thighs. He pulls me gently into his lap, letting my pussy rest against his dick. "I don't care what you want to call me as long as you know I'm yours."

I hear my subconscious already clearing her throat and raising her index finger as if to say, *well technically...* but I ignore her.

I can't keep pointing out that he is married. We both know it, and he's also been very clear of his intentions to rectify that. He'd asked for faith and time and I suppose I could give him longer than the week it's been since I walked back into his life.

Right?

The idea that I'm being silly and naive flashes through me briefly, but right now in his lap, naked in a bathtub is not the time to have this argument with myself.

"I'm yours too," I whisper, pushing myself further into his lap and wrapping my arms around his neck just before I press my lips to his.

"Oh my god!" I say grabbing his bicep and squeezing as we make our way out of the *Beckham Securities* box in the theater. "Oh my god!"

"You said that." He smiles cockily.

"That. Was. So. GOOD!" There's nothing like the high of great entertainment. A movie, play, musical, book, it felt otherworldly. Almost as if I was immersed in it and it's taking a while to float back to reality. That's how I feel right now, like I'm *floating*. "I am…amazed." I stop in front of him and throw my arms around him. "Thank you! That was…" I let out a breath. "Wow. I knew it was going to be good, and somehow, I was still wholly unprepared for *that*."

He holds me tight in his arms, like he doesn't want to let me go, rubbing my back before finally pulling back. "You're welcome, beautiful. I'm glad you liked it." He cups my face and presses a kiss to my lips, sliding his tongue along mine like we aren't in the main lobby of the theater with people moving all around us.

I'm about to pull apart to suggest going back to the room. We had dinner before the show and he is the only thing I want for the rest of the night, but the sound of a throat clearing pulls me away before my idea can fully form. I pull away from his mouth and turn toward the source of the sound to see a man who's probably older than my dad with a woman next to him who might even be younger than *me*.

"I thought that was you, Christopher!" He has an unlit cigar between his fingers which is confusing to me *because where does he think he's lighting that?* In his other hand, is a glass filled to the brim with a clear liquid that I'm convinced is not water. His salt and pepper hair is slicked back and he's wearing a perfectly tailored suit that looks like it cost more than what I make in a month.

"Mr. Blackwell," Christopher nods with a polite smile but I can sense his discomfort instantly.

"Hell of a show. Did you enjoy it, miss?" he asks me and I nod.

"It was amazing. I loved it." I look at the girl on his arm, but she looks bored and has taken to scrolling through her phone, so I turn back to him. "I've never seen anything like it."

"Well, I'm sure Mr. Holt can bring you to all kinds of shows." He points at Chris and I don't miss how uncomfortable he seems. "Tell Beckham I'll be in touch next week," he says. "You two enjoy your evening." He passes by Chris and I hear him whistle a low, "Nice."

My heart sinks to my stomach and I'm instantly brought back to reality. The high of the show is completely eviscerated as I realize that this man probably knows Chris is married and it is *not* to me. I wonder if he's even met his wife at a work function and is… praising him for…his obvious extra-marital behaviors? I notice a ring on his finger, making me feel like that guy probably cheats on his wife regularly because I'm pretty sure the woman on his arm is not the one he promised to love in sickness and in health.

I don't say anything as we make our way outside where it's dropped at least twenty degrees since we went in earlier. There's a night in September when the weather changes, usually following a few days of rain where it struggles to get up to a certain degree and you know in that moment that summer is over. I'm wearing a sleeveless black dress and I wrap my arms around myself the second we step outside because of both the weather and the discomfort of the situation I know Chris and I have to talk about. Before I can even take a step, Chris is sliding his jacket off and it's around me. "I'm so fucking sorry about that," he says as he slides my arms through the sleeves. I'm grateful for the literal warmth plus the warmth in his words as he wraps me in a hug.

"Can we talk at the hotel?" I ask weakly. That interaction felt like a bucket of cold water on the whole evening and I'm suddenly very aware that my feet hurt, they're freezing, and I am exhausted.

"Of course, there's our car." He guides me towards one of the many black cars lined up along the curb. We slide in, and he immediately grabs my hand, pulling me closer to him, like he can feel the wall I'm putting up between us. I'm not trying to; I'm just already struggling with how I feel about everything without realizing that there may be times I'll have to interact with people who may also have their own feelings or comments.

I suddenly feel like I'm wearing a neon sign that says *whore*, and I do not like that at all.

We don't say anything on our way back to the hotel, but Chris doesn't let go of my hand the entire time, dragging his thumb over my knuckles every few moments almost as if to remind me of his presence.

We make it back to the room and just the faint sound of the door closing causes the dam to burst. "He knows you're married."

He sighs as he beelines for the bar and pours himself a drink. "Yes." He holds up the bottle asking if I want a drink and I shake my head.

"So, that '*nice*' is what? Good job on your new piece of ass?"

He takes a long sip of his drink and sighs. "He's a prick, and I know you could sense that. That girl he was with was obviously not his wife, and to be honest, he has a new girl every time I see him."

"That oddly does not make me feel better," I respond sarcastically.

"That's not me, Marissa. I don't have multiple women. It's just you. There's no one else."

"Just the woman you took vows with." I blink at him. "A woman it's obvious he's met before. Not to mention, you didn't even try to introduce me."

"Did you want me to? You were triggered by me calling myself your boyfriend. I wasn't sure what you wanted in terms of introducing you to people. Also, I haven't told Beck who you are. He's not going to fire me for breaking a fraternization rule but I'd at least like him to hear it from me rather than that asshole."

Fair. I cross my arms over my chest. "Okay, I'll give you that." I scrunch my nose as I feel the tears starting to prickle there. "I didn't like how that made me feel. Like he *knew*..."

"I'm sorry," he says as he moves closer to me. I'm still in his jacket, still feeling the chill from the outside, and I pull the lapel up and run it under my nose, smelling him and I feel the slight flutter of my heart from the inhale. "I'm sorry, I couldn't stop that from happening. Or that I kissed you in public. I should have been more careful about being in a space where I could have seen people that I know. I'll be smarter next time."

Next time.

I drop to the couch and tuck my legs underneath me as he sits down next to me. "I feel a little out of my depth with this." I swallow past the lump in my throat and I wish I'd taken him up on that drink to loosen the knot. "I know you say it's different but I still feel like I'm doing something very wrong."

"I get that." He stares down into his drink. "I'm not going to try and convince you not to feel that way or tell you that this isn't complicated. But what I will say is that life isn't always so black and white."

"Trying to rationalize it isn't going to make me feel better." I wish it did. I wish I could just get on board with the fact that the man I'm seeing is in a loveless *potentially open* marriage to a woman that doesn't care that he sees other women.

Well, me.

"What will make you feel better?" he asks and I wish I had the answer to that. It would certainly make things easier.

I shrug, not knowing how I feel about any of this but I know I want more with him. This interaction aside, this has been one of the best weekends I've ever had with one of the best guys I've ever known. Chris is so considerate and charming and unbelievably generous with not just his money but everything he has to give. While I know this situation is messy, I can tell his intentions with me are genuine. I can tell he wants to be with me and I'm beginning to think the feeling is more mutual than I've been letting on.

Chapter

NINE

CHRIS

THE SOUNDS OF COUGHING AND THE BED MOVING IS what wakes me up. The room is dark, so it can't be later than five in the morning. I immediately reach for Marissa hoping she's getting back in bed and not the other way around when I see her moving towards her suitcase in the corner and pulling a sweatshirt over her tiny pajamas. She coughs again and pads into the bathroom and I'm out of bed after her instantly.

"You okay?" I ask her, as she splashes some water on her face.

"I…I think I'm sick." She groans. "I always catch something when the seasons change and the drastic change yesterday and not sleeping much the night before and wearing open-toe shoes, I think my immune system is just fucked." She coughs again. "I'm okay though. I can go lay on the couch. I don't want to get you sick."

"Absolutely the fuck not," I tell her. "Get back in bed." I pick up the phone in the bathroom to call downstairs. She starts to protest but when I point towards the bed, she huffs and leaves the bathroom to go slide under the sheets.

The concierge answers after two rings. "Hello, Mr. Holt, what can I help you with?"

"Can I get some cold medicine, pain reliever, some tea with honey, and some chicken soup please?"

"Sir…unfortunately soup isn't on our late-night or our early breakfast menu, may I suggest—"

"Find some then," I snap and I hear Marissa gasp from the bed.

"Chris!" she croaks and her voice sounds raspy. Then she blows her nose. "Be nice."

"Listen, my girlfriend is sick. Can you please make an exception?" I ask, feeling bad for the attitude I gave the concierge. I just hate seeing Marissa like this, especially after last night when she was already feeling like shit. We had sex last night and it was incredible, but I almost felt like she was holding back a little. The air had shifted slightly due to that old bastard and I hated it. I'd eaten her to two orgasms and had her come on my dick and I still felt the small wall she'd put up.

"Very well, sir. The late-night kitchen might be able to accommodate. Give us about twenty minutes."

"Thank you." I hang up the phone and move back towards her. She'd pulled her hood over her head but I can tell she's shivering because there isn't anything on her bare legs. I go to my suitcase to pull out a pair of sweatpants and move back towards the bed. Moving the covers to the side, I grab one of her feet. She gasps as I slide my sweatpants up her cold legs and pull the drawstring as tight as possible but they still look like she's drowning in them.

"Thank you," she says and I climb in next to her and bring her closer to me.

"Can I do anything?"

"I'm okay. The tea and the medicine will help." She bites her bottom lip. "That was really sweet."

I rub her arm gently as I watch the fatigue settle back over her features. "What are the chances I can take you to my penthouse tonight and you stay there with me?"

She rubs her nose before scrunching it. "Why?"

"So, I can take care of you. You absolutely do not need to come in to work tomorrow."

"Chris, it's my second week. If we weren't sleeping together, you'd be ready to fire me for calling in sick during my second week."

"I'm going to let the slight belittling of our relationship by saying we are *just* sleeping together go for now. Marissa, you are sick."

"I'll be fine. It's just a cold and the first day is always the toughest. I'll be fine by Monday."

"Will you still stay with me tonight anyway?"

"I don't have any clothes for work," she offers and I want to tell her she shouldn't even be thinking about work but I shake my head.

"I have a shopper; I'll pick something up for you," I counter.

"You think of everything, huh?" she says as I watch her eyes start to close. "I'm too tired to argue right now." She turns to her back and lets her eyes flutter closed.

I touch her forehead and while I'm not an expert, I don't think she's warm. "I don't think you have a fever."

"No, I don't think so either," she says. "Just a cold, like I said." She sniffles and pulls the covers up to her neck. "I'll think about coming over," she whispers, her eyes still closed. "But I want to go home and get my car so I can drive to work Monday and that way I can get some clothes."

"Your parents won't have a bunch of questions about where you're staying?"

"They absolutely will." She laughs before letting out another few coughs. "But I'm twenty-one. I don't have to ask for permission to do things. As long as I let them know I won't be home, they'll be fine."

"Then I should probably meet your dad when I bring you home." The thought makes me nervous, but I figure I'll have to do it at some point so I might as well get it over with sooner than later.

"That's a no."

"Why?"

"Because I'm his little princess and believe me, the first time you meet my dad does not need to be as you're taking me home for a sleepover."

"Fine," I relent, because one step at a time I guess, and she seems like she's leaning towards staying with me tonight.

"And even if the circumstances were different, it feels really early to be bringing our families into this. You met my mother by accident."

Several minutes later, I hear a tapping on the door and I get up to grab what I ordered, pleased that it got here so quickly. A lady wheels in the small serving cart complete with the tea, medicine, and soup as well as orange juice, dry toast, and ginger ale, and I'm somewhat impressed that they even added a few things despite their initial reluctance. I thank her before pushing it into the bedroom towards Marissa's side of the bed and she turns her head to look at me. "That was fast."

"It helps to be a VIP," I tell her as I sit next to her. She sits up and I hand her the cold medicine that she takes with a sip of orange juice. I finish making her tea and when I hand it to her she's staring at me. "What?"

"I just...I can't believe that there's a woman out there who doesn't appreciate you," she whispers quietly as I hand her the mug. She wraps her hands around it and blows gently before taking a slow sip. "I'm sure that must bother you."

"Not as much as it used to." I shrug. "In the beginning, yes. I couldn't understand why we just couldn't seem to get along. We were a year into our marriage and arguing all the time and it seemed like nothing made her happy. Once I realized who she really was it more bothered me that I'd let myself get so sucked in. Some would say I got married too fast, I guess." She purses her lips and a frown crosses her face like she wants to say something. "What?"

"I'm just wondering if that is kind of your pattern? I mean… you haven't known me that long and you've already said you want to marry me."

"That's different."

She takes a slow sip of her tea while avoiding my gaze before setting it on her nightstand. "How?

"I know what I want now and what I most definitely don't want. I didn't then. Once you've had the wrong one, you know how different it feels to find the right one."

Marissa seems much better when she wakes up. She isn't coughing nearly as much but I can still hear it in her voice. She sleeps the majority of the way back to Philly and though I feel bad waking her, I'm not sure where we landed on her spending another night with me and I need time to convince her if necessary.

I want another night with her.

Want all of them if I'm being honest.

I know she's still feeling off about the interaction with Blackwell and I want to show her it won't always be like that. That although there is this elephant in the room, she won't be forced to look at it all the time.

My hand hasn't left her leg for the majority of the drive and when we are about twenty minutes out, I squeeze it gently, shaking her awake. She stirs and blinks her eyes at me sleepily before darting her eyes back to the road and then back to me. "How far away are we?"

"About twenty minutes." She nods before pulling the mirror

down and wiping under her eyes. "Stay with me tonight." It comes out more like a statement than a question.

"I feel much better than I did last night."

"Still. I need another night."

She purses her lips and narrows her eyes like she's thinking about it. "We can't be up late."

I nod my head rapidly in agreement. "I can commit to an early bedtime."

"Can you?" She raises an eyebrow at me. "Because you seem to get a second wind around two in the morning."

"It's not the time. It's *you* rubbing your body against me in your sleep." I smirk at her and I can see the grin lurking behind her annoyed expression. I think she's about to respond when her phone starts to ring.

I watch as she narrows her eyes at it like she's not sure if she's going to answer it but I watch as she slides her finger across the screen where the word *Mother* is displayed.

"Helloooo?" she says. "Probably in about twenty minutes or so. Why, Mother?" she says, and then her eyes widen before she squeezes them shut.

FUCK. I watch her mouth.

"Mom, that's really not necessary." She looks at me with a worried expression. "Because it's new and I don't want you all scaring him off. I am not ready for that." I don't know what's being said on the other side but I wonder if I'm about to walk into something we may not be ready for. "Nothing in our family is a quick hello!" she huffs. "Ten minutes in what world?! Is Aunt Theresa there?" She nods. "Of course, she is. Mom, for once can you just...not?" She pinches the bridge of her nose and I can see the anxiety all over her face. Though I'm not exactly calm over the idea of meeting what sounds like a number of Marissa's extended family, I rub her leg gently. When her eyes meet mine, I give her a smile that I hope conveys that everything will be okay.

"I'm good with families," I tell her quietly and she sighs.

"Ten minutes, Mother. I mean it." I haven't heard anything from the other side of the call the entire time they were talking but I hear the response to that which is a loud cheer causing Marissa to pull her phone away from her ear.

"Do not eat or drink anything they offer you," she says when she hangs up the phone.

"Well, that's rude."

"That's how they get you!"

"I feel like that's a little insulting. How much of your family is there?"

"Probably just my parents and my uncle and aunt."

"Not your siblings?" I'm not sure if her siblings will be just as intimidating as meeting her parents, but I figure it couldn't hurt to have someone closer to my age in the mix.

"No," I shake my head. "They're both always working. I think it bothers my parents that they don't make more time for them. Maybe that's why I have it so easy." She shrugs. "They really don't want me to leave. They loved it when I was away at college but now that I'm older they like having me around. Honestly, I think they just like having a live-in designated driver." She shakes her head. "Okay, I was not prepared for this. I really was going to have you drop me off down the street but you can't do that now, can you? You won over my mom easy enough. My dad is…" She puts a finger to her temple and continues to ramble. I'm not even sure if she's talking to herself or to me at this point. "I don't even know how to prepare you for this. Just don't let him rattle you. He can smell fear and if my uncle is there it's just going to rile him up."

"Babe, I can handle it. It'll be okay," I tell her, and although I'm a little bit worried myself, part of me believes it.

Her eyes dart to my left hand that's on the steering wheel and I know what she's looking for. "I haven't worn my wedding ring in years. You think I've been wearing it this weekend?" I shoot her an incredulous look.

"No, I know. I guess it was just a knee-jerk reaction to check."

I nod before changing the subject. "Do you want them to know I'm technically your boss, or are we skirting around that?"

"I'm fairly certain you showing up to my house in a Maserati debunks the belief that you're just my co-worker with the same entry-level salary." She points at the Rolex on my wrist. "That certainly doesn't help."

"Is this your way of asking for a raise?" She glares at me and I smile. "I do have some pull you know."

She puts a hand up. "Now is really not the time."

"Will your parents have a problem with it?"

She bites her bottom lip and I'm reminded that I haven't really kissed her in several hours. I'd given her a few gentle pecks this morning but she hadn't let me deepen it so I wouldn't get sick. "I don't know. I've never been in this situation. Maybe if I tell them that we met at the wedding and that this is all just a coincidence they may back off about it for now. They *shouldn't* really give you a hard time about it. They'll save that for me later."

"Will they have a problem with my age?"

"No." She shakes her head. "You look like you could be anywhere between thirty and your actual age and being only nine years older than me isn't that big of a deal. My brother is about ten years older than my sister-in-law."

"But you're the baby." I smirk as if to say, *the rules are probably very different for you.*

"They won't sweat that," she says. "My parents are…somehow both a little old fashioned and what they believe to be *cool* at the same time."

I nod, understanding somewhat because her parents seem so much different than my mother. "Okay, anything else?" I ask her, wanting to make a good impression.

"No…" She winces. "If I coach you too much, they'll know. They can sniff out bullshit pretty easily. Just be yourself I guess." She smiles at me. "The annoying part about all of this, is that they'll probably like you."

"Annoying part?" I can't deny that it makes me happy that she thinks that her parents will like me. She doesn't answer, she just shoots me a sideways glance before rolling her eyes. I'm about to respond when my phone begins to ring, resounding through the car and connecting to my Bluetooth which just so happens to flash on the screen on my console.

Holly's name appears across the screen and even though I press the end call button before it has a chance to ring a second time, I know Marissa sees it and I watch the hurt flash across her face.

"Marissa..." I start and she shakes her head as she looks out the window.

"It's fine."

"It's not fine."

"No, it's really not. It's fucked up. You are minutes away from meeting my parents and your wife calls you." She lets out a sigh. "You said she didn't care what you did."

"She doesn't," I counter.

"She's calling you after you've been gone for two days. That's a woman who's wondering where her man is."

"I am not her—"

"According to the state of Pennsylvania, you are," she interrupts me with a glare.

"A piece of paper doesn't mean shit."

"Except hundreds of millions of dollars," she snaps and I don't even know what to say to that. "I'll make something up. I'll say you had to go. I don't want you meeting them."

I can see her shutting down quickly and I hate it. "What... Marissa, I can at least come in and say hello."

"No! I don't need them liking you because that will lead to wanting to have you over for dinner or one of my aunt's parties or my nieces' birthdays and that's not happening. You are *not* my boyfriend. You can't be while you're still someone else's husband."

"Then what am I?" I don't know why I ask because I'm not

sure I want to know her answer. I don't want to know what she considers me to be right now.

"I don't know, you tell me?"

"Marissa, you already told them I'd come in. I don't want to be rude to your family and put a bad taste in their mouths for when you are ready to call me your boyfriend," I tell her. "And make no mistake, at some point, you *will* be calling me your boyfriend."

"You can't possibly be that sure of yourself."

"I'm not sure about anything except how much I want to be with you."

She rubs her chest and I watch as the previously hard look on her face softens. "Do you always say the right things?"

"No. And the longer you're with me, you'll see that I don't."

"I still don't think the time is right to meet them. I'll tell them it was my decision."

"This is really what you want?" I ask her, because I don't want to do anything that will cause her family to see me in a bad light. I'm already planning our next date and the one after that and the last thing I want is to piss her parents off before I even have the chance to meet them.

She nods. "I'll come over later. I just…" She trails off. "They're my parents and I feel wrong letting them meet someone under false pretenses."

"It's not false," I tell her because there is nothing untrue about what I feel for her or what I *think* she feels for me.

"Fine. Complicated," she corrects.

I hate the thought that she sees me as complicated even though I understand why. "You promise you'll say it was all your idea?"

"Swear." She crosses an x over her heart.

"I don't want this to come back to bite me in the ass later."

"If it does, I'll let you bite mine as a way to say I'm sorry." She giggles and I can't stop the instant jerking of my cock in response to the thought of sinking my teeth into her perfect ass.

"I want to do more than bite that ass of yours," I tell her and she squirms in her seat.

"Oh? Like what."

I lick my lips. "Eat it, for one. Fuck it, for two."

"I've never done that."

I nod. "I didn't think so but I wasn't sure. You didn't answer when I asked you last time."

"You have a big dick." She fiddles with her hands in her lap.

"Thank you." I smile cockily and she smacks my arm in response.

"I'm worried about it being…there."

"We'll go slow," I tell her. "I'll make it feel good for you. I promise to always make it feel good for you."

Moments later we are pulling up around the corner from her house for her to get out and she stares up at the house that is obviously not hers before letting out a defeated sigh. "You know it's not about you, right?" She tilts her head to the side without looking at me. "I mean it is but it's not," she tries to explain.

"I know," I tell her. "I get it." She gets out of the car and I frown, that she does it before I have a chance to open the door for her. I grab her bag out of the trunk and put it on the sidewalk next to her. "So, I can see you later?"

"Text me the address." She nods before she wraps her arms around me. "I want to see you too."

I cup her face in my hands and press my lips to hers without another thought. I slide my tongue through her lips without a care in the world that she hasn't been feeling well or that we are in the middle of her neighborhood. I need her taste on my tongue and nothing else matters. She gives in with ease, rubbing her tongue against mine and pressing that delectable little body against me.

"What time should I expect you?" I murmur against her lips.

"Maybe an hour?" she says and I nod in response.

"I'll send you the codes for the garage and the elevator."

"Will you not be there?"

"Of course, but just so you have them. You can go whenever you want, even when I'm not there." She bites her lip nervously and I grip her jaw forcing her to release it. "I'm the only one with the codes." I rub my nose against hers. "And now you. No one else will ever be there."

She nods before grabbing her suitcase. "I'll see you in a bit."

"See you soon, gorgeous."

Chapter TEN

CHRIS

I ALREADY KNEW THE HIGH OF THE WEEKEND WITH MARISSA was going to dissipate the second I stepped foot into my house and realized Holly was home. I am actually shocked that she even called me in the first place. She rarely does unless she needs me to approve a big purchase that she's preparing to put through on the credit card. I wasn't even expecting her to be home at all. I figured I could get in and out with a change of clothes and be ready to meet Marissa at my penthouse with roses I'd already called in to my local florist and more tea in case she still has some lingering effects of her cold.

I feel rattled the second I walk through the door, as if the previous weekend of relaxation with Marissa hadn't happened. Despite what happened last night, I felt lighter than I have in weeks.

But the second I walked in, Holly is waiting for me in my bedroom with a saccharine grin masking her usual look of indifference.

"What are you doing in my bedroom?" I ask her as I drop my bag in my closet and begin looking for a suit to wear tomorrow. While I have suits at my penthouse, I know I have a meeting tomorrow and I wanted to wear one of the ones I keep here.

"Does a woman *need* a reason for wanting to be around her husband?"

"Women, no. You, yes." I look at her and she furrows her brow before tossing a curly brown strand behind her shoulder. Once upon a time, I believed Holly to be one of the most beautiful women I'd ever met and I'll admit even now, objectively she is a good-looking woman. *Despite her very ugly personality.* Long, glossy, chestnut hair, green eyes, high cheekbones, and a button nose. A nose that isn't exactly the same as when I met her but I never asked or cared what she'd done to alter her appearance once she got her hands on my money. I'm fairly certain she got a boob job at one point also, but again, I hadn't asked and she hadn't offered up the information so I figured that meant I was supposed to pretend she'd always looked this way.

She runs a hand through her hair and tucks a leg under her. "What are you doing?"

"I have an early business meeting. I'm staying in the city," I tell her without even a glance towards her.

"Wow," she says and I can hear that tone that drives me crazy. "You must really like her." I don't respond, not wanting to engage with her. "A weekend in the city plus another night? She know you're married?" I walk out of my closet and come face to face with Holly who's got the smuggest grin on her face.

"What do you want, Holly? Just tell me what it is, so you can go."

"Nothing? I'm just catching up with my husband."

I chuckle as I open the bag I'd just taken to New York. "Funny how you only call me your husband when it suits you."

"I always think of you as my husband. It's you that forgets you have a wife."

"Trust me. I remember," I grit out as I zip up the garment bag with my suit. "I'll be in the city."

"You didn't answer my question," she says. "Does she know you're married?"

I want to react. I want to tell her that Marissa does and as soon as the workday begins Monday morning, I plan to be in touch with my lawyer to figure out what I can do to change that. But I don't want to show my hand. I don't want Holly to know that her days of calling herself my wife are numbered, especially because she doesn't even care about the title past anything financial.

Feeling what I feel for Marissa has made me realize that I really can't be with Holly forever.

I want more.

"I'll see you later, Holly." I zip my weekender back up and sling it over my shoulder. She follows me out of my room but doesn't say anything. I move down the spiral staircase but I don't hear her footsteps behind me nor does she follow me into the garage. Maybe she knows that this woman means more because rarely do I spend this many consecutive days out of the house. Maybe I should be more concerned about her realizing that fact but I don't care. All I care about is being at my penthouse when Marissa shows up.

I've just finished lighting another candle in the living room when I hear the ding of the elevator and then she's walking towards me like she's confused as to how she got here. She turns around to look at the elevator and then back at me, her eyes still wide like a deer caught in headlights. "It opens…" Her mouth drops open in surprise. "Wow."

I walk towards her, my body already releasing the tension it felt over the conversation with Holly at just the mere sight of Marissa's smile.

"Wow is right," I say just before I pull her into a hug and squeeze her like I haven't seen her in days and not the hour it's been since I dropped her off. She changed into leggings and a cropped t-shirt underneath a leather jacket and the sight of her ass in that tight material makes my dick hard instantly. She has a bag tucked under her arm that I pull from her and drop to the ground at our feet before pressing my lips to hers. "I'm glad you're here," I tell her when I pull away and grab her hand.

Her eyes immediately find the crimson-colored roses on the island in the kitchen and she glances back at me. "Those for me?" I nod as she takes a sniff of them and drags her fingertips over the petals. "They're so pretty. I wish I could take them home," she says and I make a mental note to have some delivered to her house.

"Do you want a tour?" I ask her and she shoots me a wicked glare and drags her hands underneath my shirt.

"Maybe after?"

I raise an eyebrow at her. "After?"

She pushes herself against me and presses her mouth to my neck. The softness of her lips sends a shudder through me. "I think we have a problem, Chris."

"Oh?" I lift her into my arms and immediately she wraps her legs around my waist as she trails kisses down my neck. "What's that?" I ask her as I walk us up the flight of stairs toward my bedroom. She pulls her jacket off, letting it fall somewhere on the stairs, followed by her shirt which she pulls over her head leaving her in a lace practically see-through bra that her nipples are poking through.

"Just the thought of you makes me wet."

My dick hardens even more. "Is that so?"

"When I got out of my car downstairs, it's like my body knew you were close by." I walk her into my bedroom and push her hard against one of the walls just as her hands push into my hair forcing my face upward towards hers. She presses her lips to mine and I groan against hers.

"Every part of me can sense when you're close," I tell her. "Your scent is all over *Beckham Securities* and it drives me crazy." I reluctantly set her on her feet and my dick throbs painfully, like it's not on board with the idea of not having her pressed up against me. I drop to my knees in front of her, pull off her tennis shoes, and then slowly slide her leggings down. "Whenever you've been in my office, it takes a full ten minutes for my dick to go down." She puts her hands on my shoulders to balance herself while I pull her leggings off. I hadn't realized she unsnapped her bra until it drops to the floor next to me. I look to the discarded lace before I slowly drag my eyes up the length of her body and meet her hooded gaze. "It's only a matter of time before I have to bend you over my desk to take the edge off and get me through the day."

She licks her lips and I take the waistband of her underwear between my teeth and slowly move them down. My lips brush against her mound in the process and I watch the goosebumps erupt on her flesh. Once they hit the ground and she steps out of them, I not only sense how wet she is, but I can see it. Her wetness clings to her pussy and my mouth waters for a taste of it.

I stand up and I want to laugh at the pout on her face when she realizes I'm not going to devour her cunt *yet*. "On the bed."

She narrows her eyes at me before she begins to slowly walk towards the bed, her eyes still glaring sexily at me with every step. She sits on the bed, her legs slightly spread and I pull the t-shirt I'm wearing over my head. I watch as her eyes light up full of excitement the second my naked torso comes into view and it never gets old witnessing her reaction to me getting undressed. I know I have a nice body, and I'm used to looks of appreciation, but there's something different about getting that kind of reaction from the woman I'm obsessed with.

I watch as her eyes ping-pong from my eyes to my chest to my covered dick. Her bottom lip makes its way between her teeth and one of her fingers slides through her sex and I watch as a sexy shiver wracks her body. "God you're hot."

"Fuck." I groan, the visual stimulation of seeing her rub one and then two of her fingers over her clit almost too much. I'm on the bed and between her legs in an instant, wanting a closer look of her fingering herself. She starts to pull away when I grab her wrist, holding it in place. I use my other hand to push her to her back and then I let my tongue gently brush against her cunt, dragging against her two fingers in the process. She lets out a whimper as she continues to rub her clit and I slide my tongue into her opening.

"Chris…" She moans. "I need…fuck. I'm going to come." I pull away from her and grab her hand, removing it from between her legs and she cries out. "No!"

I suck her fingers into my mouth, licking all the traces of her pussy from her before setting it down next to her and settling between her legs. I take a slow lick through her sex before swirling my tongue in a circle on her clit and her hands find their way into my hair pulling me harder against her. I feel her raise her hips to get closer to me, and *fuck me*, I wish either of us knew a way to get us closer because I'd surely fucking do it.

"I want to sit on your face," she says, her voice shaky and breathy with a hint of desperation. Almost as if she's asking as more of a formality but she's not above pushing me to my back and mounting my face.

I don't think she's counting on how bad I want just that because I'm on my back and have my hands wrapped around her hips, pulling her to straddle my face all in the span of a second. She gasps when I pull her hard against my mouth, my tongue already inside of her. "Wait!" she cries as she looks down at me, and when our eyes meet, I give her a look that I hope she reads as *yeah fucking right*. "I wanted to sixty-nine, hello!?" She points behind her to my dick.

"Tough." I grit against her. "You didn't specify so I made an executive decision," I tell her between light licks on her clit. Her hands reach up to grab her breasts and she pinches both of her nipples, rolling them between her fingers as she begins to move her hips slightly against my mouth. "Seems like you're okay with it." I wink at her, and put a hand on each of her ass cheeks, pulling her so she's practically sitting on my face and she cries out when I grip her tighter, letting my nails press into her flesh.

"Oh fuck," she moans. "Between your stubble and your fingers and your tongue, it's so much." She cries out just as her hands reach behind her to grip my thighs. I'm not sure if it's for balance or to give herself some leverage to grind against my mouth but she begins moving her hips like she would if she were riding my dick. My cock tingles almost painfully, like it can feel her cunt around it and then I feel her hand on my dick, rubbing it.

"Get it out," she commands me. I take my hands off her ass and manage to slide my sweatpants down slightly to release my dick and I'm glad I'd had the foresight to take off my briefs before she got here. She looks down at me for the span of a second, long enough for me to watch her spit in her hand, and then reaches behind her. She finds my dick instantly, wraps her hand around it, and moves up and down in time with the way she's fucking my face.

"Christ, Marissa. You're going to be the death of me, you know that?" My eyes slam shut as I feel my orgasm start to build brought on by her hand and her taste. "Stop, if you don't want me to come all over your hand," I tell her and she halts her movements.

"Do you care about your blankets?"

"Fuck no," I grunt just before sucking her clit into my mouth.

"Oh!" She moans and I know she's been close for a while. My eyes dart up and I see her head tipped back and then she squeezes my dick a little harder just as her cunt pulses around my tongue. "Fuck yes," she whimpers as she jacks me off through the entirety of her orgasm. She moves her hips in a circle, "Chris, oh my god, yessss." And my name leaving her lips in that sexy voice tips me over the edge, and I feel myself releasing god knows where.

"Fuuuuck." I groan into her cunt and I hear her giggle and I don't know if it's from the vibrations against her or the hot cum trickling down her hand or maybe both.

I eventually feel her hand leave my dick and when I open my eyes, I see her dragging her tongue along her palm with a wicked smile on her face. I place another kiss on her cunt and she squeals before climbing off of me and then I'm on top of her, my lips attached to hers. I kick my sweats off, leaving us both completely naked and I fucking love feeling her smooth skin against mine. She kisses me back with equal enthusiasm like she cares more about keeping our mouths pressed together than she does about taking a breath.

She wraps her legs around my waist and even though I'd just come everywhere, just feeling the heat of her cunt against me is enough to make me hard again.

"You're hard again?"

"It seems to be what happens whenever you're close by." The kiss turns wetter and more aggressive and I don't miss all of the sexy whimpers that leave her every time my cock brushes against her cunt.

"You taste like me," she whispers just before she drags her tongue along mine.

"My favorite fucking taste," I tell her. I don't know how long we are like this, our arms and legs intertwined as we kiss like two people who are slowly falling into something deeper, but at some point, she pulls away. Her lips are swollen and pink and her brown eyes are slightly glassy.

"What is it?" I ask her and she pulls away, letting her chin rest on my chest as she looks up at me with those eyes I could easily get lost in.

"I wish I'd met you before you were married."

I move us so we are lying on our sides facing each other and prop my head up on one hand. "So do I."

"Where does she think you are right now?" she asks as she slowly blinks the tears out of her eyes.

"Here," I tell her honestly.

"Does she think you're alone?"

"No."

She sits up and I wonder if telling her that was the wrong answer. "So, she knows about me?" she asks weakly and I watch her scrunch her nose.

I sit up and reach for her, hoping I can stop her from shutting down on me. "She knows there's a woman in my life."

She lets out a sigh and drops her head to my shoulder before wrapping her arms around my neck. "I really don't want to let you go."

I pull her away from my neck and meet her sad gaze. "Who's letting anyone go?"

"I'm not that naive to think that this is going to be easy. And you stand to lose the most...I just..." She swallows nervously. "Right now, things are exciting and fun and new and sexy and I know there's a possibility that when the novelty wears off, you may rethink the choice of wanting to blow up your entire life."

"Marissa—" I start.

"No, I know you say it's not like that but...it's just hard for me to not have that thought in the back of my mind. You have so much to lose."

"Maybe, but the tradeoff is getting you. I'm gaining what I want the most," I tell her and watch the worry leave her face as she relaxes in my arms. "I get it. You think I'm just reacting impulsively to the most amazing sex of my life with the woman I haven't been able to shake for months." I grin at her and a shy grin finds her face. "But it really is bigger than that." I sigh. "I want to be with you, Marissa. But on the off chance it doesn't work out between us, I still need a divorce. I'm only thirty-four, and I can't spend the rest of my life in this marriage. Now that I've seen that *this* is possible, I want it. I don't want a life of complacency. I want to be married to the love of my life and Holly isn't it."

Chapter

ELEVEN

Marissa

THE NEXT FEW WEEKS SEEM TO FLY BY AS I GET acclimated to my new job. Even though I can feel Chris' heated gaze on me every time I pass him in the office, we've managed to keep our hands off of each other between the hours of nine and five Monday through Friday. There was one time that he'd pressed me up against his car in the garage and kissed me senseless on a night I had plans with my sister, so I wasn't staying at the penthouse. But other than that, we hadn't done anything anywhere there was a chance we could get caught. Not only do I work for him and it is against some pretty strict fraternization policies, but everyone knows he's married and I am not interested in letting the entire office think that fact doesn't faze me. *Or worse, that I'm sleeping my way to the top.* Both of us have too much at stake.

It doesn't stop us from spending most of our days texting though.

A beep distracts me from the email I'm sending and his name crosses my screen.

> **Chris:** You look so beautiful today.

I can't stop the smile from finding my face.

> **Me:** So you told me this morning.

I'd stayed with Chris last night and we were almost late for work because he tried to fuck me on his kitchen counter when he saw me dressed and ready this morning.

> **Chris:** And I'll probably tell you three more times before the day is over.

I'm about to text him back when Elise, who was just recently hired as well, stops by my cubicle. "Hey girl."

We'd bonded over going to the same college in Boston and having some mutual friends and our love for yoga and binge-watching Golden Girls reruns. She'd also managed to get on Wes Beckham's bad side on her first day, so we've commiserated a few times over how much of an asshole he is. She's sweet in that way that makes her liked by everyone, and while I'm sometimes wary of those types of women because they weren't always that nice behind closed doors, I think she may actually be genuine.

"You coming out tonight?" she asks as she leans over my short wall and lets her hands rest under her chin. I'm in a group chat with all of the new hires and we've been trying to coordinate doing something outside of work since we started, but it hasn't worked out until now. "I think a few other people from the office are coming too."

As much as I wanted to hole up with Chris in his penthouse, I should probably try to make some friends with more of my colleagues. I am not by any means shy, but I am a hard worker and I rarely leave my desk while I'm here. I'm just trying to get acclimated and prevent getting screamed at again by one of the richest men in the country.

I nod. "Yep, I'll be there. We're meeting around eight, right?"

She moves into my cubicle which I'm thankfully not sharing with anyone yet and leans against my desk. "I think I want to hook up with Liam."

I spin in my chair and cross my legs, leaning forward. "Oh?"

"I don't know. We've been flirting and…texting outside our group chat." Liam Patterson was also hired at the same time as us, and while objectively I find him attractive with his All-American boy look mixed with Southern boy charm, he really isn't my type. *The man I'm currently smitten with aside.* "I know you guys are pretty good friends and at the risk of sounding so lame, has he…said anything about me?" Liam and I typically have lunch together, *maybe because I'm the one girl in the office whose panties he's not trying to get into.*

"Ummm maybe?" I say, really not wanting to get involved. "I don't really remember," I say, but I do and he has. Something along the lines of *hot and very fuckable*. "But I don't think he's really interested in dating anyone."

"Who said anything about dating?" She fusses with her curly hair in her compact mirror before tucking a blonde strand behind her ear. "I just want to have some fun. Anyway, I'm glad you're coming. I'm probably going to text you later because I have no idea what I'm wearing," she says with a smile before she disappears.

I pull up my messages with Chris once she's gone and type out a reply.

> Me: So a few of us new hires are going out tonight. Maaaaybe we can see each other later?

I hoped he could read between the lines that I would probably be a little tipsy and probably more overzealous than usual about putting my mouth on his dick.

> **Chris:** I've been wondering when you all were going to go out. Where are you going?

> **Me:** I think we are starting at someone's house and then going somewhere in the city.

> **Chris:** Behave yourself.

I raise an eyebrow at my phone, my fingers itching to type the words, but not sure how he'll respond to it. *Fuck it.*

> **Me:** Yes daddy.

I bite down on my bottom lip, a smile pulling at my lips as I watch the bubbles appear instantly before disappearing. This goes on for a minute before two words pop up on my screen and the air leaves my lungs in a gush.

> **Chris:** My office.

I am about to protest that we really shouldn't when another message comes through.

> **Chris:** Now.

Despite the horrible idea this is, my pussy seems to disagree and the heartbeat beginning to pulse between my legs forces me to my feet and towards his office. I'm grateful Christine isn't at her desk and there doesn't seem to be anyone lurking in the hallway that will see me going into his office. Not that it's unheard of for me to have a meeting with him but it isn't usually one on one. I don't even have a chance to knock on the door before it swings open and he stands to the side to let me enter. He closes it, standing in front of it with one leg crossed over the other and his arms crossed over his chest as he drags his eyes up my body slowly.

"Sit on my desk."

"Chris…" His hand finds the handle on the door and when he turns the lock, the quiet noise resounds around the room. "We can't…we've been doing so good!" I whisper and he shakes his head.

"Say it again."

"Say what?"

"You know what."

I take a step back when he takes a step towards me and continue walking backward as he moves closer like he's preparing to pounce on me. "No. You're being reckless." I shake my head despite the fact that my body is practically humming for him. It's one of the last warm days of October, so I'm wearing a skirt and it would be so easy for him to reach his hand under it and touch me or kiss me or…*fuck me.*

"Trust me, I'm trying to," he says and I realize I must have said that last part out loud. His hands are on my hips and he has me pinned against his desk. "I need to fuck you." I can practically hear the pleading in his voice and I'll admit his constant desperation for me is fucking hot.

"Chris…" I gasp when he spins me around to face my desk. I feel his erection pressing into my back and his hands drag up my body to cup my breasts.

"My office is soundproof, stop whispering." He pushes my hair to one side, exposing my neck, and presses his lips to the space where it meets my shoulder before dragging them up slowly. "Are you going to be a good girl and let me touch you?" he murmurs against my neck before pressing his teeth to the space. His hands move down and then slowly up my skirt up. He reaches around and strokes my thighs slowly, moving closer to my pussy with each passing second. "Answer me, Marissa. Are you my good girl?"

I'm panting at this point. My heart is pounding and my entire body feels like it's on fire. His hands find the waistband of my underwear and he drags his index finger over the skin just below my belly button, teasing me. My stomach flips at the ticklish feeling and my pussy clenches involuntarily.

"Chris."

"Mmmm?" He chuckles just before he slides his hand beneath the waistband and cups me, pushing me back against him. "Say it."

"Yes, I am a good girl." I breathe out just as he parts my sex and drags a finger through the slit. "Yes," I repeat and my eyes flutter shut as the feeling of his very talented fingers rubs my clit. I fucking loved his hands. I've never been big on fingering but I realized it was because I'd never been fingered by Chris Holt who knows exactly what he is doing.

"Yes, what?" he asks.

I turn my head and give him a cheeky grin over my shoulder. "If I knew calling you Daddy would make you this unhinged, I may have said it sooner."

"Fuck," he says as he begins to rub me harder. "Say it again."

I pull his hand from between my legs and hop on his desk, spreading my legs and pulling my underwear to the side to expose my wet cunt to him. "Fuck me, Daddy."

He unbuckles his belt and unzips his slacks all within the span of a second, pulling his dick out and staring at my bare wet cunt as he drags his hand from root to tip. "We shouldn't be fucking doing this here," he says with his eyes still staring between my legs.

"No, we shouldn't. Anyone could catch us," I whisper. He swallows hard before his eyes meet mine and I can see the smile in them. "But I ache for you, Daddy." I bite my bottom lip and lower my gaze to his dick. "Make it feel better."

"Jesus. Whatever you want." He groans as he moves closer to me. He tilts my chin up to meet his eyes just as he swipes his dick through my slit once.

"I don't have time to taste you now, but tell me I can later." He pushes inside of me slowly with shallow thrusts but not going all the way inside. "Tell me you'll let Daddy taste your pretty cunt later."

My eyes widen at his dirty words and I can feel my cheeks heating. "Yes," I whisper just before he presses his lips to mine in a kiss so delicious, I feel it all the way in my toes.

"Put me all the way inside of you," he whispers against my lips and I reach for his dick, which is still tracing my opening, and guide him inside of me slowly. I clench around his head, letting my pussy pulse around him and he lets out a low groan.

"Don't tease Daddy," he says and I giggle at his obvious feeling of torment just before he pushes his dick fully inside of me and swallows the moan that leaves me. I drop a hand to his desk behind me and place a hand at the back of his neck to help me meet his thrusts as our bodies slap together frantically. "I can't believe this is happening," I murmur as my eyes flutter open. He stops thrusting for a second and stares down at me like I'm the most precious thing he's ever seen.

"I can't either," he says.

I was somewhat staying in character for our daddy fantasy and also referring to the fact that he's fucking me on his desk during the workday, but with the way he's looking at me, I think he means something else entirely. He gives me a smile that makes my heart flutter in my chest before he lowers his lips to mine again and begins moving in and out of me slowly. It's not as frenzied, but rather like he believes us to have all the time in the world.

"Marissa." He tucks his face into my neck. "I…fuck…" he starts, "I need you to come." He pushes in harder and it hits that spot deep within that makes me squirm against him.

"Chris." I let my head fall back and his lips trace the slope of my neck.

"You're so fucking perfect. Squeeze my dick, honey," he says and I can't stop the gasp that leaves my lips. He usually calls me babe and hearing this new name makes my heart thump in my chest. Like we'd somehow unlocked something different in our relationship. "Yes, just like that. Just like fucking that." His rhythm picks up and he begins to fuck me faster. "Can I come inside?"

"God." I moan, my body already too far gone to realize that I probably shouldn't let my boss come inside of me when I still have to work the rest of the day while wearing a thong. "Yes yes yes, please. Come inside me. Always fucking come inside me." I lift my head and meet his icy blue eyes. His gaze is hard and intense and I suddenly feel very vulnerable. It makes me feel like my walls are lowering even more to let this man into my heart. I blink away, not wanting his eyes and his mouth and his dick to trick my heart into thinking I'm ready to be all in.

"Look at me." I shake my head, keeping my eyes closed but he turns my chin gently. "Please." I reluctantly open them and he's looking at me with concern. He's still hard inside of me and I wonder if he'll be able to stay that way through whatever he's about to say. "We're in this together, you and me." His voice is laced with such sincerity that I have to talk myself out of crying. "Don't hide your feelings from me."

"How can it be you and me when it's you and someone else?" The words leave my lips without a second thought and I wish I hadn't said that while he's still inside of me.

"It's only you and me here." He grabs my hand and presses it to the space over his heart.

"Chris," I say, doing my best to blink the tears away but failing fucking miserably as one slides down my cheek.

"Please don't cry." His thumb wipes it away and I blink the rest away to prevent any more from falling. He rubs his nose against mine and begins thrusting again. "I need a lot more of you and this later, but I need you to come now. I only bought us twenty minutes," he says before pressing his lips to mine. He drops his fingers between us and begins rubbing them over my clit and it doesn't take but a few strokes for my orgasm to start building fast.

"Shit, are you close?" I sputter out as my toes begin to curl despite the four-inch heels on my feet.

"Been close, since you called me Daddy." He chuckles and the reminder that we'd unlocked that kink sends me over the edge.

"Oh my god, yes fuck, I'm coming," I moan as I clamp down around him.

"Oh, there it fucking is. So pretty. So fucking pretty." He grunts as I feel his dick expand inside of me. "Fuck fuck fuck, I love feeling you come on my dick." He slows his thrusts as his orgasm wanes. "Only thing that comes close is feeling you come on my tongue." I squeeze again in response and I hear a low chuckle as he slowly pulls out. "Hold on," he tells me as he tucks himself into his briefs and pulls up his pants quickly before he unknots his tie and slides it off. He spreads my cunt with his fingers and he licks his lips like he wants a taste.

"No," I tell him, pushing my hands against his shoulders.

"Just a taste."

"Good joke," I tell him, knowing the second he puts his mouth there, he won't stop until I come again and we don't have that kind of time.

He huffs. "Fine." He slowly drags his tie up my slit, trying to wipe away as much of his orgasm as possible.

"Oh my god, Chris, your tie." It was gorgeous, royal blue silk with flecks of silver and it's one I've seen him wear a few times so I assume it's one of his favorites.

"I have a backup." He continues cleaning me up with his tie. "Once I get it dry cleaned, I'll think of your pussy every time I put it on."

I cock my head to the side just before he slides my underwear back into place. "Are you ever not thinking about my pussy?"

"Rarely." He helps me off my desk and helps me straighten my clothes.

"That was so hot," I tell him as I fan my face, trying to cool my heated skin. He cups my face before pressing a kiss to my nose and then my lips.

"Yes, it was. So, I'll see you tonight after you go out? Let me know when to pick you up?"

Chapter TWELVE

CHRIS

I'D GONE TO A BAR WITH BECK IN AN ATTEMPT TO KILL TIME before I picked up Marissa and although she claims she isn't ready, her texts have slowly gotten more obscene as the night goes on. I'm lining my cue stick up to shoot my turn at our game of pool when I feel another vibration in my back pocket. I don't even care that I fucked up my shot when I see what she's written.

Marissa: I want your dick so bad.

Me: Is that so?

Marissa: Yes! You have a really fabulous dick, you know.

Me: So I've been told.

Marissa: By who?!?

Me: By you.

> **Marissa:** Uh huh. I better be the only person getting to see your fabulous dick, Christopher Ethan.

> **Me:** Don't middle name me over that. You know you are. Are you ready for me to come get you?

"You've been grinning like a fool at your phone all night. Who are you talking to?" Beck asks as he looks up at me from where he's about to take his shot. He shoots, knocking two striped balls into a corner pocket and I groan, knowing that if he beats me, I'll never hear the end of it.

"No one serious." The fewer people I involve in this the better and if I tell him I'm still talking to the woman from Owen's wedding he'll want to know more details and potentially meet her and I'm not ready for Beck to know that I'm not only sleeping with someone from work but in the process of leaving my wife for her. I haven't given him details from the weekend when we were in New York and he hasn't probed much. He probably assumes I got her out of my system and am over her.

"That smile certainly looks serious. A random girl doesn't make you light up like that."

"No, random girls don't make *you* light up because you're a hopeless romantic that has an aversion to one-night stands."

"I don't necessarily have an aversion to them." He pushes his glasses up. "I just…think they're oftentimes messy or disappointing and I'd rather sleep with someone I have a connection with." He misses his next shot and swears under his breath before pulling his beer to his lips. There's a group of women in the corner who I've caught staring at us on more than one occasion since we started playing and when one of them meets my gaze, I pan my gaze to Beck. I'm most definitely not on the market, but maybe Beck could be interested.

The eye contact must have been all the confidence she needed because two of them are standing next to our table within a minute.

A blonde and a brunette, blue eyes and green eyes and neither one of them Marissa Collins.

"Care for a friendly game," one of them asks and then they are both pulling sticks off the wall like we already agreed.

Beck looks at me and then at them from over his glasses and gives them a polite smile. "Hello ladies, we are actually about to wrap this up for the night." He points at me. "He's also married." Rarely does he play that card so he must know I'm not interested.

Right on time, my phone vibrates and the reason I'm not interested flashes across my screen with an incoming call and I can't even stop the smile from crossing my face.

"Just a second," I say and Beck glares at me for leaving him alone with the women that are still hanging around. I hear one of them ask about his relationship situation and I shake my head at Beck's inability to ever be dishonest because he surely should have told them we were both married.

"Hi beautiful."

"Hi," she says and I can tell she's been drinking but I'm not sure how much.

"How much have you had to drink?"

"Not much!"

"What's not much?"

"Hmmm."

"Didn't I tell you to behave yourself?"

"I am! I only had a few shots."

"Shots?"

"Remember when we did shots at Lex and Owen's wedding?"

"I do remember." I lean against a wall. I look over my shoulder to make sure Beck hasn't snuck up behind me to be nosy and I see he's on his phone and the women have retreated to their table. "Should I be expecting a repeat of that night?"

"Yes," she murmurs. "Plus, your dick in my mouth." My cock throbs. "And maybe somewhere else if you're nice." *Fuck.* My mind is already coming up with a way to blow Beck off and the fastest way to get her into bed.

"I'm always nice. Especially to you," I tell her.

"Elise is waving me over, I should go."

I look at my watch, noticing the time inching closer to midnight. It's not necessarily late, but I want as much time with her as possible. "I can't wait to see you."

"Come in an hour."

"You got it, beautiful." I hang up and make my way over to Wes who's staring down at his phone.

He looks up at me and a smile pulls at his lips. "Since when can't you take a call from a woman in front of me? Quite frankly I've heard more than I care to know about you in the past."

I rub my hands together. "Okay, if I tell you something, can you not ask a bunch of questions?"

He narrows his eyes at me. "Is it legal?"

"What? Yes, of course it is. I'm talking about the woman, Beck."

"Okay, shoot."

"I had divorce papers drawn up. I'm serving Holly on Monday." All the air leaves my lungs in a rush because Beck is the first person I've told. I haven't even told Marissa this yet, or my mother or my sisters. All of whom I know will be thrilled, but I know this is just the first step. I was planning to tell Marissa this weekend and I didn't want to tell my family until Holly had at the very least been served.

"I've been with you for the past two hours and you're just now telling me this? Why aren't we celebrating?" He clinks his glass to mine. "I'm so fucking happy for you."

"Because this is only the first step. You and I both know this is not going to be easy. She's probably going to want me to make about a hundred addendums." I rub my forehead. "She's already getting a fuck ton more than I had hoped but I want out. It's time."

"Is this all because of the new woman?" He nods at my phone. "The 'not serious one,' which I knew is bullshit by the way."

"Yes and no," I tell him as I think about what Marissa said on our first date about wanting to get out of my marriage for me and not *just* to have a shot with her. "I like her a lot." I slide my hand into my pocket and drag my finger over her hair pin. It reminds me that she doesn't even know I've been carrying it around. "She's not crazy about the fact that I'm married, obviously."

"You tell her you're working on that?"

"Not yet. You're the first person I've told."

He puts a hand over his heart. "I'm honored."

"Shut up, dick." I chuckle as I pinch the bridge of my nose thinking about the chaos I'm preparing to bring into my life. "Holly is going to lose her shit."

"Probably." He drops to a seat in the corner. "But what is she going to do, force you to stay married?"

I sit in the adjacent chair and take a sip of my beer. "Bring up every time I've ever been unfaithful in attempts to get more money, I'm sure."

"Maybe if you just talk to her calmly and explain to her that you know she's not happy also and you're trying to do the right thing by you both. We know how she is but maybe there's someone else better suited for her."

"You mean like Satan himself?" I put my hands over my face. "I feel like I'm about to go to war." I shoot him a glare. "Why did you let me marry her?"

Beck chuckles and shakes his head. "Oh no, you're not putting that on me. I believe I tried to talk you out of it more than once. Even before she turned into..." He trails off, because there really wasn't one way to describe the person Holly became after we got married. "I still didn't think she was right for you."

Wes rarely likes to be out past midnight, so he's ready to go before it's even time for me to pick up Marissa. I know where they are so

I decide to go early and wait for her. I had planned to wait in the car, but my curiosity gets the best of me and I wonder if there are any men in the office who may be interested. I'm not worried she'd do anything, but some of these *casual* outings become breeding grounds for interoffice hookups, and I'm curious if anyone in the office is trying to shoot their shot with my girl. I find street parking relatively close and make my way into the club, not even glancing at the line down the block before giving the guy at the door a hundred dollar bill. I hate doing that but hate the idea of anything standing in the way of seeing Marissa even more.

I make my way into the club and it is loud and hot and I've already stepped in something sticky reminding me that most, if not all of them are in their early twenties. The music is EDM and there are clustered groups of people everywhere dancing. *There's no way I'll be able to find her.*

I am not that far removed from the party scene, but even this is a bit too much for me. I haven't been to any bar or club in at least three years where there wasn't at least an option to sit down. I don't even see a space for reserved tables which most clubs have nowadays. I chuckle and shake my head as the DJ says something and everyone cheers.

A group of girls stumble by me and one stops in her tracks causing one to bump into the back of her. The first girl, clearly drunk, blinks her eyes several times and takes a few steps towards me. "Are you a model?"

I look around me. "Not that I know of?"

"You are hot. You should be a model," she says as she drags her eyes over me.

"B!!" The second girl that almost tripped over her smacks her arm. "Leave him alone."

B or drunk girl number one, cocks her head to the side. "Do you have a girlfriend?"

"I do." I nod at her, wishing like hell she'd somehow manifest.

"And she let you out without her? Looking like that?" She

blinks up at me and I definitely do not remember girls being this bold in my early twenties even after multiple shots. "Is she here?"

I'm about to respond when my eyes move away from her and I see Marissa staring at me with her arms across her chest and a look on her face that I can't quite decipher. She's wearing a black strapless jumpsuit and her hair is pulled up into a messy ponytail on the top of her head, like it had been down earlier but she'd gotten hot. She looked fucking sexy and maybe a little jealous over what looks like me entertaining another woman. *I hope she knows better.*

I look at the woman, who hasn't moved, but is now talking to her friend. I turn my eyes back to Marissa and raise an eyebrow at her and I hope she sees it as a dare to come over here and stake her claim despite the half dozen people running around this club that also work for me. The music shifts to something sexier and I watch as she takes a long sip of her drink before setting it on a high-top table on her way towards me.

Her eyes don't leave me the entire time and the second she's within arm's reach, I hold my hand out for her. She glances at it briefly before turning her head over her shoulder and doing a brief scan of who's behind her. She shakes her head slowly but when I drop my hand, hers brushes against mine and I feel her pinky link with mine. I turn to look at her before the two girls in front of me follow suit. "Hi," she says.

"Hello." I look her up and down salaciously, not sure how she's planning to play this and wanting to play along however she wants.

"You here with them?" she asks and the two girls look at her.

"Nope," I tell her, my eyes never leaving her.

"He said he has a girlfriend," drunk girl number two says.

"Did he now?" She narrows her eyes at me. "Well, I won't bother you then."

"You are definitely not." I tell her as I shake my head slowly.

"Marissa," she says as if introducing herself.

"Chris."

One of the drunk girls, *don't know or care who,* asks, "Do you two know each other?"

"Nope," we say in unison, grins pulling at both of our lips.

"Can I come home with you?" she asks as she makes an obvious show that she's looking at my dick.

"I'm already in the car waiting."

"I think that's his girlfriend," I hear one of them say and then I sense movement in my periphery and while I am enjoying our little show, I am more than ready to take her home.

"You ready?"

She nods and then she's moving towards the door and I'm following no more than an inch behind her. "Is anyone from the office still in there?" I nod behind us as we step outside and guide her to my car.

"A few, but the majority went home. They're pretty drunk though."

"You tell them you were leaving?" I know Irish exits are popular, but I'd like to think we've cultivated an environment where people would look out for each other while they're out drinking.

I nod. "I sent a message to the group chat once I saw you. I wasn't expecting you to come in."

"Was just curious if there was anyone in the office I had to worry about."

She turns her head towards me confused as we turn the corner. "Like…another guy?"

"I didn't think you'd be interested but…this is the time where a man shoots his shot with women he works with."

We make it to my car and I reach for the door but she leans against it, preventing me from opening it, and pulls me gently by the t-shirt I'm wearing under my leather jacket. "I would say I have a boyfriend."

I was not expecting that. "Oh?"

"Well, don't I? You said you have a girlfriend."

I take a step closer to her, resting my forearms on the top of my car and pressing myself against her. "I think this is the first time you've called me that."

She shrugs. "I just didn't want anyone hitting on me. I always say that when I don't feel like warding off men's advances even when I don't have one." She licks her lips. "I told another one of the groomsmen at Lex and Owen's wedding I had a boyfriend."

Annoyance flares through me that one of Owen's friends tried to make a pass at her, but I also want to beat my chest with pride that she didn't tell me the same thing. "What happened to him?" I ask her. "The mystery boyfriend."

"I broke up with him when you approached me."

"You're really stroking my ego, right now."

"I'd rather be stroking something else." She says just before she leans forward and presses a kiss to my lips.

Chapter

THIRTEEN

CHRIS

MARISSA IS ON ME THE SECOND WE GET OFF THE elevator, her hands down my jeans as best as she can and her lips on my neck as she grinds her sexy body against me. She takes her hand out of my pants and slides them slowly up my shirt dragging her nails over the skin which sends a spark to my dick.

"You are so fucking hot," she murmurs against my skin before licking a trail up my neck. She's not so much shorter than me that she struggles to reach my neck but I lift her into my arms anyway so we don't have to break apart as I walk us to my couch. "I have a proposition for you."

I drop to the couch with her in my lap, my dick already hard at whatever sexy thought she has running through her head. "Is that right?" I ask her as I reach behind her and slide the zipper of her jumpsuit down. She'd already discarded her jacket but she's still wearing entirely too many clothes. Lace covers her delicious tits and I lean down to drag my tongue between them. "Tell me."

"I will be willing—" She gasps when I bite her nipple through her bra and grabs my face to make me look at her. Her eyes are still a little hazy and I wonder just how filthy her words are about to be. "To let you fuck me in the ass," she puts a finger on my nose, "*if…*" she trails off and I raise an eyebrow at her, "you let me do something to you first." She bats her eyelashes and puts her hands under her chin, giving me the most innocent expression.

I snort at her, because as cute and sexy as she is, nothing in the world would make me agree to what I think she's asking. "I am absolutely not letting you peg me." I chuckle.

She rolls her eyes. "Who said anything about pegging? What if I just put a vibrator there…" She puts her hands up in front of her face to indicate something small. "Just for a little."

"No." I shake my head.

"Come on. You want to put something up my ass! I've never had anything up there either."

My dick throbs at the thought of being the first dick up her tight little ass. "That's different."

"How so?" I don't respond because she's a little intoxicated and I'm fairly certain she'd be able to refute any argument with drunk logic. "Please?" She tilts her head to the side. "Daddy?"

My eyes flash to hers, wide and unblinking because *Jesus fucking Christ*. I wasn't prepared for her to know that those two words when used together may be able to make me do anything she wants. I feel like my heart is suddenly pounding and I can feel it in my dick and I can feel the agreement sitting on the tip of my tongue. "I'll blow you while I do it."

I rub my tongue over my teeth and breathe out through my nose because I don't really know what to say. I move her off my lap despite my dick screaming to keep her rubbing against it and get off the couch. "I need a drink."

"Oh yes, get on my level." I glare at her and she gives me a sexy smile as she follows me to the kitchen. When I turn around, I see she's discarded her whole jumpsuit leaving her in only a bra and her barely existent underwear as she hops up on the counter next to me. "I'll be gentle." She shoots me a wicked grin. "Are you worried you won't like it? Or you will?" She lets her fingertips dance up my arm. She presses them to my cheeks, tapping it a few times like she's trying to get me to smile.

I pour myself a double pour of scotch and take a healthy sip. "I've just never been interested in ever having anything back there."

"And yet, you're considering it now?"

"Because I'm interested in giving *you* whatever you want," I tell her and the smile that lights her face is enough to agree but I have some questions. "So, just a vibrator?" She grabs the drink from my hand before I can protest because I recall her referring to my drink of choice as nasty. She scrunches her cheeks while it sits in her mouth before letting it slide down. I chuckle at the face she makes and rub a hand over her cheeks hoping that will ease the burn. "Do you want something else?" Her tongue darts out to lick a stray drop from the glass, her eyes never leaving mine as she shakes her head.

"Just a vibrator." She twists her mouth. "One of the smaller ones I've fucked myself with while I thought about you."

Thoughts of her thrusting a toy inside her pretty little cunt has my dick thickening in my jeans and I raise an eyebrow at her. "Fine."

Her eyes widen and her lips part. "Really?"

I let out a breath and rest a hand on either side of her, brushing my lips against hers gently. "Do you know how crazy I am about you?"

"Because you're letting me stick something up here?" she asks as she reaches around and taps my ass before squeezing one of my cheeks.

"Yes, but even if I didn't agree, would you still know how I feel about you?" I trail my index finger down her cheek before dragging my knuckles over it. "I know things moved fast and our situation is far from ideal, but I've never felt this way about anyone." I cup her face and rub my thumbs along the apples of her cheeks. "I've known for months that I've felt differently about you."

Her eyes glisten slightly and I don't know if it's my words or the alcohol or a combination of both making her emotional. "I'm pretty crazy about you too. I *obsessed* over that interaction at Owen and Lex's wedding for weeks...months. I couldn't figure out what I'd done wrong." She looks down at her hands, removing her face from my grasp almost like she's embarrassed to admit that.

I lift her chin to look at me and tuck a hair behind her ear. "I'm still obsessing over that interaction." I smile at her and she gives me a bashful look. "And every interaction since." I pour myself another drink and down it before letting out a sigh of defeat because I can't believe I agreed to this. "You better suck my dick like a pornstar, Marissa Lee, I mean it." I point at her before I tap her nose.

She scrunches it before giving me an innocent grin. "Oh!" She bats her eyelashes at me again. "Yes, Daddy." She hops off the counter and walks out of the kitchen. "Okay, come on!" She's half naked and walking towards my bedroom, so I'm likely to follow her anywhere, but it has just registered that she's potentially ready to do what we've been talking about *right now?*

"Wait..." I down the rest of my drink and follow her towards the stairs. "You have one here?"

She's halfway up the stairs when she turns around and gives me a nod. "A couple, actually."

"You planned this?" I narrow my eyes at her as I meet her on the step below her and grip her waist to pull her hard against me. "You knew I'd give in?"

"No," she giggles as I bite her nipple again through her bra, "but...I wanted to be prepared in case you did! I knew if you agreed, I'd have to strike while the iron was hot!" She slams her fist down on her open palm before she leans down and pecks my lips twice. "Even if you never agreed, you could still use them on me."

"Oh, believe me, I will be using it on you," I tell her as we make our way up the rest of the stairs to my bedroom. Before she gets too far into the room, I grab her wrist and pull her to me. "Before we do anything, I need to put my mouth here." I cup her and slowly move her underwear to the side so I can slide two fingers through her slit. She's fucking soaked and my dick throbs painfully when I drag them over the wet silk. "Fuck, you're wet." I rip them from her and unsnap her bra, leaving her completely nude. My eyes devour her like I'm staring at her for the first time. "You're so beautiful."

She takes a step closer to me and unbuttons my jeans to push them down my legs before she pulls at my shirt like it's offensive. I pull it off and toe off my shoes all while her hands have made it into my briefs. "I want to sit on your face while I deepthroat you," she says with her hand wrapped around my dick and rubs it from root to tip.

"Do you now? You're going to take all of me in your pretty little mouth?" She nods. "Are you going to be able to focus while I'm rubbing my tongue against your clit?" I guide her towards the bed. "Or while I have two fingers deep inside you?" I whisper before I let my lips brush against hers. "Get your vibrators."

Excitement fills her eyes before she hops off the bed towards my closet. She brought a small suitcase over the first time she stayed and I assume they're in there. She brings out three vibrators. One looks like a wand, one like a bullet, and a third is pink and more slender and oddly shaped. Even though I know where it's going, it's not as intimidating as I thought. "I got this one…in case you were interested. It's supposed to massage your prostate." She deposits all three on the bed.

"Which one is your favorite?" I ask as I remove my briefs and toss them to the side. "Which makes you come the hardest?"

She holds up her bullet, a toy no bigger than a tube of lipstick, and gives me a shy smile. "This tiny little thing is dangerous."

"Dangerous, huh?" I hold the tiny toy in my hands and move to lie on my back. "Get up here," I tell her. She wastes no time straddling my face and leaning over to grip my cock in her hands. I was already rock hard but the scent of her sinfully sweet pussy makes my dick feel like granite.

She gasps when she hears me turn on her toy like she knows what's coming before it even touches her. I lick her once, sliding my tongue through her cunt that's practically dripping before I touch the vibrator to her clit.

"Oh fuck," she moans out. "I…I don't think I can handle that and your mouth. I'll come too fast."

"Good. Give me more than one." I begin circling my tongue around her entrance as I rub the vibrator in circles against her clit at the same speed. She clenches around my tongue and grips my dick harder as she pulls me to the back of her throat. I hear her sputter around me and then the sexy sounds of her sucking.

"Chris," she moans and her hips rock against my face. I smile at how quickly her orgasm is building. "Oh my god, right there," she breathes out.

"Keep your mouth on my dick when you come. I want to feel you scream around my cock while you come on my tongue."

She lets out a moan that tickles my dick just as a hand begins to rub my balls. I'm so focused on the sounds of her tiny vibrator in my hand that I don't realize she's turned on another one until I feel the vibration on my balls.

"Oh, fuck me, Marissa." I groan into her pussy and she lets out a sexy squeal just before she drags her tongue up my shaft. I've never had a woman use a vibrator on me at all and I'm shocked by the instant electricity that moves through me. My balls are tingling, my cock aches with every suck of her mouth and I find myself raising my hips to fuck her face in time with her sucking. "Babe, you're going to make me come. Your fucking mouth, goddamn."

"Mmm," she moans.

"I need you to fucking get there," I grit out as I move a finger to rub her clit along with the vibrator. "Stop what you're doing and focus on coming," I tell her because I am close and I don't want to come without her.

"No." She moans as she pushes herself all the way to the base and sucks me hard just as she turns the vibrations up on the toy she's still rubbing against my balls. She moves it lower to stroke the space behind my balls and I fucking explode down her throat.

"FUCK!" I grit out as I pump my dick into her sexy little mouth. Her lips are still wrapped around me when I feel her clench around me one final time and then she lets out a low moan that makes my dick feel like it's ready to go again. Like the sounds of her coming is all it needs to get hard for a second time. She squirms around on my face and I slide the vibrator away, wanting every part of her pretty cunt against my mouth while she climaxes.

I can't tell if she's moaning or crying out or saying a garbled version of my name as she comes but she does hard and long all over my face. Some of it slides down my chin and my neck, and I relish the feeling of being covered in her orgasm. I want more. I want all of it all over me. She pulls me out of her mouth and grips my thighs hard as she sits up slightly but continues to rub her cunt against my mouth.

"Fuck yes, you want to go again?"

She doesn't answer, but I feel her clench against me so I take that as a yes. I grab the vibrator again and pull her away from my face. "I am going to lick you here this time," I tell her as I grip her ass and squeeze. "I've spent more time than I care to admit staring at your ass, Marissa. It's about time I taste it." I spread her cheeks and lick a trail between them, rimming her hole as I turn up the speed on her vibrator. "Gonna make you come all over my fingers while my tongue is in your ass."

"Oh my god." She groans. "I-I've never...fuck." She whimpers and I smile at the thought that she has no control over what's coming out of her mouth. "So fucking good. Oh fuck, Daddy," She moans and my dick jerks in response.

"You like Daddy's tongue here?" I circle her hole with my tongue as I grip one of her ass cheeks.

"Fuck yes," she whimpers as she moves so she's lying against me.

"I do too. You see how hard it makes me? How hard *you* make me, honey? Fuuuuuck." I moan when I feel her hand wrap around my dick again. "I want to come inside you this time."

"Not yet."

I land a hard slap on her ass and squeeze one of her cheeks. "What do you mean not yet?"

"I...I want to try something first." She starts to pull away from my mouth, and I stop the vibrator just as she manages to climb off of me and sit between my spread legs. She gives me a mischievous look before she drags her gaze down my body slowly, before settling those gorgeous eyes on my dick. She still has a vibrator in her hand and she drags it slowly up and then down my shaft once before moving it towards her opening. She's sitting back on her heels with her knees spread. I watch enraptured as she slides the toy through her slick cunt, first through her slit and then I watch as the tip disappears inside of her. "I won't go too far," she says as she slowly pulls it out. The toy is wet and shiny and I'm already picturing my dick looking the same way after it's been inside of her. With her eyes locked on mine, she lets a trail of spit fall onto it to serve as more lubrication.

Nerves course through me but also excitement over the thought of trying something new, and I realize that those back to back drinks I had are starting to hit me. I'm feeling looser and more uninhibited than I did twenty minutes ago. She grips my dick and begins to stroke it slowly as she lowers the vibrator. I'm still on my back so I lift my hips slightly just enough for her to push it between my cheeks and cum already begins to pool on the tip of my cock.

"Fuck, that feels good," I manage to sputter out just as she circles the tip of it around my opening. My hands find her breasts and I rub my fingers across the soft supple skin before tracing her nipple. "You're so incredible."

She beams under my praise. "I think you're pretty incredible too." She leans down and wraps her lips around my dick just as she pushes the vibrator slightly inside. I gasp at the foreign feeling but already feel myself being pulled under by the force of her mouth. She sucks hard, lowering herself slowly down my shaft just as she pushes the vibrator an inch further.

I clench around it, and I feel overstimulated but in the best fucking way. She pulls off of my dick and a trail of her spit connects her mouth to my cock before her tongue darts out and licks it away. "Are you okay?" she whispers, and I nod.

"More," I grunt and surprise reflects on her face. She pushes a little bit further and I let out a groan that I wasn't expecting. "Fuck me." I throw an arm over my eyes. No more than a second later, I move my arm when I feel her weight on top of me and I watch as Marissa slides herself slowly down on my cock. I can still feel the vibrator in my ass and the feeling of her snug cunt wrapped around my dick has me chasing my climax.

"I couldn't wait anymore. I wanted your dick inside me." She spins her hips every time I bottom out inside of her all while she has one hand behind her keeping the vibrator in place. She continues to fuck me, bouncing her sexy body up and down on me and I feel my balls starting to tingle with the need to release.

"You're going to make me come, I need you to get there. You need some friction on your pretty little clit?" I reach for the vibrator I was using on her earlier and press it against her clit causing a part squeal part moan to leave her lips. *Fuck, there is something so hot about us both using vibrators on each other while I'm inside of her.*

"Oh, fuck yes!" she screams, and then I feel her pulsing around me and pushing the vibrator a little further into my ass. I thrust upward one final time just as my climax sucks me under like a tidal wave. She moves the vibrator out of my ass and just rubs it around the opening again and I swear it extends my orgasm. My dick just keeps pulsing, shooting god knows how much cum inside of her.

What if I get her pregnant?

That thought floats through my head at the peak of my high and I'm instantly flooded with images of a baby that looks a little more like her than me but enough that people would know I'm the father.

"You're looking at me like you want to do that again," she says as she hovers over me and presses her lips to mine gently. Both of the vibrators are off, quieting the room of the low hum of the sex toys.

I'm still thinking about what it would be like if she were to get pregnant despite the high wearing off and I realize that it might actually be something I want at some point. I want every single thing I haven't had before, *with her.*

I slide my tongue into her mouth and flip us so that I'm on top of her. She wraps her legs around my waist and my dick slides through her slit. "Many many more times, in fact."

Chapter FOURTEEN

Marissa

I WAKE UP THE NEXT MORNING TO SUNLIGHT STREAMING through Chris' window and the sound of his soft snoring behind me. I'm on my side, still naked from last night, with his arm wrapped around my waist and his chest pressed directly against my back. Our legs are entwined and one of his hands rested over mine like we have to be attached at every point possible. I'm grateful for the two glasses of water he made me drink before we went to bed because I feel fine and not like I had multiple shots of tequila last night. I manage to turn in his arms without waking him and I take a moment to stare at him. I'm pretty sure I will never get tired of looking at him and I'm happy to have a second to do it uninterrupted.

Whenever we are together, I can sense that he's lighter, almost like he gets to take a break from his life but there are still moments where I see the tension all over his face, When I feel his anxiety radiating off of him, but right now he looks so peaceful and I wish it could always be like this. When I reach up to move the hair off his forehead and drag my hand gently down his face, a small smile pulls at his lips and I realize he's awake.

"I can feel you staring at me," he murmurs, tugging me closer. Then with his eyes still closed, he presses his lips to mine like he already knows me by heart.

"Sorry for waking you," I whisper and when he finally opens his eyes, he smiles immediately.

"I love when your face is the first thing I see in the morning."

My heart flutters in my ribcage. "You waste no time wooing me, do you?" I slowly untangle myself from him. "Be right back," I tell him with a peck on his lips. I slide on the t-shirt he was wearing last night to cover up my naked form before heading towards the bathroom. "Don't move."

It takes me a few minutes to brush my teeth and wash my face and when I head back into the bedroom, Chris' demeanor has changed dramatically. His face is angry and he's furiously texting on his phone before he lets out a sigh and rubs his forehead. I move towards the bed, wanting to do whatever I can to de-stress him, but as soon as I drop to the bed, he's off of it and I frown in response.

"Hey, what's wrong?" I ask as I look up at him, but he shakes his head and leans down to press a kiss to my lips.

"Nothing." He pulls away as I reach for his hand and give it a squeeze.

"Want to try that again?"

"Marissa…" He trails off and I let go of his hand because I think I know what the problem is. My eyes drop to his phone that's still in his hand and then back up to his eyes.

"It's her?"

He nods and grabs his briefs from the floor, pulling them up over his dick, and I feel that wave of guilt I try to pretend isn't there every time I'm with him. He's right; it really does seem like she doesn't care. She rarely calls or texts from what I've seen. She's never shown up here and I assume she has to have at least a hint as to where his penthouse is located. He really seems like a single man everywhere except on paper. At this point, I'm sure it would appear from the outside that if Chris were married at all it would be to me because of how much time we spend together. "I just... give me ten minutes, please."

"I can go," I say.

"No." He holds his hand out to stop me from getting off the bed. "Please," he adds, and I nod reluctantly.

I watch as he leaves the room, shutting the door behind him and I fall to my back and stare at the ceiling. *This was exactly what you were trying to avoid by not getting involved. Now, I'm half-naked in his bed while he argues with his wife.*

His wife he still lives with.

It doesn't matter that he spends most of his nights here with me. He still owns a house with her. A house that probably has her name on the deed as well. My mind begins to spiral thinking about their shared closet spaces and their toothbrushes that shared a holder once upon a time. Matching monogrammed towels and maybe framed pictures hang in the foyer from their wedding day.

I swallow, trying to stop my brain from thinking about all of the ways she has him that I don't. He said they sleep in separate bedrooms but what if that isn't true?

What if they've slept together since I came back into his life? I'd like to think he wouldn't initiate it but what if she seduced him and he just went along with it because he felt like he couldn't say no?

Okay, you're freaking out. Relax. Chris is crazy about you. He tells you this all the time.

He was probably crazy about his wife too at one point.

I put a pillow over my face and let out a low groan, trying to quiet the arguing in my head. I sit up and reach for my phone to call the only person I can talk to about this.

"Hi, do I know you?" my sister answers as soon as she picks up and I should have expected a bit of passive aggression after not seeing each other in a few weeks.

"I know…I know," I say. We've been texting the same as always but it's been the longest Autumn and I have gone without seeing each other and it hadn't really hit me until this moment.

"Look at you. You get a man and just drop me."

I run a hand through my hair in exasperation. "I've been busy!" I huff.

"Getting turned out, I know." She chuckles.

"No. Work has been—"

"Oh, I know how work has been," she says in reference to the sex in Chris' office yesterday.

"I'm sorry," I tell her. "Let's do something next week."

"I'm giving you a hard time; I know you've been busy and I have been too, but I'm glad you called. Texting is not the same."

I dart my eyes to the door. "I'm at Chris' house."

"I assumed. I talked to Ma this morning and she said you weren't home. She's really itching to have him over, you know." She says it in a way that makes me think our mother put her up to this.

"I know. She only asks me twice a day."

"Well, what's the holdup?" I can hear the excitement in her voice like she can't wait for it either.

"Ummm, what do you think?"

"Well, I wouldn't suggest telling them he's married, but you could still introduce him to dad. He's beginning to think there's something wrong with him."

"There isn't!"

"Well, yes, I know, but you remember how long it took for him to come around to Eric?"

"That's because you two were horny teenagers and he caught you guys dry-humping outside the house at one in the morning. Like…more than once." I shake my head, still in disbelief over that because I would have surely expired after the first time.

"We weren't dry humping!"

I roll my eyes at her trying to rationalize it. "Semantics, you were sitting in his lap."

"Aaaaanyway, you need to stop hiding your boyfriend. He's met mom, and she's given dad the rundown. Apparently, he's even okay with his age and the fact that you obviously work for him."

"He's not even that much older!"

"They think he's thirty, Marissa, which I believe is still what—four years younger than what he actually is?" She laughs and I hear the sounds of her treadmill starting up.

"I don't know if I'm ready to bring him home," I blurt out when she finishes laughing.

"Why?"

"Well, for starters, because he's currently in the other room arguing with his wife."

She's silent and all I hear are the sounds of her walking on her treadmill. "Seriously?"

"Yep." I sit up in bed.

"I thought you said they had an open marriage or something."

"I never said that. I said that he said that his wife didn't care if he slept with other women." I groan as soon as the words leave my lips. "I can't believe I just said that."

"Okay, why are they arguing?"

"I don't know."

"Okay, maybe they're arguing over something house related."

"What does that matter?"

"I just mean it's different if she's calling him to complain that he's not home or that she misses him or something. Then yes, I would say that's a bigger problem, but if she's just calling to pick a fight with him because their coffee maker broke or she needs money or something then…that's different."

"Do you hear yourself, Autumn? He's married and that *is* the bigger problem." I sigh. "I should not have gotten in so deep with him."

"Okay, come back from the dark side please. Do you love him?"

"I…it's too soon to tell." My knee-jerk reaction is to say yes but I can't admit that to myself yet, let alone anyone else because I cannot be falling in love with a married man.

"Okay then maybe...maybe you take a step back." I don't say anything but the painful feeling in my chest leads me to believe that I am definitely in the process of falling for him. "Not forever, but just let him figure out what his plan is long term for leaving her and being with you. This doesn't sound like it's just sex for either one of you, but it's impossible for you guys to really move forward unless he's completely unattached and free to do so."

I sigh. "How long does it take for a divorce to be finalized?" I ask, hoping she can provide some legal insight.

"It depends on so many things. If she were the one filing, she could obviously cite infidelity and that expedites the process but if he's filing without a reason other than he doesn't want to be married anymore and *she's* not on board with that, it could take a long time."

"What's a long time?"

"A year of separation. Maybe longer?"

"Ugh, awesome." I sigh.

"And if they have a lot of property and assets to divvy up, who knows. Him not having a prenup is going to make things dicey."

"Yeah. I think that's what the holdup has been this whole time."

"Well, you're twenty-one, Marissa, and if this guy is worth it, you just wait."

"He hasn't even taken any steps to do that though."

"Which is why I said you need to talk to him and figure that out," she says just as the door opens and Chris enters the room looking even more annoyed than before. He sits on the bed in front of me and gives me a sad smile.

"Can I call you back?"

"Of course, love you."

"Love you too," I tell her as I slide my phone away from my

ear and toss it to the side. He looks at the phone and then back at me. "My sister."

He nods and lets out a sigh. "I'm sorry about that." I nod not really knowing what to say. I want to ask if everything is okay, but that feels like a ridiculous question because nothing about this is okay. "I uhhh…I need to run to my house." His words feel like a punch in my stomach. Goosebumps pop up everywhere and I feel the tears building in the back of my throat. "Marissa, please just stay. I'll be an hour tops."

I shake my head. "No…" I let out a shaky breath. I want to ask him why he's leaving but it really doesn't matter.

"She tripped an alarm in one of the garages where I keep my vintage cars and I have to go disarm it," he says as I get off the bed.

"It doesn't matter," I tell him as I grab a pair of leggings from one of the drawers. I've started leaving clothes here and I just realized I should probably take them back with me as this may be the last time I'm here.

"It does. Baby, please—" he starts and I snap my gaze to his because it's the first time he's ever called me that and I hate that it's under these circumstances.

"No." I bite my bottom lip. "It's fine."

"Marissa, there's stuff you don't know. Please just let me go home and deal with this and then I'll explain everything."

"What's there to explain? You're married," I whisper as I begin to pull more of my clothes from the drawers. "And I knew that, so I'm not blaming you—"

"I'm serving her, Marissa." He stands in front of me, slowly pulling the clothes out of my hands and putting them back in the drawer. I frown, because I'm trying to do the right thing by leaving and ending this, and he seems to be derailing my plan. "I'm serving her divorce papers." He rubs a thumb over my bottom lip. "Monday."

I narrow my eyes, confused because I was not expecting him to say that. "W-what?"

He sighs. "The papers are drawn up and she's being served. I didn't tell you because I wanted to wait until everything was done. My lawyers have been working nonstop for a week."

"Mon...day?" I struggle to get the word out and when it leaves my lips, I feel like my heart has started to race.

"One hour, please." He grabs my hands and brings them to his lips. "Don't leave." I nod slowly because that does change things. I don't think he'd lie straight to my face just to keep me here, so I do believe him, but I think I'm in shock. "You'll stay?" I nod again because I think I've lost the ability to speak. "If you leave, I'll come after you." He rubs a thumb over my bottom lip again. "I'll always come after you."

Chapter FIFTEEN

CHRIS

It takes me less than twenty minutes to get back to my house which has to be some sort of record and I'm pretty sure I got at least two camera tickets in the process, but I'm not sure what kind of headspace Marissa is in and I know the longer she sits with her thoughts the harder it will be to talk her out of it. I know I dropped a pretty large bomb on her and basically told her to *trust me*. I'm also not exactly sure what Holly was doing by trying to get into that specific garage but I'm fairly certain it isn't anything pleasant. Those cars are in perfect condition and very valuable and fury spikes in my veins that she could have potentially been trying to damage them or begin the process of trying to sell them.

I pull into my driveway and am already irritated when I see her coming out of the main house still in her pajamas with a cup of coffee. I'm actually surprised she's not already dressed for the day. It's Saturday, which means she normally spends the day shopping and then lunch with her friends, and that usually turns into dinner and then a night out.

"You still haven't told me why you were going in there in the first place," I tell her as I make my way toward the other garage where there's a loud incessant beeping. The alarm is through *Beckham Securities*, so I was able to cancel a dispatch but I made it so I couldn't disarm this particular alarm virtually. *Something, I'm regretting at this moment.*

She puts her hands on her hips and gives me a look of annoyance. "I don't see why my fingerprint doesn't work just like it does for everything else."

"Because there's nothing in here that belongs to you," I tell her as I press my finger to the keypad to disarm the incessant beeping.

She scrunches her nose in disgust. "So? It's still a part of my house."

"Answer my question. What were you doing?"

"I just…wanted to see something."

"Bull," I snap.

She huffs. "Fine. Marcia Bradley was bragging that her husband had just purchased some rare car. I think she said only like thirty of them were made or something. I just wanted to see which ones you had."

At any other time, this may have had my attention, because I am curious about which car and where Bradley bought it, but as there is a zero percent chance he'd sell it to me, I certainly don't give a fuck at the moment. "You could have asked instead of trying to break in."

"Like you would have responded," she says in a tone that makes it seem like she's bothered or hurt by that fact.

I choose not to dignify that with a response either. I'm not willing to feed into that considering there have been more times than I can count when Holly hasn't answered my calls or texts while she was out shopping or at a spa with friends.

Unless I was in a meeting, I always answered. Or at the very least sent a message that I'd call her back if it wasn't an emergency.

I start back towards my car when I hear her speak. "You're leaving?"

I turn back to face her, surprised and a bit confused that she even cares. "Yes?"

She sighs. "You've barely been home."

"Have you?" I ask, because it's not that unheard of for her to stay out either.

"Yes."

"Okay, well that's a first."

"I wasn't staying out fucking around with a guy every night."

I shrug, because to this day, I'm not sure I believe that she's never been unfaithful. I don't have proof; it's just a feeling. "I don't know that."

"I've never cheated on you."

I shoot her an incredulous look. "Do you want a medal for that? That doesn't just absolve you from all the other shit you've done."

"Can't you just…stay?" *Deflecting, of course.*

"For what, Holly?"

"Because I'm your wife and I'm asking?"

I look back at the garage and then at her when a thought smacks me in the face. It's so obvious that I'm shocked I didn't think of it sooner. *In what world does Holly give a shit about cars in general?* Even if she's just trying to one-up her frenemy. If she cared about my hobbies, she'd know exactly which cars were in there, and where in our house to find which ones they are without even having to go into the garage. *God, I'm stupid. How did I not realize this?* "Did you…trigger the alarm on purpose?"

"No," she says and I know she's lying based on her body language.

I shake my head at her. "You're joking, right?"

"You're way off base, Chris." She gives me her back as she walks toward the house. "Forget it. See you whenever." She waves a hand over her head.

I want to go after her and get the truth out of her but I know she and I are in for a long road of uncovering truths. Now, I just want to be with Marissa. I told her an hour and I'm already dancing pretty close to that if I happen to hit any traffic on my way back into the city.

I'm back at my penthouse in a little over an hour, and when I enter, Marissa is sitting on the couch in the living room watching a movie. I sit on the coffee table in front of her, grabbing the remote to mute the television, and give her a smile. "Are you mad?"

"I don't know," she whispers, her eyes not meeting mine like she's avoiding my gaze.

"Sorry I was longer than an hour."

"Is everything okay?" Her voice is soft and filled with something I can't quite detect.

"I think she did it on purpose." I sigh. I rarely talk to Marissa about Holly, but it might be time that I start.

She frowns. "Why?"

"Couldn't tell you. She never cared about me being home before. Hell, she's rarely home."

"You're saying it's because she wanted to see you?"

"I don't know. She tried to get me to stay once I got there." I can see the discomfort all over her face and I move to sit next to her and pull her closer. I expect her to fight me but she lets me wrap an arm around her. "Ask me what you want to know."

"What happens after you give her the divorce papers?"

"I have to wait and see what she says."

She runs a hand through her hair and I can feel the tension radiating off of her. "What if she doesn't agree?"

I let my head fall to the back of the couch with a groan. I don't even want to put that in the universe. "I don't know. There's a waiting period." I run my fingers down her shoulder. "Will you wait?" I ask her the question I've wanted the answer to since she walked back into my life. I've been thinking about it since I first slept with her, if I'm being honest.

She turns to face me. "Are you sure you want to do this?"

I nod. "Yeah. I know you think I'm just doing this for you but it really is for me too. I want to be happy with someone." She nods and I grab her chin and tilt it towards me. "With you if you'll let me." She's staring at the muted television with her lip trapped between her teeth. "What?" I drop my hand to her leg and rub it gently, trying to alleviate the tension I can feel coursing through her.

"It's just hard not to feel like a homewrecker."

It would be easy to tell her that she's not. That she had little to do with the demise of my marriage. That although she may have been the final push, she certainly wasn't the catalyst. I turn her face gently to mine and brush my lips against hers. "I don't know what to do to change that."

She looks up at me and though I can see the apprehension all over her face, she leans into me and rests her head against my chest. "A part of me wishes I wasn't already in so deep."

"I'm glad you are," I whisper against her forehead.

The door of my office swings open without so much as a knock and just when I'm about to reprimand whoever thought they could just barge in here unannounced, I'm met with the very angry eyes of my *hopefully* soon to be ex-wife. "I am absolutely *not* signing this." Holly stares down at me, her green eyes full of fury as she waves the divorce summons I had served to her this morning. I knew this wasn't going to be easy.

In the state of Pennsylvania, if she doesn't consent to a divorce, we are required to stay married and live apart for one year before I can be granted one. My lawyer didn't think the fact that she makes my life miserable was necessarily enough for a fault-based divorce that wouldn't require us to stay married for a year. So, I need Holly to cooperate, and I know she isn't going to.

"This is not the time or place for this conversation and I don't appreciate you just showing up here unannounced." I pull my gaze away from my computer and turn towards her. "What do you want? More money? This already gives you half and monthly alimony payments. That is more than fair."

"*That* is not half," she says pointing at it and I can't believe whatever I fucking saw in this woman. I'd do anything to go back in time and do everything differently.

"My statements are provided. It's half, Holly," I tell her. I want to be done with this marriage so I already resigned myself to the fact that I'm going to be giving her a pretty significant amount of money. There is no point trying to get around it or lowball her. Holly is going to take me for everything she can and I'm at the point where I'm not going to fight her. I'm exhausted and I want to be free of all the bullshit I've dealt with over the past six years. "What, are you going to keep me in this marriage against my will? I want out, Holly. We aren't in love. We aren't happy. I made the stupid fucking mistake of not making you sign a prenuptial agreement, so fine, you get half, but I am *not* staying married to you."

"You cheated on me. *Multiple times.*"

"A fact that my lawyer has been made aware of." *It's also why we offered alimony payments that are higher than standard.*

"How can you do this? I've given you six years. You wouldn't even give me a baby—"

"Because bringing a baby into this dysfunctional marriage would have been the worst idea. Are you kidding me? Holly, you don't love me. You've said it on numerous occasions. You love the idea of me and what I do for your socio-economic status, but you don't love *me*."

I turn back to my computer, hoping she gets the picture that I am done with this conversation just as there's a knock on the door. My heart momentarily stops. While I assume it's my assistant, I can't be completely sure and I haven't had a chance to text Marissa to tell her to avoid my office. Holly hasn't been here in months so there hasn't been a chance for them to run into each other and I really fucking hope this isn't about to be the first time. Marissa's desk is on the other side of the floor and my hope is that she stays there for the foreseeable future.

"Come in," I call out, and I try to hide the worry from my voice just as my assistant, Christine, comes in with a cup of coffee that I assume is for Holly. I notice immediately that it's from the coffee shop down the street and I'm even more irritated that she's managed to send my assistant on a fucking errand. That means she's been here longer than I thought.

Fucking hell. Could she have already run into Marissa?

I pull up my text messages with Marissa and I hate myself for what I'm about to send.

> **Me: Please avoid my office. Stay at your desk if you can, please.**

I dart my eyes up just as I see Holly taking a sip of her coffee.

Christine tries her best to smile. "Is there anything else I can get for you?"

I am very aware of how Christine feels about Holly so I know she's trying her hardest to be polite.

"Oh, this is cold," Holly says as she attempts to hand the cup back to her. "I'd like it warmer, please."

"It's fine," I grit out. "You can warm it up at home."

She looks at Christine, her arm still held out and I shake my head. "Christine, you can go. Thank you." She nods at me, giving me a small smile before she scurries out of the room and closes the door behind her.

"So, I can't even get a hot cup of coffee?"

"It could have been hot if you didn't send her two blocks away to get it," I snap.

Holly is smart enough to ask her before she entered my office or I would have told Christine she absolutely did not have to do that.

She waves a hand dismissively. "It's her job, Chris."

"No, her job is not to leave the premises to get you goddamned coffee."

"We are getting off-topic," she says slamming the papers down on my desk. "Not. Signing. This." She taps a finger against the manilla folder with each word before crossing her arms over her chest. "This is all about your newest mistress? You're that obsessed with what's between her legs that you're willing to just blow up your entire life? If you think I'm going to go quietly, I'd think again." She picks at her nail beds as if the conversation is starting to bore her before her eyes flit up to me. "Marissa, right?" I've never been so grateful for a soundproof office because I am sure this is about to get ugly. Anger flashes in my veins and I ball my hands into fists under my desk in an attempt to temper the fury. She pulls her phone out and looks up at me with a raised eyebrow and a smug smile on her red lips. "A little young for you don't you think?" She drags her finger across the screen and turns it to show me a picture of Marissa from her social media. I am very well versed in all the pictures on her Instagram, having scrolled through it several hundred times.

Fuck. How did she find out about her? Is she having me followed? She doesn't have access to my phone or any of my communications and even if she were to have somehow hacked into my email, Marissa and I have never communicated that way in any way that wasn't professional.

"So, can I meet her? According to my sources, she works for *Beckham Securities*." She blinks several times. "Tell me, is Wes helping you hide your little trysts? I'm surprised she went for you and not him, if I'm being honest." Even though I know Marissa wants to be with me, jealousy floats through me that she may have been interested in Beck had it not been for our history. "Or wait...are you sharing her?" She presses a hand to her chest as if in shock.

"Stop." I grit out. The thought of anyone but me touching Marissa makes me irate. "What do you want, Holly?" I ask, refusing to confirm or deny anything.

"I want us to work on things." She blinks rapidly at me. "Give up your girlfriend and give our marriage a shot."

I am trying my best not to lose it but the thought of not being with Marissa is making me feel like I don't have any control over my emotions. "You've lost your mind. I've been trying to go to counseling for five years. I've suggested divorce more than once and you chose to call my bluff. And what? Now that you realize I'm serious you want to work on things? I think the fuck not."

"Then I destroy your little plaything." She shrugs before she points towards the door. "She shouldn't be hard to find. I know you have fraternization policies in place. She'll be gone by the end of the week."

I shake my head, feeling like the walls are closing in on me as I scratch my jaw knowing that the more I show my hand in regards to Marissa the more she'll realize how important she is to me. "You don't even love me, Holly. Why are you doing this?"

"We took vows, Chris, and I do love you." Tears pool in her eyes and if I hadn't known her for the better part of a decade, I'd think they were genuine, but she's manipulative as hell and I know her games. "I'm your wife."

My eyes fall to the folder on the desk wishing like hell she'd just sign them. "You sure as hell haven't acted like it."

"I never cheated on you, Chris," she scoffs.

"There's more to a healthy marriage than just not cheating on your spouse."

"It's a big part!"

"Fine, I destroyed this marriage, Holly. If that's what helps you sleep at night, fine, but you're going entirely too far. Blackmailing me into staying married? Are you insane?"

"It's not blackmail and it's not forever," she says shrugging.

"We can argue the definition of blackmail in a minute. Spit out what you fucking want from me." I can feel my anger rising and I really don't want to get into a screaming match in the middle of my workday but she's fucking pushing me with this back and forth.

"I'm willing to wait the year needed for us to file under *irretrievable breakdown*. Until then, you can move out, and we start going to counseling."

"Oh, *I'm* moving out?" I blink at her, confused as to how she thinks she gets to keep the house I pay for.

"You surely don't expect me to?" I let out a breath through my nose and press my fingers to my forehead to attempt to alleviate the pressure building. "No more Marissa, Chris. I mean it."

"What gives you any fucking right—"

"The state of Pennsylvania?" She blinks at me. "And if you don't play by my rules on this, I swear to God, Christopher." I don't say anything and she shakes her head. "I knew you were sleeping with other women. I was stupid to let it go on for so long but…you actually think you're going to leave me for another woman?" She scoffs. "I don't fucking think so."

"So, you were okay with sharing my dick, but not me. When *you* don't even want either." I'm out of the chair, my body feeling tense and anxious over the thought of breaking up with Marissa.

Maybe Marissa would be willing to quit working here. I'd write her a stellar recommendation to go anywhere. Hell, our competition if she wanted to. Beck would understand. I think.

I run a hand through my hair as I begin to pace the length

of my office. "You're the fucking worst for this, you know that? I knew you were hateful, but this is on another level."

"I'm hateful? You've fucked half the city behind my back and I'm hateful?"

I glare at her because I wasn't about to let her make me feel like she was sitting at home crying over it. "You certainly never had a problem with it before."

She takes a compact out of her purse and pulls the clip out of her hair before starting to fuss with it like she's bored with this conversation. "You're saying that makes it okay?"

"Actually, that is exactly what I'm saying. You didn't give a shit so long as you still had access to whatever you wanted. The only reason it's suddenly a big deal is because I'm asking for a divorce."

Her green eyes snap to mine as she closes her compact with a hard smack. "And I'm not saying you can't have one!" Her tone is bordering on shrill and it makes my skin fucking crawl.

"But you're going to make me wait a year when you could just sign it now and we could be fucking done with it! You know nothing is going to change, Holly. We are not meant for each other."

I want to tell her that based on how she acts she may not be meant for anyone until she does some serious reflection, but I refrain.

She takes a step closer to me and puts a hand on my arm. "I think we owe it to each other and this marriage to try."

I pull out of her grasp as I shake my head. "It's a waste of time."

My time and Marissa's. The thought that she wouldn't wait the year flashes through my mind.

She's already mentioned that men don't leave their wives and she was worried about me making her promises I didn't intend to keep. How can I tell her that I have to wait a year for us to be together? "I'm not firing her, Holly, and I swear to God if you so much as breathe in her direction, I will find a way to destroy you."

She grits her teeth and bites out a bitter, "Fine." She picks up her purse that she'd dropped on a chair when she entered my office. "I'll leave her alone, for *now*."

"Forever, Holly. She hasn't done anything wrong." I'm not even sure if I'm on board with these new terms, but I'm not agreeing to shit if she can't adhere to my only term which is to leave Marissa out of this.

"Except knowingly screw a married man?" She scoffs in disgust. "I'd be willing to give her the benefit of the doubt if she didn't know, but she works here, so she fucking knows."

"She didn't. I didn't tell her," I argue, and a part of me wishes I had told her when we first met. I wish she'd somehow known I was married and then she wouldn't have gotten mixed up with me. I'd made my bed but I asked Marissa to join me and now she could get hurt when I've convinced her that this isn't a problem.

"And it hasn't come up since? Bullshit. You think no one here has mentioned it in passing?"

"Most people that work for *Beckham Securities* do their best to forget you exist at all. So, it's possible you haven't come up." I make my way to my office door.

"So, she's not just a whore but she's dumb as well because how is it possible that she hasn't figured it out? Is she just not asking questions?"

"Watch your mouth, Holly. I know it's your jealousy talking but lay the fuck off. Green really isn't your color." It's a bit below the belt given the color of her eyes, but I'm fucking enraged and it's taking everything in me not to explode.

I open the door, annoyed that I haven't succeeded in getting her out of my life, but I can at least send her out of my office. "This is not over, Holly. I just don't want to get into this any further while I'm at work."

"I'll start looking into a marriage counselor." She gives me a saccharine grin and rubs a hand down my arm.

"You need to start looking into a lawyer," I tell her, low under my breath. I'm grateful Christine isn't at her desk, but I don't know who else may be within earshot.

She rolls her eyes in that placating way as if she's saying, *yes, dear.* "So, I should expect you home tonight? I was thinking of making your favorite." She leans forward to press a kiss to my cheek and pats it in that way she does when she's trying to patronize me. "Goodbye, honey," she says, and then she's moving down the hallway toward the elevator without another look back at me.

Fuck. FUCK. I take a deep breath as I try to calm my racing heart wondering what the hell I'm going to do and more importantly how I'm going to explain all of this to Marissa. I'm about to move back into my office when I notice movement in my periphery, only to find Marissa staring at me with an expression that shatters me.

Chapter

SIXTEEN

Marissa

I knew what Chris' wife looked like. As much as I wanted to live under the veil of ignorance, my curiosity got the better of me and I looked her up. It's pretty easy to find pictures of them together from events or galas and there were even a few from their wedding that I stumbled on because her Instagram is public. It takes all of the restraint I have not to stalk her social media more often, but I've looked at a few pictures and scrolled long enough to know that she and Chris rarely spent much time together.

I knew the second he sent that text what he meant and I should have listened, but I was stubborn, and the morbid curiosity over what this visit possibly entailed had me moving towards his office. I stay out of sight when she walks out of the office so there is no chance of her seeing me but I can still see her. Polished, beautiful and put together and exactly what she looked like in her pictures. I know designer clothing and she is decked out in it, making me jealous of her for yet *another* reason.

I know he asked me to stay away from his office, and I mostly believe that he said it for my sake, but a part of me, albeit a small part, wonders if maybe Chris has fed me a bunch of bullshit. That he doesn't want me to witness them behaving like a perfect couple. That maybe he's led her to believe that they are blissfully happy and all those nights he spends with me she believes is really him 'working late.' Maybe she's here to surprise him with lunch and an afternoon delight. Maybe there aren't even divorce papers. Just words to keep me happy that will in turn keep his dick happy. I only know what Chris tells me, after all.

There are an infinite number of maybes.

I wince as I watch their interaction like a car crash in slow motion that I can't pull my eyes from. A hand on his arm, a kiss on his cheek. Witnessing another woman's familiarity with him makes me feel like shit. Although it doesn't necessarily seem like Chris is too excited to see her, it certainly doesn't seem like behavior from a woman who was just told her husband wants a divorce.

Once I see that she's out of sight, I take a few steps from where I'd been watching so that he'll see me if he looks my way, and after only a few seconds, he meets my gaze. His shoulders deflate almost instantly and I can see the apology all over his face. I tilt my head to the side and he takes a few steps toward me before looking behind him. When he doesn't see anyone, he holds out his hand and I shake my head before taking a step back. I feel the tears building in my throat. Not just because I saw his wife in the flesh but because it's a painful reminder of the choices I've made that have led to this. That I've made a fucking mess of my life and I don't know how to see my way out of the storm. That ultimately, I chose to be in a relationship with someone who is already in a relationship with someone else and now there is a very good chance I'm about to have my heart broken.

"Please, Marissa." The two words are quiet but I hear them clearly.

"Not here," I tell him. This isn't the place for this conversation. This past weekend was the first time I had really learned anything about his wife, and I assume I will be learning quite a bit more. "Later."

I feel like he wants to say something but he just nods once before sliding his hands into his pockets. I turn on my heel and move back to my desk without another word.

I don't know how I make it through the rest of the day. I feel like a bomb is about to go off and I'm not prepared for my entire life to go up in flames. I'm walking towards my car in the garage that evening when I spot his car next to mine. He has his own spot with Wes and the other members of senior leadership so I'm surprised to see it there, but as I get closer, I realize he's actually in the car. He rolls his window down just as I step between our cars and I hear his voice. "Can you follow me?"

No greeting or term of endearment. No sign that this conversation is going to be pleasant. I feel the guards around my heart that I was slowly letting down to let him in move back up.

Men never leave their wives. We knew this.

After only a few miles of driving, he pulls into a shopping center with a pretty crowded parking lot. I'm just about to get out of the car when I see his door open and then he's sliding into my passenger side. It had started raining earlier this afternoon and hasn't stopped. It has actually picked up. The sky is dark and ugly and the air has a chill that can only be brought on by October precipitation.

"Hey, beautiful," he says and the tenderness in his words makes my heart ache.

"Did you know she was coming?" I ask quietly.

"No." He's not looking at me; his gaze is trained out my front window. "She knows about you," he says in a way that feels like he's ripping off a Band-Aid.

My heart falls so far into my stomach for a moment I feel like I might be sick and I let out a shaky breath. "Me specifically or just that you're seeing someone."

"You. Specifically." He rubs his jaw and leans his head back against the headrest, letting his eyes shut. Despite this conversation we are having, I wonder if this is the most relaxed he's been all day. "She won't give me a divorce without going to counseling." My eyes widen and I dart my gaze away from him to my window because I am certain if our eyes meet, I'll burst into tears. "Marissa, look at me, baby."

"No," I grit out. *And damn him for calling me that AGAIN.* "What did you say?"

"Nothing. I wanted to talk to you first."

I'm still staring out my window, so I know he can't see the confused look on my face. Like I somehow have a say in a decision between a man and his wife. "About...?"

"What do you think?"

I furrow my brows, anger flaring through me when I turn my gaze to him. "About what? You think we're going to be together while you and your wife go to counseling to fix your marriage?"

"It's not going to fix anything." He shakes his head.

I shoot him a look that isn't quite a glare, but I hope he can see that I'm annoyed by his flippant response to therapy. "I am sure you're not the first husband to feel that way."

"She asked for a year and then she'd give me the divorce."

"So, a year of what exactly? Playing house?" I'm not trying to be a smartass, but what exactly would they be doing?

"No, I talked to my lawyer and he thinks we can push for a trial separation, but if she pushes for counseling, a judge may side with her on that."

"So, you just don't get a say at all in it? Is that what you're telling me?"

"Marissa..." He sighs. "I cheated on her a lot. I don't have a prenuptial agreement and I make a lot of money. Unfortunately, her wanting to work things out means I have to play by her rules on some things." He sighs. "Plus, she said she'd go public about you and me."

My heart begins to pound in my chest at the thought of being fired from my first job. *After only a month.* I'd carry that stigma with me for my entire career if anyone ever called *Beckham Securities* for a reference. "What's to stop her from doing that now?"

"She won't if I do what she wants." He reaches for my hand and despite my flinching, he rubs his thumb over the knuckles. "I want to ask you to quit. Go somewhere else. Anywhere else. I'll write you a recommendation," he says.

"So, you want me to give up my job for you. For us." I shrug.

"I don't mean it like that. If I could walk away, I would. It's not as easy for me."

"I get that. I didn't ask." I pull my hand away from his and cross my arms over my chest. "You told me not to worry. That she didn't care. I already gave up my moral compass to be with you. Now, you're suggesting I give up my job? I made all these rationalizations so I could still look at myself in the mirror every morning. I already feel like a different person than I did months ago, and I don't want to risk waking up in another few months and not even recognize myself." I shake my head. "We have great sex and we make each other laugh and I like who I am around you, *whole mistress things aside,*" I whisper because I can feel the tears building, "but you're married and I think it's best we just end things now…" My voice is calm despite the fact that my insides are screaming. "Before we go further down this road and it's even harder to stop."

"It's already fucking hard, Marissa."

My heart thumps painfully and I wince in response. "I know. For me too—but this is so complicated and the only thing that will make things easier for us both is if we walk away."

He turns in his seat and lets his back rest against the door to stare at me. "How am I supposed to look at you every day and know that I can't touch you or kiss you?" I turn to look at him and

I see the anguish all over his perfect features. "Would it be that easy for you to see me?"

"Nothing about this is easy, Chris, but what do you want me to do? Even if she didn't know who I was, I don't know that I could do this for a whole year. We've hardly been sneaking around, but if you're trying to work on your marriage, I can't imagine you'd be able to spend every night out of the house with me, if any."

"I wouldn't ask you to put up with that. I shouldn't have asked you to put up with as much as you have." He sighs.

"Being with you is not a tough feat." I give him a sad smile as I blink away the tears forming in my eyes. "I have been very into you since you bought me that shot of tequila."

"Will you wait? Until I'm divorced?"

I've been waiting for this question. He's asked it in so many ways before but now this is explicit and attached to a specific timeline. "I think it's best if you don't expect me to," I tell him. In a perfect world, I'd tell him yes and we could spend the entire year shooting longing looks at each other from across the room, send each other secret love notes, and maybe even take a secret trip under the guise of business, but how is that different from what we're doing now? "You can't give your marriage a valiant effort if you're just counting down the days until you can be with me. It'll drive you crazy."

"So, that's a no."

"What happens if in a year she wants another year *or* you two decide to reconcile? What if the last few years were just a bump in the road to your happily ever after with her?"

"It—"

"You don't know that," I interrupt. "So much can happen in a year. Maybe *she* decides to go to therapy and changes. You loved her at one point; what happens when you start to see glimpses of that person she used to be that made you fall in love?"

"I...it won't be the same. It has *never* been the same," he murmurs. "I'm not the same." He offers as his lips form a straight line.

Full lips I've grown accustomed to feeling against mine. I'll miss the way they move against mine and the way his stubble scrapes against my cheeks and everywhere else he puts his mouth because he can't keep his lips off of me. "We could have really been something." He laughs, but I can hear the pain in it. "It's crazy to think that in another life where you don't work for me and I'm not married, I'm probably convincing you at this very moment to move in with me."

"Chris…" I start, but he shakes his head.

"I get why you feel this way, but it doesn't mean I like it."

"I'm not crazy about it either," I tell him honestly.

"Try not to break too many hearts out there, yeah?" he asks as he opens his door. A part of me thought he'd try to kiss me one final time, but he's out of my car, letting the rain beat down on him.

"Wait…aren't you going to kiss me goodbye?" I know I shouldn't ask but if I'm never going to kiss him again, I'd like the last one to be memorable. He hesitates at first like he's not sure he wants to before he moves back into my car.

He reaches for my cheek and I ignore the fact that his hand is wet because his mouth is an inch from mine. "For the record, this is not goodbye because this is not the last time I'll ever kiss you." He gives me a smile and then he pushes his lips to mine. His tongue darts out and rubs against mine once before he pulls back, not even giving us a chance to sink into it. "That's all you get for now." He winks and then he's out of my car.

I don't know how I got home. Or how I made it to work the next day or the one after that. In theory, I know I did the right thing, but the way my heart throbs in my chest every time I even hear Chris' name makes me feel I've done all the wrong things. Chris had our one on ones switched to emails for the time being but that wasn't a permanent solution. When it had only been three days, it felt like I'd been avoiding him for months. It was pretty hard to avoid the CFO of the company that works on the same floor and it felt like I'd been working overtime to do so. It wasn't until a meeting at the end of the week when Mr. Beckham announced they were ready to send a team to Paris for six months to open the new office that I realized the best way to avoid the CFO for an extended period of time.

By the following week, I was in Europe.

Chapter SEVENTEEN

Marissa

```
I'll admit I wasn't thrilled about you
leaving to begin with, but you actually
left without saying goodbye?
```

C

I open the email for the hundredth time that's been sitting in my inbox before I even landed in France *two days ago*. I notice he's sent it from what I assume is a personal email address and he'd sent it to my personal email that he must have gotten from my resume.

What did he want me to say?

It's not like he didn't know I was leaving. It's also not my fault that he was in Seattle the day I left. I'm sitting at one of the many cafés on the same street as my temporary apartment staring at the words on the screen. I don't know why I keep opening his email because I have it memorized at this point. I pick at the croissant in front of me, suddenly wishing I hadn't ordered it; I've already had four in the two days I've been here. It's going to be a long six months if I'm already overloading on carbs.

But fuck they are so good. They're my weakness at home. I knew I wouldn't be able to resist them here.

I fell in love with the look of this café instantly because it reminds me of one at home—*Avery's*—which I know the owner modeled after a Parisian café.

I open the email again, finally deciding to respond because I've had two espressos and my caffeine anxiety won't allow for it to go unanswered another second.

```
You said we weren't doing the whole
goodbye thing.
```

His reply is almost instant. It's noon here which means it's six in the morning at home—*on a Saturday* for that matter—so I'm shocked at the swift reply.

```
There she is. I was beginning to think
you were ignoring me. It's a good thing
I'm getting updates, or else I'd think
something happened to you.
```

I want to reply something sarcastic along the lines of *something had happened to me. Him.* But I decide against it because I'm the one that walked away. It's strange, but I haven't cried very much. Maybe because I haven't let myself stop moving since he left my car that day. I went home, deep cleaned my room and three others in my house, listened to two audiobooks and started binge-watching *Sex and The City* immediately so I wouldn't have to be alone with my thoughts, and then spent a week going through my closet as well as my mother's and Autumn's for a perfect wardrobe for Paris. *I didn't have time to be upset over our breakup.*

```
Nope, I'm fine. Just been busy since I
got here.
```

I type out as I lazily scroll through Instagram. He probably knows that's a lie. We don't technically start until Monday but they wanted us to get here a little early to get settled and adjust to the time difference. So, for the past two days, we've been on our own with optional dinners with the team every night.

> Hope you're having fun. But not too much.

Another email comes through a second later.

> I miss you.

I don't respond to that and the next day, while I'm taking a bubble bath in a tub worthy of an aesthetic Pinterest page, my phone beeps indicating a message. I set down the book I'm reading and grab my phone, sighing when I see that he's texted me this time.

Chris: My apartment isn't the same without you here. I hate sleeping in this bed without you.

Me: Are you alone?

I type out the message and send it before I can tell myself I shouldn't ask because it's not my business and I shouldn't care.

Chris: Yes. I moved out. My lawyer is pushing for an official separation. We start counseling this week. We'll see how that goes.

Me: Good luck with everything. I hope it works out the way you want it to.

Chris: That would mean I get the girl in the end.

Me: Which girl?

Chris: You know which girl.

Me: I have to go.

Chris: It's almost eleven-thirty there and you have to be up early tomorrow. Where are you going? Or are you out?

Me: Those are a lot of questions that a normal boss wouldn't be entitled to know.

Chris: Maybe, but your very jealous and possessive ex-boyfriend would like to know.

Me: Emphasis on the ex

Chris: Don't make me come out there.

Me: Please don't. I took this job to put distance between us. We need to get over each other.

Chris: I didn't agree to that. I'd prefer you didn't get over me.

Me: That's not fair.

Chris: Why isn't it? I'm not going to get over you. Am I an asshole because I want you to be miserable with me?

Me: I'll submit that question to Reddit for confirmation, but I would say yes you are the asshole for that.

Chris: Ha. I know you went there for space which is why I told Beck I didn't want toc ome out there this week. You'll have to deal with him though so try not to get yelled at. If I keep defending you, he'll start to suspect we're sleeping together.

> **Me: We aren't sleeping together.**

> **Chris: Don't remind me.**

The next morning, I'm getting ready for my first day when there's a knock on my apartment door. It's barely seven in the morning, so I can only imagine it's someone from the team asking if I want to walk to the office together. I open the door to someone holding a massive and gorgeous bouquet of white and pink tulips in a glass vase. The person lowers their face and I see Emma giving me a knowing grin as she walks through my apartment with them in her hand. Emma is from Beckham Securities as well, but she works in legal which is on a different floor, so we hadn't met until the flight here. She's a few years older than me and recently broke up with her fiancé. Well, *I suppose he recently broke up with her.* So apparently, she's using this trip in a similar way that I am and while I didn't give her any details, we bonded on the flight over here about our failed relationships.

"We've been in Paris less than a week and you already have someone sending you flowers?" She blinks her hazel eyes at me several times. "Where have you been going and why are you not taking me?!" She sets the vase on my counter and puts her hands on her hips. She's wearing sunglasses perched on her nose and she's looking at me from over the tops of them. She fits in so well in Paris, it's almost like she's from here. She pulls the sunglasses off her face and places them delicately on her head before she fusses with her bangs. *An impulse decision in response to the breakup. Zero out of ten recommend,* she says.

Emma is gorgeous and turned at least twenty guys' heads just in the airport alone. With legs up to her ears, and always wearing no shorter than four-inch heels, she has the kind of skin that is sun kissed year round with raven-colored hair making it a conundrum where she's from or what's in her DNA.

For the record, I've seen pictures of her ex-fiancé. I don't get it. But love or whatever.

I don't see a card with the flowers, thankfully, so I go for the easy lie because I have an inkling as to who they're from. "I think they're from my parents. They know it's my first day. Trust me, I haven't met anyone here." *Well, that part is true.*

"That is so freaking cute." She runs her finger over one of the petals. "It's been forever since someone has sent me flowers," she muses sadly before turning to me. "Okay, I want to stop for coffee, so hurry up!"

While I'm in my room grabbing my coat because November in Paris is anything but warm, I text who I believe to be behind the flower delivery.

> **Me: Safe to assume the flowers are from you?**

Again, he responds instantly. *When does this man sleep? I guess it's only one in the morning at home, but still.*

> **Chris: Should I be worried about anyone else sending you flowers?**

> **Me: You never know. I could have Parisian admirers.**

> **Chris: I'll bet you do. As long as I'm still your favorite.**

I roll my eyes just as I hear Emma calling for me to *move my ass.*

> **Me: Thank you for the flowers.**

> **Chris: Have a great day, beautiful.**

> **Chris:** Heard things are going well. Glad to hear it. I can't stop thinking about you.

I'm sitting at lunch with Emma a few days later when his message comes through and I guess the smile that crosses my face is a dead giveaway because she squeals.

"Who has you smiling at your phone?" she asks, and when I look up, I see her straining to look at my screen from across the table. "And you expect me to believe your *parents* sent you those flowers?" She scrunches her nose and points her spoon at me before taking a bite of the best parfait I've ever had. "Let's go out tonight."

"It's my ex," I confess hoping that will get me out of trolling the streets looking for a European fling.

Her eyes widen and she shakes her head. "All the more reason to go out! You said you guys were done."

"I believe I used the word 'complicated.'"

She readjusts her beret and cocks her head to the side. "'Complicated' just sounds like a fancy way to say we're in that toxic in-between where we just go back and forth hurting each other on the path to breaking up." She uses air quotes before she takes a sip of her sparkling water.

If Emma worked for *any* department other than legal, I may have trusted her to tell her about Chris, but I value my job. I also don't know her well enough to know her stance on women sleeping with married men. *Hell, I barely know my own stance on it.*

"You're right, but the feelings are still there."

"They always are." She sighs. "Garrett won't stop calling ever since I got here. Probably assuming I'm already fucking my way through Paris." She pushes a strawberry around her bowl. "I made a mistake, blah blah blah, but it's a very firm *fuck no and fuck you* from me."

"I wish I could be that firm."

"Oh, honey, did he cheat on you with four different women?" She snorts. "Maybe I wouldn't be if he wasn't such a lying cheating asshole. Also, he's not even good in bed! I don't know how he got four women to consistently sleep with him." She scoffs. "I had this so I had to by law," she jokes holding up her middle finger with her enormous diamond engagement ring.

"Why are you still wearing your ring anyway?"

"Because it's four and a half carats with perfect clarity and I haven't decided what I want to do with it yet."

"I get not giving it back, but why are you wearing it?" I raise an eyebrow at her and she rolls her eyes.

"It's pretty." She holds it up. "It's not the ring's fault that the person who bought it was awful. It's too gorgeous not to show off." She rubs it sadly before dropping it into her lap. "So…tonight?"

It's only Wednesday and we have an early meeting on Thursday so I was able to convince her it would be a better idea to go out this weekend, which is why I'm home by seven-thirty doing yoga in my apartment. It is my favorite thing to do to relax but I'd stopped for a while and just recently incorporated it into my *trying my best not to think about Chris plan*. I get up from my mat when my phone starts to ring and see his name across the screen.

So much for my plan.

"Yes?" I answer and a chuckle from the other end makes my nipples hard. *Fucker.*

"Hello to you too." I haven't heard his voice in almost two weeks and now my mind is flooded with all of the times I've heard it. All those times he groaned low in my ear when he was about to come. The times he'd grunted out my name while he spilled inside of me. When he fucked my face and exploded down my throat. The times he'd stroked my hand and told me how beautiful I was while we had dinner.

"Why are you calling?"

"I'm checking in with my favorite employee."

"Fuck off." I want to hang up and my finger hovers over the end call button but I can't bring myself to do it.

"Trust me, I wish I could," he says and I take a sip of my water wishing I had just let this call go to voicemail. "Are you thinking about me at all?"

"No," I lie at first before I decide to go with the truth. "I mean…I am trying not to but you are making it hard."

"I can't help it. I wasn't expecting to be cut off from you almost completely. I thought I'd still be able to catch glimpses of you in those dresses you wear or hear you laugh…maybe catch your smile during a meeting even if it wasn't directed at me."

"This is better."

"For who?"

"Both of us."

He sighs. "We started counseling." I hear the clink of a glass and I wonder if he's drinking.

"Isn't it like three p.m. there? Isn't it a little early for a drink?" I can hear the joke in my voice and I hate that I'm right back in it. Flirting with Chris Holt.

My boss.

My married boss.

Fuck me.

He laughs. "Careful. Nagging me over day drinking is girlfriend behavior."

I grip the phone and try to calm my racing heart over the thought of being his girlfriend. *No, Marissa.* "I just mean…you're at work."

"I'm working from home."

In the two months I've worked for *Beckham Securities*, I don't think there was a day he wasn't in the office so that's surprising. "Are you sick?" I ask immediately, wondering if maybe that's why he's home for the day.

"No. We had our first session this morning and I just decided not to go to the office after."

I try not to let myself think about him and his wife in therapy 'working on their marriage.' "Oh. I guess I've just never known you to not be in the office."

"I used to work from home once a week, but then this new woman started working for me and I wanted to see her as much as possible."

"You can't be serious." I chuckle.

"I'm always serious when it comes to you." I can hear the smile in his voice and the question is sitting on the tip of my tongue. I know I shouldn't ask but he did volunteer the information.

"How was...counseling? I mean..."

"Are we on the path to reconciliation?" He snorts. "Yeah, I'll invite you to the vow renewal."

I frown and narrow my eyes. "Did you forget who you were talking to?"

"No, did you?"

"I don't appreciate the sarcasm."

"My apologies, I'll be clearer since maybe I wasn't the first time. I don't want to be in counseling. I want a divorce, but the woman I married is forcing me into this charade because she doesn't want to divorce a man on track to join the Forbes List of billionaires. I also want to be with a woman—that's you by the way—that not only works for me, but said wife knows about because I cockily didn't do better at hiding the fact that I fell in love with my mistress. So, she told me she'd blow up her life if I didn't give my girlfriend up. So, excuse me for drinking after a bullshit marriage counseling session and for my sarcasm."

I blink my eyes several times because what did he just say?

"Wait, you're in love with me?" I'm not going to beat around the bush or try to be coy over the fact that those words may have momentarily stopped my heart.

"Don't tell me you're surprised by that."

"Can we stop the smartass remarks for one second, please?"

He sighs. "Yes."

"To which question?"

"Both." He sighs and then I hear the clink of ice against glass again.

"You've just never said it before."

"It didn't seem fair to tell you that when I wasn't free to."

"I feel like we hardly know each other," I whisper. "I mean… past the sex."

He doesn't say anything for a minute and I pull my phone away from my ear in case the call dropped. "I think I know you pretty well. I know you like white tulips with pink and that you've probably had three croissants a day since you've been there. I know your coffee preferences, your drink preferences, what you like to eat, and what you're like when you're sick. I know you like to read smutty books in the bubble bath and that you like to take them with me." His voice lowers. "By the way, are you enjoying the tub in your apartment? Do you think about me when you're touching yourself in the bath? Do you miss sitting on the edge of the tub while I lick the water away from between your legs?" I don't respond and he continues. "I know everything you like in bed. I know a lot about you, Marissa. I even know the things you haven't quite figured out yourself yet." I drop to the couch, yoga completely forgotten and I briefly wonder if he's going to take this conversation in a more salacious direction.

"What haven't I figured out?"

"That you like that I can't leave you alone." I go to protest when he beats me to it. "You could have ignored my call, you know."

"It's still the work day in the States, it could have been about work," I offer, but even I know that argument is weak.

"When have I *ever* called you about work?"

"Well, maybe you should. You call yourself my boss," I quip.

"Imagine if I wasn't. It would be much harder for me to take care of you while you're there."

I narrow my eyes curiously. "What does that mean?"

"Do you really think everyone has a thousand-dollar daily allowance?"

"That was you!" I shoot to my feet. I was shocked when I saw how much I was allotted for daily meals. "Chris, I don't even put a dent in that every day."

"Well, you should. Where have you been eating? Go somewhere nice. Take Emma."

"Wha—how do you know I've been hanging out with Emma?"

"I know everything."

"Stop spying on me!" I tell him but somewhere deep in my subconscious, the thought brings me a bit of happiness that he's so curious about how I'm spending my free time in Paris.

"Oh, relax, I'm not."

"Don't you tell me to relax. It sounds like you are and can we back up for a second? How did you get me such a high stipend? And isn't that setting off alarm bells that I'm the only one?"

"No. I said anyone that reports directly to me needs that much."

"I'm the only one here that reports directly to you!"

"Funny how that worked out." He chuckles. "Though to be fair, Liam and Elise will be there in a few weeks and they'll get the same. Feel better?"

"Not really. Are you spying on me?"

"No."

"Christopher," I warn.

"Fine. I may have looked at the cameras for the building and I see you two together most of the time."

I dart my eyes around my apartment, suddenly very aware that I work for a security company. "Are there…cameras in my apartment? Don't lie to me. I swear to God, Chris."

"No." He laughs. "I swear. I'm not that crazy. The cameras just show who's coming in and out of the building. We own the building and it's only for our employees, we just want to make sure everyone is safe."

"So, if I brought a guy home, you'd know?"

"If you brought a guy home, I'd be on the first plane to Paris." I can hear the growly edge in his voice and it has a direct line to my clit.

"Really, now? Should we test that theory?" I tease, and my pussy clenches at the thought of his jealousy.

"Let's not."

"Emma wants to go out tomorrow," I tell him.

"Mmmhmm."

"I think she wants to get laid."

"Do you?"

I could torture him but he did just say he's in love with me, so I decide to throw him a bone. "Yes, but the guy I'm interested in isn't exactly available."

I hear him exhale. "Is that so? Should I be worried about this guy?"

I snort in response. "That's an awfully loaded question. Are you having an existential crisis?"

"Daily."

I chew on my bottom lip as I try to think of something witty to say but I come up empty. "I can't stop thinking about you either," I tell him, referencing his comment from earlier. "But I can't help feeling that I'm being stupid. That maybe this is just a right person, wrong time thing but we aren't respecting it by still talking and flirting while you're married. Especially now that it sounds like your wife is a bit of a ticking time bomb. What if she finds out you're still talking to me? Does she know I'm here? If you have to come here, is that going to be tough for you?"

"I don't care about what's tough for me, Marissa. I care about *you*. And I hate that I can't be with you. I hate that there may come a time when you'll be over this because you'll get tired of waiting. You're twenty-one and gorgeous and smart and far too fucking charming and mature for someone your age, and I know there are men just waiting for you to be over me."

My eyes well up with tears and before I can stop it, one slides down my face. I haven't let myself dwell on this situation with Chris. I hadn't cried other than briefly on the way home after we talked in my car because what use was there in crying? It's a shitty situation that I have no control over, but hearing him tell me he's in love with me and there's nothing we could do about it for at least a year makes my heart feel like it's cracking in my chest. A year feels like an eternity. "It's really not fair."

"You're telling me."

I pull the cork out of the wine I opened last night and pour myself a glass. I take a healthy sip of it as I contemplate what I want to say next. "I don't know that a year is enough time to get over you…so maybe you're safe."

He lets out a deep breath that sounds like relief. "Best news I've heard all day."

"You know, if there ever comes a time that you're single and unattached…how are we going to tell people at work?"

"Once Wes realizes that you and the woman I slept with at Owen's wedding are the same woman, he's going to know that I'm serious about you."

I smile. "I did that much of a number on you, huh?"

"Did you." He chuckles. "I never told you this but I took one of your hair pins that night. You had your hair up with these silver hair things. I took one off the nightstand while you were sleeping."

My mouth drops in shock as I remember that I couldn't find one of them when I was leaving his room that morning. "Wanted a souvenir, did you? What if that was a family heirloom!"

"Was it?"

"No," I chuckle, "but that's not the point!"

"I wanted something to remind me that it happened. That it was real. That you were real. I've been carrying it with me in my pocket ever since."

I gasp. "What?"

"That's how Beck found out about you. Aside from the fact

that I couldn't shut up about you. Whenever I had too much to drink, I'd take it out and mess with it."

"Wow."

"Still think I can't be in love with you?"

My throat feels suddenly dry and I take a long sip of my wine before licking my lips. "No."

"Good. Now, tell me what you're doing."

"Well, I was doing yoga when you called."

"I'm sorry I interrupted you, I'll let you get back to it if you'll let me watch."

"You want to watch me do yoga?" I look down at what I'm wearing and I imagine most men wouldn't mind watching a woman do anything while wearing skin-tight leggings and a bra.

"I'd watch you do anything."

A wicked idea floats through my head and I drag my teeth over my bottom lip. "Okay, I'll FaceTime you from my iPad in two minutes."

"Really? Fuck, I haven't seen your face in almost two weeks. Okay, I'm ready."

No, you are definitely not.

I hang up the phone and strip out of my clothes leaving me completely nude before propping my phone up on the coffee table and in perfect view of everything. I start the call but I'm not in the frame.

"Let me see that gorgeous—" He starts but immediately stops talking when he sees my bare ass walking towards my mat. I turn around and his mouth is ajar as his drink hovers near his lips. He takes a long sip before I see him bite down hard on his lip. *Fuck,* I see him mouth.

"Are you breathing?" I ask as I cock my head to the side and he shakes his head, his eyes still wide and unblinking. "You have seen me naked before, yes?"

He scratches his jaw and lets out a chuckle. "I am trying to talk myself out of getting on a plane right now."

"No." I shake my head before shutting my eyes and trying to center myself.

"That's how you do yoga?"

I lift one of my legs to my knee in a tree pose as I put my hands over my heart. I open one eye to look at him. "Shhh."

He lets out a breath. "You're so fucking beautiful. And your body makes my dick fucking hard as a rock."

I drop my leg and move into a different position, forcing one leg back into the warrior position. I've never gotten wet doing yoga before but I can feel his eyes trained on my pussy and I'm getting turned on by my exhibitionism. We've only been on for a minute but I can already see him adjusting himself in his seat.

"Take it out," I tell him as I move closer to the camera and move into the goddess pose which completely opens me up.

"Fuck." I hear him grit out and then I see that he's propped his phone up somewhere and I hear the sound of his slacks being unzipped. "You have the most gorgeous cunt, baby. I'd do anything to taste it right now."

He pulls his shirt off leaving him completely naked as well and I'd somehow forgotten how chiseled his body is. "Your body is insane," I whisper as I continue on to another stretch.

I turn my back to the camera giving him a view of my ass before bending over into a stretch called forward fold that's basically downward dog but my legs are spread giving him a very up-close look at my wet pussy. "Fuck me, you're wet," he grits out. "Does your pussy always get hot from yoga?"

I look at him from between my legs. "When I have an audience."

Jealousy flashes across his face and he runs his tongue over his teeth. "I better be the only person in your fucking audience."

I move one hand up my leg slowly and let it ghost over my pussy before I stand up just as a guttural groan comes from the screen. I turn around to face my iPad and I watch as his hand slowly pulls at his dick as he drags his eyes slowly up my body. "Your nipples are hard."

They are aching at this point, and when he licks his lips, they pebble even harder under his gaze like they're desperate to feel his tongue. "I want to run my lips over them…and then my teeth. I want to leave bite marks all over them." His eyes meet mine and a smile pulls at his lips. "Touch them."

I do as he says and roll both of my nipples between my index finger and thumb. My sex is getting slicker and I want him to instruct me to touch it so badly. "What else do you want to do?"

"Every. Fucking. Thing." He runs his hand from root to tip with each word. "Sit down and spread your legs." I do as he says and adjust the iPad so he has a better view. I open my knees and it feels almost obscene how wet I am. "Look how gorgeous you are." The lips of my sex are slightly spread and I can feel my clit pulsing with each passing second. "Put your fingers in your pussy. Don't touch that hot little clit yet." I groan in frustration because *fuck I'm close* and I know just a few brushes against my fingers will have me coming already. "I know you want it, but not yet." I put two of my fingers inside of me, careful not to rub my clit even though I'm dying to. "How's that feel?" he asks and I nod.

"It would feel better if they were your fingers, but it'll suffice," I tell him and he begins to pull harder on his dick.

"Fucking hell, I wish. I can almost feel how wet you are just by looking at you. I love when you drip down my hand while I'm fingering you."

"I never…really liked fingering until you," I tell him as I continue to move my fingers slowly in and out of me. "I love your hands."

"Well, they love being buried in your wet cunt." He leans forward. "Almost as much as my tongue does." My sex gets even wetter and I feel a wave of butterflies moving south. "Kiss me." I bite my bottom lip and he raises an eyebrow sexily.

"Where?"

"My pussy."

"Fuck yes. I'd devour your fucking pussy if I were there. Would have you screaming while you came all over my tongue. Start at your opening and drag your fingers slowly upwards to your clit." I do as he says. "Good girl."

Fuck.

"That's me dragging my tongue through your slit. How'd it feel?"

"Amazing," I whisper through a shaky breath.

"Now rub your clit. Slowly." I start doing it, already feeling my body building when he speaks again. "Stop." His nostrils flare sexily and his tongue darts out to lick his bottom lip and I almost convulse at the thought of him licking me fucking anywhere. "Use one hand to open yourself up, I want to see everything." I swallow, slightly nervous at the thought of being so completely exposed to him. "Don't be nervous." He gives me an encouraging smile. "If I were there, I'd do it myself." And this is true; he did have a habit of spreading me open while he ate me out, so I don't know why this feels different. *Almost more intimate.*

I nod and open myself up to him, spreading the lips of my sex and it suddenly feels like the most erotic experience of my life. "So perfect," he whispers and I watch as he takes another long sip of his drink. "God, I want to fuck you." He nods at me. "Use your other hand to rub your clit. Do it slow." He begins to fuck his hand again and I drop my eyes away from his hungry eyes to his fist pumping his dick. "That's right," he groans. "I'm giving you long, languid strokes. You think you like it fast, and sometimes you do… but you come the hardest when I lick you slow and hard. Right now, you'd be pressing your cunt harder against my mouth." He lets out a breath. "I can almost taste you on my tongue right now, Marissa. Fuck me."

"Do you like my taste?" I whisper.

"Fucking love your taste. Would die for it right now." His eyes shut and he lets out a groan. "Christ, I miss you."

"Me or my pussy?" I respond cheekily.

"Both. I miss *you*, but the fact that you're attached to the only pussy I've ever been addicted to doesn't hurt," he says and a smile pulls at my lips.

I stop rubbing myself for a second. "That was both kind of romantic and hot."

"My specialty." He grins and I roll my eyes as his gaze drops to my cunt. "Keep going. I need you to come."

I go back to rubbing, pushing myself closer to the edge. My eyes flutter closed as I feel my climax brewing beneath my skin and a moan rips through his throat. "Open your eyes, let me see you."

I shake my head. "I can't…I'm too far…" My mouth drops open, feeling the first wave of my orgasm wash over me.

"Tell me how it feels. Tell me how good my mouth feels."

"So fucking good," I moan.

"Good girl. I'm going to suck your clit into my mouth now. Pinch it for me, honey." I do as he says. My body lets go of the mounting tension and my orgasm hits me hard and fast. My clit quivers under my fingers and I hear a groan that sounds more like a growl and then an almost pained, "Oh my god," and then nothing else registers except for how good my fingers feel on my clit. I don't know how long my orgasm goes on, but eventually, I stop pulsing and my eyes flutter open. His blue orbs are locked on my face. He drops his gaze between my legs and then back up to me. "That was the sexiest thing I've ever seen." He rubs his jaw and lets out a chuckle. "And I spent most of my adolescence watching porn." He sits back on the couch, his dick still hard and pointed straight up but his hand is no longer touching it. "You get so wet and…your clit was…" He lets out a breath. "I will never get that image out of my head."

I giggle. "I'm glad you enjoyed the show."

"So fucking much."

I grin just before I drag my wet fingers across my tongue, tasting myself. "I think it's your turn to come now."

Chapter

EIGHTEEN

Marissa

BEFORE I KNEW IT, I'D BEEN IN PARIS FOR A MONTH and I felt like everything was going well both at work and in my personal life. I talked to Chris practically every day even if it was only a few texts or an email. Then other times were two-hour long phone calls that oftentimes led to phone sex or FaceTime sex. *Yes, I'm right back in it but I couldn't stop and it seems like he couldn't either.* I haven't told him I love him yet but I feel it and I'm sure he can too.

I'm one of the last people to leave work one day and I'm rushing home to change before I meet everyone for dinner. It's still light out but I have my face buried in my phone which is how I manage to miss the woman standing in front of the door to my building. I look up just before I collide with her and my heart almost flies out of my chest when she lowers her sunglasses and looks at me with a smug grin.

"Miss Collins, correct?" She's wearing white satin gloves that she slides off slowly before tucking her clutch under her arm. She looked like old money, chic and sophisticated, and I hate how gorgeous she is up close and in person. "I believe we have some things to talk about."

I blink several times in shock because of all the people, I certainly was not expecting Chris' wife to show up at my apartment…in Paris. "I…I don't think so." I try to take a step around her but she blocks me from entering and gives me a look that lets me know that she is definitely going to get her way on this.

She cocks her head to the side and gives me a look. "Oh, honey, I've seen your nudes. We are far past coy, wouldn't you say?"

WHAT? My mouth drops in shock. "If you think you can do something with those, I can assure you that's illegal, but I'll be sure to ask my father who's a retired judge or my sister who's one of the best litigators in the state." I raise an eyebrow at her because I refuse to let her blackmail or intimidate me over that.

Her eyes widen and she looks almost impressed by my words. "You have some bite to you. Good for you. But relax, I won't leak your nudes. Between the two of us, only *you've* proven to not be a girl's girl." She points to the door. "Now, I have an appointment to get a massage in an hour. So, are you going to let me in or what?"

She can't be serious. "Or what."

"Fine." She shrugs. "We can have this conversation out here if you want. Might be kind of weird to be seen talking to the CFO's wife outside your building though. Can't think of anyone who would believe *we* are friends." She looks me up and down before pointing to where I believe the cameras are and I wonder how soon until Chris starts blowing up my phone. *Or hers.*

I don't think she'll do anything to harm me, but I'm still not in love with the idea of having her in my apartment. I turn my head and point at the coffee shop across the street. "I'm not letting you in my apartment. I don't know you and I can't imagine you're my biggest fan. We can go there."

She huffs indignantly and begins walking towards the café.

She's far shorter than I am and practically glides across the cobblestone despite her heels. She's carrying two shopping bags, one from Chanel and one from Hermés, and I wonder if Chris has already put it together that she's here.

Maybe he's on his way here himself.

We sit at one of the outside tables and she removes her sunglasses again before running a hand through her shiny chestnut hair and tucking it behind her ear. "I don't know what he's told you but we are not divorced." I don't respond to that. "So, you knew that? My, aren't we classy?" she digs and I resist the urge to respond. "We are trying to work on things," she continues, and I grit my teeth so I don't say anything that maybe Chris wouldn't want repeated.

"I've been here in Paris. We haven't seen each other. We broke it off."

She laughs in a way that I think she actually finds my comment amusing. "Hardly. You're talking. Constantly."

I've been under the impression that he was at his apartment that she supposedly had never been to when we were talking. *How does she know?*

I don't want to say too much or confirm or deny anything. "We are talking because he's my boss."

"Do you think I was born yesterday? I know *you* practically were, but I don't know why either of you are underestimating me. Do you not care about your career?" I bite my bottom lip. "You're just a baby and you're letting a man—or I suppose just his dick—control your decisions? I know you probably think I'm just the worst human in the world, but I'm still his *wife*. No matter what either of you seem to think, you're the other woman. Not me."

Shame washes over me and I hate the feeling. "Why do you want to be…his wife?" I ask. I hope this to be the only interaction I have with this woman, so I figure I might as well see if there is more to the story. "You say I'm letting him control my decisions but you stay with him? I know I wasn't the first and I know *you* know that. Kind of seems like you're letting something control you also."

She narrows her eyes at me. "You think you know everything."

"I actually don't. I feel like I've been kept in the dark about a lot of things."

"Well, feel free to ask me whatever you want to know." She raises her hand toward the waiter. "Two waters please and a cappuccino." She points at me. "Would you like anything?"

I shake my head before he walks away.

"Do you even love him?" I blurt out.

"In my own way, yes." *Not sure what that means.* "Do *you* really want to be a woman responsible for breaking up a marriage?"

"I didn't break up your marriage."

"Funny, he was never serious about divorce before." I don't say anything and she continues. "I've warned Chris what I would do if he continued his affair with you but seeing as how he didn't listen, I wanted to come and talk to you in person." Our waiter brings over our waters and her coffee. "Thank you, dear," she says handing him her credit card. She turns her eyes back to me. "Stay away from my husband. Stop communicating with him."

"Can I ask what your bottom line is? Do you *want* to be with him?"

"For now," she says before she takes a sip of her drink. "We are in counseling for a reason, but if it doesn't work, I'll give him a divorce. But he needs to give it an actual effort. I don't know what Chris has told you but I'm not unreasonable. He's been cheating on me for god knows how long and now he wants a divorce and expects me to roll over and take it? No. He's been a terrible husband, and now I'm making him pay for it. So sure," she shrugs, "I'll give him a divorce eventually, but I'm going to make it hurt first."

She takes an envelope out of her purse and slides it across the table with a smile. "What is this?" I reluctantly open the envelope and my mouth falls open when I see that it's a check for…
FIVE MILLION DOLLARS?!

I slide the envelope back across the table. "You think…? I don't want…I can't be…" I sputter, unsure of what to say. "I do not want this."

"Fine, name your price." She shrugs.

"It's not even your money!"

She snorts. "Clearly you don't know how marriage works."

"Fine. Legally, sure, but I would never do that. Do you know how…how bad this looks that you are offering this to me?"

"Ten million." She counters and I feel like I'm going to be sick. She can't actually think she can pay me off? *No. Fuck no.*

"Mrs. Holt, I'm sorry for my part in hurting you, and more importantly, I'm sorry I got myself caught up in your very dysfunctional relationship. Neither of you are happy and you're not about to use me to try and even the score with him." I grab my purse. "Please just leave me be."

"Trust me, I would love to. We never have to speak again so long as you stay away from Chris."

"I'll be here at least five more months and I'm contemplating staying the year."

"Cease all communication with him."

I frown. "He's my boss, you can't expect us not to talk."

"I'll know when it's anything but business."

"What did you plant a listening device at the penthouse?" *This woman may be more calculated than Chris thought.*

"Not your business."

I shake my head. "How did you even find out about me?"

"I have my ways."

I sigh as I stand up, accepting the fact that she's not going to give me any more information. "Fine, but for what it's worth, I hope you find happiness at some point, because if and when all of this is over with Chris, will you be happy? Rich, sure, but will you be able to look at yourself in the mirror for trying to destroy another person? I'm not saying he's absolved from guilt, but do you think you'll feel better in the end?"

She yawns and looks up at me as she slides her sunglasses back on. "Are you done? I'm really not in the mood to be lectured by my husband's whore. Like your moral compass is so perfect."

"I love him," I tell her and I hate that she's the first person to hear that but I want her to know that this isn't a game to me. The person that stands to get hurt the most is me because at this point, I am convinced she doesn't even love him and that this is more about her ego and getting revenge than her protecting her heart.

"Oh, please spare me." She chuckles as she stands up. "You think he loves you?"

"I don't know." I lie, because I'm pretty sure Chris didn't lie to me about that.

"I can assure you he doesn't. He likes young pussy. I'll admit he's more enthralled with you than he's been with the others but you're all the same." The thought of him with other women makes me irate but I do my best to quell the anger raging inside. "You think he's been sitting at home pining for you while you've been here? Please. I wouldn't be surprised if he was balls deep inside some other girl before you were even fully across the Atlantic Ocean." My heart sinks at her words even though I don't believe it. *There isn't anyone else. Just you.* I can practically hear his voice in my head but her words still sting. She stands up and stares into my eyes. "He's not a good person, Marissa. Get out before you get hurt." She picks up the envelope and slides it into my hand again. Then she's moving across the street towards a town car that has suddenly appeared outside of my building.

Chapter NINETEEN

CHRIS

"*You've reached Marissa. Leave a message.*"

I end the call after trying her back to back, each going straight to voicemail. She should already be done for the day, but it's possible she got stuck in a meeting.

> **Me: Thinking about you, baby. Call me.**

A few hours go by and I still haven't heard from her, which is unlike her. In the past month, we've talked every day, and often several times during any given day. I'm just about to text her again when I see the dots indicating that she's typing. I watch as they appear and disappear a few times over the course of a minute. I press the button to call her and put the phone to my ear. "What the fuck?" I muse aloud when the call goes directly to voicemail.

> **Me: Why are you ignoring my calls?**

> **Marissa:** I can't do this anymore.

> **Me:** What's going on? Talk to me, baby.

> **Marissa:** Please, just let me go. It's better this way.

> **Me:** What are you talking about? And why aren't you answering your phone?

My phone begins to ring in my hands and I answer it on the first ring. "What's wrong?"

"Where are you?" she asks without answering my question.

"My office. Where are *you*?"

"My apartment." She sighs. "But I'm about to go out. Your office at home or at work?"

She sounds like she's had a drink and the thought of her upset, drunk, and in a foreign city is making me feel like a caveman. I resist the urge to text my assistant to prepare the jet until I have more context. "Work. Tell me what's going on."

"I met your wife."

Of all the things she could have said, I was not expecting that, and part of me thinks I may have hallucinated and heard her incorrectly. "Excuse me? Run that by me again?"

"She's here in Paris. Tracked me down." I hear the uncorking of a bottle through the phone and the sound of her pouring. "Outside our building."

I immediately pull up my credit card app. I didn't have alerts set up for the card Holly uses so I wouldn't have necessarily known if she was out of the country, but normally she at least sends me a text when she's traveling.

Probably not if she's planning a trip for the sole purpose of accosting your girlfriend.

I scrub my jaw, my body feeling tense and anxious as I scroll through her last ten charges. She'd checked into the Four Seasons

Hotel in Paris last night and done quite a bit of shopping today. *Fuck.*

I'm pulling up the feed to access the cameras outside of Marissa's building when I realize I haven't said anything. "Baby, I'm so sorry. What did she say? Are you okay?"

"Yes."

"Did she touch you?" Holly isn't a violent person but if she flew to Paris, that means she assumes I'm still talking to Marissa and I am not sure how she'd react to meeting her in person.

"No."

"I need more than one-word answers."

"What you'd expect. She told me to stay away from you. Called me a whore. That I'm ruining my life by messing around with a married man I work for. Pretty much everything I already think about myself." She sniffles and I wish I could crawl through the phone and hold her.

"Marissa, you are not a whore."

"I don't think your vote holds that much weight here. Also, I think she may have tapped your apartment or something so just be careful. She knew we were still talking and I don't know how she'd know that unless you haven't really moved out."

I frown, wondering how in the hell Holly would know that. "I don't lie to you. I've been at the penthouse." I look around my office, wondering if maybe she'd been bold enough to leave something here and immediately call for a sweep of my office. I walk out of my office toward one of the conference rooms that has a balcony for the rest of this conversation to try and give myself some privacy. I close the door behind me, leaving me alone outside, and sit on one of the chairs. "I can't lose you."

"You were never free to have me, Chris."

"Please don't do this." My hands begin to shake. I hear the sound of a door opening and when I look up, I see Beck staring at me. *You good?* he mouths and I shake my head before putting a hand up. He hovers in the doorway before going back inside. "I'm coming to Paris."

"No, don't!" she exclaims. "Are you insane? She's probably still here! I'm sure she's expecting for you to figure out—"

"I don't care—"

"I do! You and Holly are hell bent on making each other miserable and I just can't be involved in it anymore. There's nothing about this separation that's going to be amicable and you being with me is just going to make things harder for you."

"I'll deal with it."

"Okay, but I can't. And I can't deal with any more run-ins with Holly. That was..." She trails off and lets out a breath. "Awful and I feel like shit. But I welcomed this, right? I did this to myself by getting involved with a married man. I deserve every single thing she said."

"No, you don't. I deserve whatever she has to say, not you."

"I knew you were married. Maybe not the first time, but I eventually learned the truth and actively continued being with you. I'm just as guilty. I slept with her husband. I wronged her." She starts to cry and I know there's only so much I can do while I'm almost four thousand miles away.

"Please don't cry. I'm so sorry, but you won't have to deal with her again. I'll be sure of that." *I have no idea how I'm going to deal with Holly because I am fucking furious at her for this. Part of me wants to turn off her credit card while she's in Paris but I want her out of the same city as Marissa right now.*

"Somehow, I doubt you can. I'm going to assume you had no idea that she was in Paris until I told you." She sighs. "I'm not saying this is the end forever but you need to be single before I can go back down this road with you. Not separated either. I mean the ink is dry on your divorce papers."

I was afraid things would come to this. I guess I was stupid to think that if Marissa was in Paris, Holly would assume we were over. *Could she have really planted something in my apartment? When would she have even gotten in?*

"I should go," she says and I remember that she's planning to go out tonight. A single girl with a broken heart, drunk, and in Paris sounds like a recipe for there to be a line of guys waiting to talk to her tonight and the thought makes me sick.

"Wait." She doesn't hang up but she doesn't say anything either. "I'm sorry."

"I know. I am too," she says so quietly that I almost don't hear the last part.

"For what?"

"For not walking away sooner before we both got in this deep." She pauses before taking another breath. "I'm going to request to stay here for the full year."

I think about the fact that I won't see her for twelve months if I don't go out there. It has only been a month and I already miss her like she's been gone for years. My body has been tense and every time my phone beeps my heart squeezes in hope that it's a message from her. If this is over, that means she wants at least twelve months of no contact.

"We can't talk at all?" I ask her even though I already know the answer.

"What's the point?"

"Because I love you?" I answer immediately because that seems like the only reason that should matter. She doesn't respond so I ask the question I've been wanting to know. "Do you love me?"

"I don't think it's fair for you to ask me that."

I hear the implication but the fact that she doesn't say it makes me feel like she never will. "One year, Marissa. I'm not letting you stay there longer than that. If I have to come out there and get you, I will."

"Please don't come for me until there's no longer a ring on your finger."

By no surprise, I haven't been able to get in touch with Holly for the past two days and I feel like I am ready to explode by the time I pull up to my house. She's due home in an hour and I want to be here so she can't avoid talking to me for another second. I walk through my house, brimming with anger as I think about the shitstorm that's become my life. I don't know how long I've been pacing when the front door opens and I hear Holly on the phone. Based on her bubbly tone, it sounds like one of her friends and when she sees me in the foyer she gasps. "Oh my god, let me call you back. There's a situation at my house," she says before she hangs up. She tosses her keys on a nearby table and pulls off her wide-brimmed hat.

"Christopher," she says the word like it disgusts her. "I'm sorry, don't you not live here?"

I cross my arms over my chest. "Where have you been?" I nod at her.

"Out." She meets my gaze and offers a shrug but her face remains impassive.

I walk towards her. "Of the country? So, I heard. I've locked your credit card by the way."

Her eyes widen and she gives me a confused look. "Excuse me?"

"As of about five minutes ago. I wanted to make sure you could at least get home." I shrug. "But for the time being, you are not able to use your cards. Either of them."

"You're insane." She pulls up her phone and while she's trying to appear dismissive, I can hear the panic in her tone.

"For putting up with your shit as long as I have? Yes. Definitely."

She glares at me. "Oh, this means you must have talked to your girlfriend. Did she tell you that we had a nice cup of coffee? Lovely girl." She looks at her nails. "For a whore and all."

I ball my hands into fists to try and temper my rage. "Call her a whore one more time, Holly, I swear to God. Why would you go out there?"

"Because you were not listening. You were still talking to her after I told you to end it with her. So, I thought I'd have better luck getting through to her. Which I guess worked if you're here and you cut off my credit cards. I guess that means she cut *you* off then?"

"What did I say I was going to do if you breathed in her direction? Access to my money is the only thing you give a shit about so it seems like the only way to get my point across."

She shrugs and I'm surprised at her cavalier attitude to not being able to blow through my money. "Fine. Does this mean you'll give counseling an actual effort now?"

I snort. "Did you think scaring Marissa off would make me want to be with you? You couldn't have seriously thought that. She didn't cause the problems in our marriage."

"No, I suspect you think I did that all on my own."

I want to tell her that she certainly jump-started everything but I am trying to keep things from getting out of hand and turning into a screaming match. "I know I didn't help."

"And counseling will."

"Do you really think going to counseling will just magically fix everything? We don't work, Holly. I want a divorce."

She stares at me for a second. "What is so special about this girl anyway?"

"I love her," I tell her honestly. "And maybe that makes me an asshole for saying that to you but it's been obvious for years that you're not in love with me, and…"

"You think *she* is?" She snorts. "She's not." I grit my teeth in annoyance because while I know I have to take anything she says with a grain of salt, I also know Marissa hasn't said it. "She's young and *you're* rich," she spits out, and that nagging insecurity that I'm nothing but a large bank account with a dick attached flares up.

It's not true. You know it's not, I hear Marissa's voice so clearly, it's almost as if she's standing right next to me.

"She doesn't care about the money." I want her to know that while Holly was probably quick to notice all the ways that she and Marissa are different, *this* is probably the biggest.

"They all care about the money. Even when they claim they don't. I'll be honest, I was surprised she didn't want to take the money I offered at first, but—"

My heart plummets. "What the fuck? You offered her money?"

Holly cocks her head to the side and a snide smile pulls at her lips. "She didn't tell you? Well well, that's certainly not expected. I wrote her a check for five million dollars to stay away from you. She said she didn't want it but"—she points at me—"she did keep it. Maybe she just needs time to mull it over."

I take a step back because... *what?*

She begins her way up the stairs and points at the suitcase still in the foyer. "Bring that up, will you?"

My eyes snap to her suitcase, staring at it as I try to get my thoughts together. *Marissa wouldn't cash it. Even if she took it. She ripped it up. If there was even a check at all. But why didn't she tell me?* "You're lying."

Holly turns on the stairs and narrows her eyes at me. "I'm not but think whatever you want."

"She'd..." My mind is racing, and at this moment I know I won't believe anything until I talk to Marissa. "She knows I'd give her whatever she wanted; she wouldn't take money from you."

"And maybe she won't. I can't imagine she'll be able to cash it in France, but she did take it. Maybe she's waiting until after she gets back. How the hell should I know? Can't say I really know how twenty-one-year-old girls think." She scrunches her nose. "Frankly, it's a little creepy that you do," she says and then she's moving up the stairs.

> Me: I need to talk to you.

I text her after a series of unanswered calls. We haven't talked in two days, since Marissa ended things, and I'll admit that even though I'm annoyed by the events that have transpired, I want to hear my girl's voice. I walk into my apartment and drop to my couch before texting her again.

> **Me: Marissa, it's important.**

> **Marissa: What's there to talk about?**

> **Me: Answer the phone.**

> **Marissa: I'm out and this isn't a work call.**

> **Me: Why didn't you tell me about the check, Marissa?**

She doesn't answer right away and that doesn't do anything for the mounting anxiety in me or the uncertainty over whether she's planning to cash it. I don't give a fuck about the money. I'd give her double, triple, whatever she wanted. I just hate that she didn't tell me. I hate that Holly knew something about her that I didn't. That there was a part of their interaction that I wasn't privy to and I want her to tell me it wasn't like that.

> **Marissa: Because it didn't matter.**

> **Me: Yes, it absolutely matters.**

> **Marissa: You can't possibly think I'm going to cash it. Don't fucking insult me.**

> **Me: Why did you take it at all?**

> **Marissa:** She shoved it in my hand and walked off and it has my name on it! I figured it would be better if I had it rather than her. I ripped it up.

> **Me:** You should have told me.

My phone starts to ring and the second I answer it, I hear the sounds of loud music and talking, and then those sounds become muffled like maybe she went in the bathroom.

"You can't actually be mad at *me*." She laughs and I can already tell this conversation isn't going to be productive.

"I'm mad that Holly threw that shit in my face and I was unprepared for it."

"*You* were unprepared?" she snaps. "I can assure you the shit *your wife* threw in mine was worse."

I sigh, remembering the interaction that set all of this in motion in the first place. "I'm sorry. Again. I'm dealing with it."

"That's not my business."

"Yes, it is."

"No, it's not!" she yells. "It's between you and your wife."

"Anything about me is your business. Just like *you* are my business."

She lets out an exasperated sigh. "Chris, you are not getting it. You're married. We are done."

"Stop saying that because you know it isn't true. You already said when I'm single—"

"You're not though."

Anger flares through me because she knows it won't be forever and it's beginning to sound like she's not planning to wait. "I will be eventually! Stop acting like you and I are not the fucking endgame here."

"Look," she says before letting out an exasperated breath, "I don't want to get my hopes up, okay? And neither should you."

"What the fuck does that mean?"

"It means I don't want to get caught up thinking about a future with a man who's currently in the present with someone else."

"I'm getting out of it," I argue and I feel like I'm starting to sound like a broken record.

"We're going in circles," she says. "I'm out right now. I have to go."

"Marissa—"

"Don't," she warns.

"I love you." I don't think she wants to hear these words but I say them anyway because I want her to know that despite this shitty situation, I knowingly brought her into, *she* is in fact my endgame. I want her, and at this point, I don't care who knows it.

"I said don't." Her voice is tiny and I can hear the tears in it. "I can't say it back," she says and I'm hoping that even though she can't say it she does feel it.

"I hate this," I tell her.

"Me too. I have to go."

"Yeah," I say. "Be safe. Keep yourself out of trouble until I'm around to do it myself."

"Goodbye, Chris."

"We aren't—" I start but then I hear the beep indicating the end of the call and my heart fucking sinks.

Chapter TWENTY

Marissa

Two and a half years later
May 2021

"Welcome to the United States, we hope you enjoyed your flight," are the first words I hear when I'm back on Pennsylvania soil for the first time in almost two years.

"I did, yes, thank you." I smile at the flight attendant as I get off the plane and make my way through the terminal. I can't believe I haven't been home in two and a half years. My parents came to visit a lot, using the fact that they had a daughter abroad to travel to Europe multiple times. Autumn and Shane came a few times too, and we even spent last Christmas in Paris together. I contemplated staying another year, but Autumn is finally getting married after what my parents dramatically deemed the longest engagement in the history of the world, so it was time to come home.

I tried to tell myself that it had nothing to do with the fact that my married ex-boyfriend is finally no longer married. The year of separation somehow turned into almost two years of back and forth, but I've heard through the grapevine that he's finally divorced. I half expected him to show up on my doorstep the second he was free but he didn't.

Maybe because you've barely talked to him.

There was a change in structure, and the Paris team had its own in-house senior leadership, so I didn't report directly to Chris anymore, and with there being no reason for us to have any contact, we haven't talked. There were a handful of multi-person Zoom meetings we were on at the same time where I'm sure his eyes were trained on me the entire time, but we hadn't uttered more than a few business-related words on a group email chain in over two years.

I didn't stay away just because of Chris, but I'll admit he was an incentive. I didn't want a front-row seat to his messy divorce. I knew one look from him or one drunken night from me would have had us back in bed together. Neither of us had the power to stay away from each other, so I kept an ocean between us to prevent the temptation.

On top of that, I thrived in Paris. I've moved up substantially in *Beckham Securities*. I'm coming home to a promotion and I'm preparing to train some of the new hires. I left home as a way to escape my life but somewhere along the way, it actually became my life.

I had the majority of my things shipped home, so I easily make it through the airport toward my sister who I see bouncing up and down next to her car with a sign that says, *Welcome Home! You're never allowed to leave me for this long again.* She pulls me in for a hug and squeezes me tightly before letting me go with a smile.

"I'm so happy you're back," she says with a watery smile, and I nod.

"I am too."

"You should also be happy that I talked Mom out of a huge welcome home party for you."

"Bless you." I sigh as I slide into the passenger seat and she pulls out of the pick-up lane. "I know we talk all the time, but I feel like I have so much to tell you."

"Since we talked last night?"

"I know...it's just...you're here! And thank you for coming home in time for the shower."

"Of course. I'm your maid of honor." I haven't done most of the basic maid of honor duties while I was in Paris, but I at least want to be here for the party this weekend.

I'm exhausted and a little bit jetlagged, so Autumn doesn't ask me too many questions but just as we are turning onto our street, she asks me the one I know she's been dying to ask.

"So, how is tomorrow going to be? Seeing him and all?"

"I don't know."

I stayed up practically half the night last night, my nerves and anxiety disallowing me from sleeping soundly over the thought of our first interaction. *Would it be awkward? Uncomfortable? Tense? Sexually tense?*

"Are you going to call him?"

Part of me wants to break the ice but maybe he thinks there's nothing to talk about. Maybe he's moved on.

Am I being immature for not contacting him?
Why hasn't he reached out to me?

"Do you think I should?"

"I think a simple call to see where you two stand wouldn't hurt. You don't want to run into him tomorrow in mixed company and neither of you know how to act," she says as she pulls up to our parents' house.

"What if he has a girlfriend?"

She raises an eyebrow. "You were doing a lot more while he had a wife; I don't think you calling him after two years will be a problem."

"No, I know. Just…what if he has a girlfriend?"

Her lips form a straight line, realizing what I'm saying. That I may not be ready to be thrust back into a situation where Chris Holt isn't available for me. She reaches for my hand and gives it a reassuring squeeze. "Then he has a girlfriend."

I'm staring at my phone later that night, trying to decide if I should call him. He must know I'm back in town and he hasn't reached out to me either. I've already unpacked most of my things and my closet is practically overflowing with stuff I bought while I was there. I reorganized my closet twice as a way to distract myself from obsessing over my first interaction with Chris and I have come to the realization that I need more space.

It might be time to start thinking about my own place.

I grab my phone and hover my thumb over his contact before pressing the button to call him. I'm used to Chris picking up on the first ring so when it rings more than once, I'm already convincing myself that he doesn't want to talk to me. His generic greeting comes through the phone and I know I only have a few seconds to decide if I'm going to leave a message before the beep comes through the line. My mouth opens but no words come out and I shake my head as I end the call cursing myself knowing that now he'll have a missed call and a voicemail from me.

I wish I'd just sent him a text instead.

I barely sleep that night, my eyes refusing to close at the thought of what the next day will bring. He hasn't called or texted me back and I'm already picturing all of the potential awkward conversations we could have tomorrow. Around three in the morning, I manage to drift off to sleep with the potential interaction of him telling me his new live-in girlfriend didn't appreciate my nine o'clock phone call playing on a loop in my mind.

12:00 p.m. One on One Touchbase (1 hour)
Marissa Collins, Dana Ashcroft-Human Resources
Location TBD

The email with the update to my calendar is the first thing I see when I wake up the next morning, and I assume it's a follow-up about my promotion and my new position and everything it entails, but I still feel a slight pang of worry that it could be about something else. The rest of the email states that I don't need to come into the office before the meeting in case I'm still feeling a bit jetlagged, so it's on my mind for the entire morning. At noon, I'm walking into a bistro across town, my mind still on the fact that Chris hasn't been in contact. I'm being led towards the back where there's apparently a private room and I have a moment of déjà vu. I shake the memory of my first official date with Chris from my head just as the hostess gives me a smile and motions toward the room.

I push through the door and all of the air leaves my lungs when I see Chris sitting at the table, a small smile pulling at his lips as he rests his forearms on the table. My mouth drops open in shock as I move slowly through the room, and he stands. He looks just as gorgeous as I remember, dressed in a gray suit like maybe he'd come from a meeting. I was so unprepared to see him that I can't even speak.

"Remember me?" He gives me a cocky grin and my heart squeezes at the look he's giving me.

I move quicker to close the space between us, dropping my bag in the chair, and then I'm in his arms. I wrap my arms around his neck and press my face to the skin, the tears building in my eyes as he holds me tight against him. My heart feels like it's beating so fast it could pound out of my chest, and I am struggling to control my breathing. I inhale deeply which does nothing for my nerves because I'm just breathing *him* in.

Breathing in his scent that has the power to turn me on and also make my heart flutter. His hand trails up my spine, pushing me harder against him and then his lips are dragging across my forehead gently.

"I guess that's a yes," he jokes and I pull away, trying to wipe the tears from my eyes but he swats my hands away so he can do it himself.

"Chris," is the only thing I manage to choke out as he guides me into a seat. He sits in the one closest to me and somehow it doesn't feel close enough. I want to be in his lap. *Hell, I want to be naked and in his lap.*

"Welcome home, baby," he says and my eyes snap to his because if this is his reaction to me coming home, what was last night about?

"I called you last night."

"I saw." He chuckles as his index finger traces my knuckles. "Thought I might give you a taste of your own medicine for ignoring me for over two years."

I frown. "What are you talking about?"

"Not a peep out of you for that long? Drove me fucking crazy."

"It's not like you reached out either," I argue.

"Yes, I did."

"When?"

"I emailed you. Constantly. I figured at first you weren't responding because I was still married, but I wanted you to know I was still thinking about you. I was always thinking about you. *About us.*"

I frown. "I...I never saw an email from you?"

It's his turn to look confused as he pulls out his phone and looks through it for a moment before he hands it to me and I see an email chain of at least fifty emails all addressed to me. I scroll through a few of them, some of them long and some of them short but all of them unfamiliar.

"I...I never saw these." I grab my phone out of my purse and pull up my emails.

"Sounds like you blocked me." He laughs and I look at my phone and then back at him trying to remember if I had at some point.

I scroll through them for a minute, unsure of how I would have even done it before setting my phone down, prepared to look into that later. "Why didn't you call?" I ask because I know for a fact that I didn't block his number. I'd gone to text him at least half a dozen times over the past two years.

"I thought you were done with me," he says sadly. "Especially after all the unanswered emails, but more importantly, you asked me not to try to get you back until I was divorced. I've only been officially divorced for about a month and I knew you were coming home. I figured it would be better to do this in person."

"You're...officially divorced?" I need him to say it again. Maybe a few more times to believe it. To believe that this man that I've been thinking about for almost three years now is finally single.

"I am." He nods. "Fucking finally."

"Where do you live?" I ask him.

"My penthouse. We sold the house." He sighs. "One of the many things she got half of."

I bite my bottom lip. "I'm sorry."

"I'm not. All of that was just stuff. Replaceable. I wish it didn't take me so long to get that."

"Was it messy?"

"If you bothered to read any of my emails, you'd know," he teases and a smile pulls at his lips. "I gave you a play by play."

"I don't know what happened," I tell him honestly. "I must have blocked you? Maybe when I was drunk?" I wince as I rub my forehead, trying to trigger a memory of blocking him. "I'm sorry. I have to check when I get home. You can only access blocked emails from your computer, I think."

"I guess I deserved that." He laces his fingers with mine. "It doesn't matter."

"Yes, it does. I hate to think that you spent that long thinking I didn't care about you or us."

"I didn't think that. I figured you were being true to your word. You didn't want there to be any contact between us until I was divorced."

"Where's Holly now?" I ask. "Do I have to worry about running into her?"

"For now, maybe," he says and I hate the thought of potentially running into her while we are together, "but don't worry. Part of our divorce agreement states that she can't speak out publicly about any of the women I was rumored to have had an affair with."

"Because of me?"

"Yes," he tells me honestly. "I'm trying to be the person who protects you for the rest of your life. I had to start somewhere." My skin heats and I tuck a hair behind my ear. Then there's a hand reaching out to drag my chair closer to his, and I feel the vibrations of the chair scraping against the floor through my entire body. Then his hand is on my cheek forcing my gaze to his. "Do I still have a chance at being that person?"

I look at his lips and then into his blue eyes which are so full of sincerity. "Yes."

The grin that crosses his face is so devastatingly beautiful, it takes my breath away. He presses his forehead against mine and lets out a slow breath. "Finally," he whispers and then he presses his lips to mine. It starts slow and gentle. His tongue licks at the seam of my lips, asking for access to my mouth, and then he's inside, rubbing against mine slowly. He flicks his tongue against mine and then grabs my hands, pulling me into his lap to straddle him, allowing the kiss to deepen. My hands are in his hair, his in mine. I grind down hard on him and he groans into my mouth at the pressure. He pulls away from my mouth after some time, his lips finding my neck and the space behind my ear which he must have remembered is one of my favorite spots because he drags his tongue upward before nibbling on my ear.

"Chris," I moan.

"Fuck, I missed hearing my name on your lips."

"I missed saying it."

"I missed *you*," he counters and I pull his face out of my neck so I can press my lips to his again. I don't know how long we make out, but at some point, the door opens and when I turn towards the sound, I see someone bringing in two salads. I am slightly embarrassed over being caught making out in a public restaurant, but Chris seems unfazed as he nods at the waiter before he leaves.

"We should stop before I let you fuck me here." I giggle as I try to climb out of his lap.

He holds me tighter against him and places a gentle kiss on my nose. "As much as I would love that, I have plans for the first time we make love again and it doesn't involve this restaurant."

"Do I get to know these plans?"

"Stay with me tonight?" I nod without a second thought because there is no place I'd rather be. His hand slides between my legs and under my skirt, pushing my underwear to the side so he can rub his finger over my clit. I gasp at the friction and he smiles up at me. "I've barely touched you and you're already wet." He nods and gives me a cocky smile. "Did you get wet when you saw me siting here?"

"No."

He pinches my clit and I squirm against him, as the feeling shoots through me like a bolt of lightning. "Liar."

"I still don't like being asked questions you already know the answer to." He rubs me for a few more moments before he lets his hand slide out from between my legs. I assume he's going to slide his fingers into his mouth but what I do not expect is for him to swipe his wet fingers across my own lips. After only a second of him coating my lips with my own cum, he drags his tongue across my mouth before kissing me again.

"Do you have to go back to the office?" I flutter my eyelashes at him and he chuckles.

"As much as I want to say no, I do and so do you." He raises an eyebrow at me.

He eventually lets me out of his lap to sit back in my chair, but one of his hands continues to rub mine almost like he doesn't want to stop touching me after all this time of no contact. "I assume we have to keep it quiet at work?" I ask.

"For now, yes. Until I figure out how to get around the fraternization policy." He drops his hand to my knee and rubs it gently. "But I'll figure it out. I'm not hiding you or this forever."

I nod. He was able to get through a messy and difficult divorce, so I know he can figure this out.

"Speaking of not wanting to hide, one of the reasons I came home early is because of my sister's wedding in a few weeks but they're doing a couple's shower this weekend. They've been together forever and have practically all the same friends so she didn't want to do just a bridal shower. It's more like a second engagement party." He nods before taking a bite of his salad and I lean an elbow on the table. "I don't think anyone there would know I work for you, if you'd like to come."

He laces our fingers together and brings mine to his lips. "So, you're ready for me to formally meet your family then?"

"If you are."

"I was ready to meet them two years ago."

"And imagine if you had! You've already got some work to do because my dad is still confused as to why he didn't meet you back then."

"Oh, I'm blaming you for that." He laughs. "I would love to go with you. When's the wedding?"

"Next weekend?" I wince, knowing that it's kind of late notice. "Sorry, I know that it's kind of last minute."

"My schedule is wide open for you."

Later that day, I'm at the office, and after going through all the pleasantries of being welcomed back, Christine is walking with me to my cubicle.

I'm not surprised to see someone sitting on the other side.

"Oh! This is Raegan Graham." Christine points just as the woman with dark brown, almost black hair turns around and gives me a shy smile and a little wave.

"Hi." *Oh my gosh, she is so cute and tiny, I just want to put her in my pocket.*

"Mr. Beckham's new assistant. She just started a few days ago," Christine explains.

"Oh." I let out a breath and take a step towards her. "Are you okay?" I whisper. "Blink twice if you need help," I joke and Christine giggles behind me.

"No, he seems to like her," Christine says and when I turn around, I see she's looking down at her phone. "I've got to run, but drinks tonight? I've missed you!" she says with a final hug before turning to walk away.

I turn back to Raegan who's still looking at me like she's nervous. "I'm Marissa."

"Collins. Right. They told me." Raegan points at her desk and then toward mine. "They said you sit at that one, but if you would prefer this desk, we can switch," she says. "I'm sorry that you're coming back after all this time to someone in your space," she rambles as I set my purse on my desk.

"Oh my god, please breathe. I am happy to have someone to talk to." I cross my arms over my chest. "How old are you?"

"Twenty-one."

"Oh, fresh out of college then. Where'd you go?"

"Penn State." She fiddles with a pen in her lap.

I cross the cubicle to her side and lean on the desk. "Okay, enough of the basics for the moment; what I want to know is how you got Mr. Beckham to like you after only a few days." I sigh. "You should be training half of us."

"Oh." She blinks her blue eyes a few times as if she's confused. "He's very nice. A little direct and terse at times but…" She trails off, "He's been great. I heard he's had quite a few assistants before me, but he's not too difficult."

As if his ears were burning, I hear his voice down the hall and when I peek my head out, I see he's walking towards our cubicle.

"Miss Collins, I just wanted to say welcome back. I'm very pleased with the work you all did over there," he says to me but I don't miss that his eyes flit to Raegan every few seconds.

"Well, I appreciate the opportunity. Thank you."

"And I see you've met Miss Graham?" He gestures towards Raegan. "I hope you can offer any assistance she may need." He looks at her again and Raegan smiles.

"Of course, I'll take care of her," I tell him. He nods in response, and if I'm not mistaken, I see a hint of a smile on his lips.

"Thank you," he says before he disappears.

"Oh my god?" I blink at her. "I never thought I'd see the day." I chuckle as I shake my head and she looks up at me confused.

"What?"

"Wes Beckham has a crush on someone."

She stands up and peaks her head out of the cubicle, presumably to make sure he's far enough away to be out of earshot before turning back to me. "Who?" she asks in a hushed tone.

I raise an eyebrow at her because she can't possibly think I'm talking about me. "Ummm you?"

"Me!?" she exclaims while still keeping her voice low. "He said like three sentences and they were to you!"

"He was so nervous and kept looking at you. Oh my god."

I blow out a breath. "Phew, the tin man has a heart. Go figure," I joke and she's still staring at me with a stunned expression like she doesn't quite believe me. "Do you want to go out for a drink tonight ? I'll invite Christine too, so I can catch up on everything I've missed and we can give you the lay of the land in the office."

Chapter

TWENTY-ONE

CHRIS

I'M BACK AT THE OFFICE AFTER MY LUNCH WITH MARISSA ran almost two hours longer than it was supposed to and within minutes of me sitting down at my desk, Beck is coming through my office door looking distressed and almost nervous. He's usually pretty calm and collected so his demeanor seems out of left field. He drops to my couch and rubs a hand over his chest. "I fucked up."

I frown because Wes Beckham rarely fucks up. He's good at everything to the point it's almost annoying. "How so?"

"My new assistant." He pinches the bridge of his nose, lifting his glasses in the process before he pulls them off and tosses them on my coffee table.

"Oh god, what's wrong with this one? I swear Beck, you need to find *someone* you can tolerate. You've gone through, what, four assistants in the last month? Make it work. I'm beginning to think *you're* the problem." I guess I got lucky with Christine because the turnover rate of Beck's assistants is fucking insane.

"Fuck off," he grits out. "It's not...that." He runs a hand through his hair and I notice his leg bouncing slightly. "She's incredible."

"Holy shit." I can't stop the chuckle from leaving my lips. "Are you...into her?"

"She's been here three fucking days and I can't stop thinking about her. You know I was actually late getting on a call because I was in the copy room because *she* was there and I just wanted a reason to talk to her?" He gets up off the couch and begins to pace the length of my office. "One look at her and I'm a fucking goner. No concept of time or anything." He doesn't say anything for a second before he turns to me. "I think I black out every time I talk to her."

I chuckle thinking about my best friend who always has it together and is in control of every situation tied up in knots over his assistant. "This is Theo Graham's daughter, right?" I was shocked when I saw that the daughter of an ex-NFL football star had applied to work here and even more surprised that Wes had hired her. She's younger than his usual assistants and has little to no experience, but now I'm starting to see why he might have given her the job.

"Raegan," he corrects and I nod. "She looks so gorgeous today." He stares at the door before turning back to me. "She's wearing this blue dress and it brings out the color of her eyes and...I know how crazy I sound."

I smile because it's the same way I think about Marissa. "No, you don't sound crazy. I'm actually happy for you because you haven't really been interested in anyone since you broke things off with Hannah."

He shakes his head. "This intense attraction I feel? I didn't even feel this way about Hannah." He clears his throat and shakes his head. "I shouldn't have hired her."

"Why not?"

He shoots me a look. "Because I want to ask her out and I can't? I'll bet she has a boyfriend. There's no way she can't. She's fucking stunning and smart and charming and her fucking smile..."

He trails off. "Liam Patterson is already up under her all the time and it's pissing me off."

"Sounds about right. He does love to fuck the new hires," I joke and he glares at me.

"You know, once upon a time, you were sleeping with our subordinates too. You're the reason we even drafted the first fraternization policy if I recall."

There was a time I did sleep with women who worked for us, but I haven't since I met Marissa. He knows that even if he doesn't know that it's Marissa. "You know I haven't done that in years." I haven't explicitly stated that I haven't fucked anyone since the girl at Owen's wedding, but I haven't told him I have either and the thought that I've never told Wes about Marissa sends a wave of guilt through me. For a moment I consider it, but I should probably talk to Marissa about it first.

"Besides, what if she doesn't have a boyfriend? And she has a crush on you too?"

He shakes his head. "I can't pursue her. I just signed off on an updated policy that Dana put together."

"Oh?" I ask because I hadn't heard about this and this could very well make things even harder for Marissa and me.

"I haven't felt like this in a while. Maybe ever." He scratches his jaw and while I want to circle back to the updated rules, I decide to just look them up myself later. "When she looks at me...*fuck*."

"Damn." I chuckle. "You already have it bad."

"Since the second she walked into my office." He picks his glasses up off the coffee table and slides them onto his face. "I'll get over it though. I have to. I mean...I can't have her, right?"

The sound of my elevator dings and Marissa walks through the door wearing a jacket that stops mid-thigh. I raise an eyebrow at her because it's May and there's not a need for a jacket unless she's naked underneath which I suspect she could be.

"I ordered in for dinner. It should be here in an hour," I tell her as she wheels a small suitcase behind her and sets it in the corner.

"Really? Because I brought dinner also." She giggles as she pulls at the belt holding the jacket together revealing her in nothing but a sheer white thong.

"Goddamn," I grit out. "You are so sexy." I lick my lips as I move towards her and when I'm within arm's reach of her, I grab the waistband of her underwear and pull her towards me. She comes to me with ease as a squeal leaves her lips and when she's pressed up against me, I run my hand down her back to cup her bare ass. "It's been so long since I've been inside you…I can't wait another fucking second without tasting your cunt."

She runs her hand down the length of my body and cups my dick, "Well, considering you're the last person that's had their mouth on it, I'd say I can't wait another second either."

The fact that I'm the last person that's touched her makes my dick even harder. I push her against the wall and tilt her chin up to look at me. "In the spirit of transparency, you're the last woman that's touched my dick."

Her eyes widen and she lets out an exaggerated gasp. "What?"

I pinch her nipple playfully eliciting a sexy little squeal from her. "Don't act so shocked."

"It's been over two years. I just figured…" She shrugs.

"That I haven't been thinking about you nonstop this whole time?"

"I knew you were thinking about me but…" Her brown eyes look away and I guide her face back to look at me. I can see the vulnerability all over it and I've always loved how honest she lets herself be with me.

"Let me be clear. My dick has also been thinking about you nonstop. I haven't wanted anyone else. I *don't* want anyone else." I don't wait for a reply before I press my lips to her neck and begin a trail of open-mouthed kisses down her body. When I get to her nipples, I suck one into my mouth before the other, letting my tongue roll around the bud and she lets out a moan when I bite down. "These have gotten bigger."

"Maybe," she whimpers as I drag my tongue between her breasts.

"I know your tits as well as I know my own dick. They're bigger." I palm them in my hands and press myself against her. "They're fucking perfect." She shivers when I roll both nipples between my fingers. "They're still so sensitive."

"I…" She lets out what sounds like a frustrated sigh and grabs my head, pulling my mouth away from them. "Probably because I'm on my period." She scrunches her face slightly and I look down at her and then slowly drag my eyes up her frame.

"I don't give a fuck." And I don't. I'm so desperate to be inside of her, I would do anything.

"Why am I not surprised?" she murmurs with a cheeky eye roll.

"Because you know that I haven't touched you in two years and nothing, not even a little bit of blood will deter me." I put one hand up over her head and tuck a strand of hair that had fallen over her eyes behind her ear with the other. "That thought make your pussy wet?"

I can see the arousal in her eyes and I can't stop the grin from crossing my face that I'm right. "You are not eating me out," she says and I raise an eyebrow at her because she's never told me I couldn't do anything in regards to her body.

"If it's something that really bothers you, I won't push it," I slide my hand down her body and into her underwear and drag my thumb over her clit, "but nothing is going to stop me from running my tongue over this until you come." Just the feeling of her under my hand has cum already leaking into my briefs. I press a kiss to her lips before moving slowly down her body and when

I look up at her I see lust mixed with nerves all over her face. "Are you in any pain?"

"No, I'm just annoyed." She rolls her eyes. "I was planning a very sexy reunion after we had lunch today and the universe really said, *haha fuck you*."

I press my lips to her satin-covered slit before dragging my tongue through it, penetrating her slightly through the fabric. "Oh, believe me, baby, we are still having a very sexy reunion. And I will definitely be fucking you." I grab her underwear with my teeth and slide it slowly down her legs leaving her naked in front of my eyes for the first time in far too fucking long. I take one slow lick through her slit and my dick hardens instantly.

She lets out the sexiest, breathy sigh and then my name leaves her lips in a whisper when I flick her clit with my tongue. I had every intention of taking my time but when I spread her open, revealing her wet, pink clit, I fucking lose it. I suck it into my mouth and roll my tongue around it and her hands drop to my head. "Fuck, I missed you." She moans as she begins to rock her hips slowly against my mouth. I grab my dick and begin to rub it. I want it out and in her hands or in her mouth. I move my tongue, gliding it once over her opening and she gasps and tugs on my hair when I gently pull on the string with my teeth. "You said my clit." She glares at me but I can see she's turned on and I can't stop the chuckle that leaves me that she has the nerve to scold me even while my mouth is on her pussy.

I move back to her clit, lapping at her hard with long strokes and then she tightens her hands in my hair and lets out a moan. "Fuck, I'm going to come."

My hand slides up one of her legs and I pull it over my shoulder, opening her up as I continue to devour her cunt. "Good. Do it fucking now so I can get my dick inside you."

I look up at her and I'm surprised to see her eyes open and on me. She gives me a sexy smile that makes my dick throb and with one final flick of my tongue her eyes flutter shut and she goes over the edge while she cries out my name.

Her clit has barely finished pulsing under my tongue before I have her in my arms and I'm carrying her upstairs to my bathroom my lips attached to hers the entire time. I reluctantly pull away from her mouth when I set her on her feet before I shed the rest of my clothes. "I don't want you to be uncomfortable about anything," I tell her as I turn on the shower. "Will this help?" I ask and she nods and pulls her hair back into a low bun at the nape of her neck. "Take it out," I tell her and I can see the hint of embarrassment on her face before she turns around and disposes of her tampon.

I pull her into the massive shower and immediately wrap my hands around her, pressing her against the wall while I rub my hands over her perfect tits. Every part of her is so fucking soft and I want to kiss every inch of her skin with my mouth. I grab one of the handheld attachments hanging from the wall and spread her cunt. Before she has a chance to protest about being this exposed I have it turned onto the most concentrated pressure and hold it between her legs.

"Oh!" she cries out but I don't leave it on for more than a few seconds before I put it back on the wall.

She frowns and turns her gaze to what I think may become one of her favorite new toys. "I just wanted to get rid of some of the blood so you'd feel more comfortable. You can play with it later." I smirk at her before I spin her around so she's facing the marble wall with her back against my chest and after running my hand under the water, I glide my hand down her torso and begin to rub her gently between her legs. I start at her clit and make my way down, sliding two fingers into her and she gasps.

I frown, wondering if I'd somehow hurt her. "You, okay?"

"It's just…I'm not used to…"

"Relax, baby. It's just you and me," I murmur in her ear as I turn her face slightly so I can press my lips to hers again. "Bend over for me, stick that pretty little ass in the air." She does as she's told, putting her hands on the wall for support and I take a second to appreciate the fact that I finally have the love of my life back, who also happens to have one of the most gorgeous bodies I'd ever seen in my life and is now naked in my shower.

I don't wait another second before sliding my dick back where it belongs. *Fuck.* I jacked off twice when I got home earlier so I had a prayer at lasting longer than a few thrusts and I still feel like I could come already. I haven't moved yet. I'm just seated inside of her, and when she moves her ass against me and squeezes her cunt around me, my eyes slam shut.

"Baby, give me a second," I grit out. In response she clenches her pussy around me and moves her hips in a circle I think as an attempt to grind her clit against me. I drop my hand to her ass with a smack. "What did I say?"

"*Please*," she begs, "I want to come again." Her pleading does nothing for the ache in my balls or the tingle already forming at the base of my spine as it prepares for my orgasm. My mind and body are already trained to give her whatever she wants and my dick is about ready to explode inside of her at the thought of her coming around it. I pull out and the bright red all over my dick sends a feeling of possession through me that I wasn't expecting.

"Fuck." I grunt. I can't take my eyes off of her ass or the sight of my cock drilling into her slick cunt. I begin to fuck her faster and she meets my thrusts eagerly, letting out a sexy moan each time I bottom out inside of her. I tighten my fingers around her hips, pulling her harder onto my dick every time I drive into her.

"Oh god, I'm already close." She starts to pant and I notice her hands are balled into fists on the wall.

I land another slap on her ass, this time the other cheek. "Not god."

"Fuck…Daddy!" she cries out and that one word sends me even closer to the edge.

"Damn, you take my cock so fucking well."

"Yes!" she cries out. "Fuck me harder."

I slam into her a final time just as I feel my climax rip through me. "Fuck fuck FUCK." I groan, as the first orgasm in over two years not brought on by my fist pulls me under. I keep fucking her through my climax and when I pull out of her, there's a mixture of her blood and her cum and my cum all over my dick. The visual makes me hard again instantly and fucking feral for another one of her orgasms on my tongue. So, while I'm still in the high of one of the best orgasms I've ever had, I drop to my knees behind her, rub my wet fingers through her slit a few times before sealing my mouth over her cunt.

"Chris!" she squeals, I think in protest, but her body disagrees with her words and comes all over my tongue in seconds. I taste mostly her cum and water but there's a hint of metallic that just makes my dick even harder and she pushes her hips harder against me while I continue to lap at her clit. "Holy fuck, you're a god," she moans as I finish fucking her with my mouth and stand up behind her. She turns around slowly and looks up into my eyes just as a smile pulls at her lips.

"You were determined to do that."

"I barely tasted anything but our cum."

"Liar." She narrows her eyes at me as she rubs her thumb over my bottom lip. "I was not expecting that to be so…hot." She lets out a breath. "Wow. I would not be opposed to doing that again."

I drop my forehead to hers. "The food should be here soon, and then we are definitely doing that again."

Chapter TWENTY-TWO

CHRIS

"Wow," Marissa says when she opens the door to her parents' house and looks me over with a grin. It's the day of her sister's party which is at a venue downtown later tonight, but I'm formally meeting her parents now. "You look great," she tells me as she looks at me in a way I wish she wouldn't five minutes before I'm supposed to meet her father.

"Do not start," I tell her, but she closes the front door behind her leaving us alone on her porch, and then she's in my arms. It takes no more than a second for our lips to be pressed together, something we've done for the better part of the last three days.

Every time we have a moment alone, my hands are on her. We've gone from trying to keep things quiet at work, to me fucking her against the wall in my office or over my desk or against my window. It's as if we're making up for lost time after being apart for so long. "Baby, we should stop," I whisper between kisses, very aware that there's only a door between myself and her father and maybe even her brother and who knows who else.

"No, we shouldn't," she whispers in my ear as she presses her lips to my neck and bites down gently. Even though she's pressed against me, I feel her hand between us and then she holds it flat against my dick through my pants.

"Fuck. Baby, not here."

"Why? We do it everywhere else," she says just before she squeezes me through my slacks.

I manage to pull away from her and grab her hands, pressing my lips to them. "Because I'm not afraid of HR, but I am a little afraid of your father."

"It'll be fine," she says with an eye roll.

"Yes, but I'd rather his first impression not be with your hand holding my dick." I rub my hands down her body slowly. "You look gorgeous, by the way." She's wearing a pale pink dress that stops just below her knees with a corseted top that highlights her breasts and accentuates her tiny waist. It hugged her curves so fucking deliciously and when she turned around to open the door, my dick hardens at how low the back goes and how it clings to her perfect ass.

"Fuck," I whisper and she giggles. The second we're inside I hear chatter from the kitchen followed by a bunch of shhh's and *I think he's here!*

"You guys are not quiet!" she calls out as she clasps our hands and leads me through the foyer towards a kitchen area where I see way more people than I expected all very well dressed with a drink in their hands.

"Okay, let's do this quick and there aren't going to be a bunch of questions," Marissa says as she points her finger around the room.

"Everyone, this is Chris," she starts slowly. "My Aunt Theresa and my Uncle Bill, my brother Shane, my sister-in-law Megan, you've met my mother, and this is my father." Marissa turns to look at me. "You'll meet Autumn later. She's very excited to meet you."

"It's really nice to meet all of you," I say as I shake all of their hands. "Marissa talks about all of you all the time." Though they are all giving me somewhat of a smile, no one has said anything yet.

"It's so nice to see you again. I think you somehow got even more handsome." Marissa's mother steps forward and wraps me in a hug. She's much shorter than Marissa so I have to lean down to reach her but she gives me a hug that reminds me of the ones my mother gives. "Do you want something to drink? Honey, get him a drink," her mother says, smacking Marissa's arm. I want to tell Marissa that I'd rather not have a drink in favor of her not leaving my side but she disappears in an instant walking towards the bottles on the bar cart in the corner of the room. She picks up a bottle of scotch and points at it in question. I nod before turning back to her mother.

"It's nice to see you again as well, Mrs. Collins."

"Let's not go so long next time? And Mrs. Collins is so formal! Please, call me Kim." I manage to catch a glimpse of Marissa in the corner who's shaking her head as if to say *absolutely do not call her that*.

"How old are you, hon?" Marissa's aunt asks me from over her glass of wine. "We've had a pool going for quite some time and I'm ready to collect."

"Are you kidding me?" Marissa asks as she hands me my drink.

"We're just curious!" she says while she runs her finger around the rim of her glass.

"Well, how old do you think I am?" I ask.

"Too old for Marissa," Marissa's father interjects and Marissa rolls her eyes.

I tense at his comment when I feel Marissa's hand on my back rubbing in circles. "He's joking," she says before she glowers at her father. "Dad…"

"What?"

"You said you'd be nice," she says and her father gives her a look that seems like he probably did *not* say that.

"I'm thirty-five," I say in response to their question. *Very close to thirty-six but no need to get into specifics.*

"Hmmm, and how old are you again?" her aunt asks Marissa.

"Old enough," Marissa responds with a fake smile before she reaches for my hand and gives it a gentle squeeze.

"For what!?" her uncle chimes in. A chuckle follows right after and I like to think that they're all just giving us a hard time.

"Kimmy says you're Marissa's boss. True or false?" Her aunt asks and I can tell she's going to have a lot more questions for me as the night goes on, especially if she continues to consume alcohol at the speed she is.

Marissa groans. "Aunt Theresa…didn't I say no questions?"

"I didn't agree to that." She takes another long sip of her wine and picks up her purse.

"Neither did I," her father says. "You mind if we have a little chat?" he asks me.

I shake my head. "Not at all."

Marissa gives my hand one final squeeze before I follow her father towards the back patio. I look over my shoulder and notice she mouths to me, *You'll be fine! Relax!* She taps her cheeks and gives me a smile that makes me chuckle.

He closes the door behind us leaving us alone on their back patio and despite being outside the air feels tense around us. There's a table and quite a bit of patio furniture with standing lights illuminating the space, and he takes a seat at the table.

"Take a seat," he says, gesturing towards one of the chairs. "So, naturally I have a few questions."

"Of course. I would imagine so." *I just hope I'm able to answer them truthfully without giving any information that Marissa doesn't want them to know.*

"My wife met you two and a half years ago."

"That's right."

He scratches his clean-shaven jaw and leans back in his chair. "Why am I just meeting you now?"

"Well, Marissa has only been home from Paris for a few days."

He raises an eyebrow at me. "Don't insult my intelligence." Marissa always described her father as lighthearted so I'm a little surprised at his demeanor, but I understand his skepticism.

"We weren't together while she was in Paris, if that's what you're asking."

"Hmmm." He taps the side of his glass. "Your company doesn't care that she works for you?"

"They…don't know about us."

He frowns. "I see. So, then what's the endgame here? If you two continue down this road, she has to quit her job? What happens if people find out? I assume that would all blow back on her."

"I wouldn't let that happen."

"You're the CFO, are you not? I assume you won't be the one getting fired."

"I wouldn't let her get fired."

"Do you have that much of a say?" He raises an eyebrow and I can see his wariness to believe any answer I plan to give all over his face.

I want to tell him that I do, but I don't know if he'd even buy that. "I'm just asking that you trust me."

"I don't know you."

"Fair, but she does and she trusts me," I counter.

"She's twenty-three."

I'm not sure how exactly to reply to that because it sounds like the go-to argument when parents want to underestimate their children. I go with the truth. "I love her."

"Does she know that?"

"Yes."

"You've told her?"

"I have, more than once."

He narrows his eyes before he stands up. "Marissa seems to like you as does my wife, but I'm not that easy to win over."

"Believe me, neither is your daughter," I say and while I'm sure he can hear the humor in my voice, I hope he knows that I'm very serious about the fact that Marissa has made me work for her and I would do it all again for her.

"I don't give more than one chance. Don't hurt her," he warns just as I hear the sound of the door opening and Marissa's brother steps out. I was hoping it was Marissa and I'm wondering if now I'm about to get the same talk I just had from her brother. A wave of discomfort washes over me thinking about how my father and I never had the chance to interrogate my sister's boyfriends in the same way.

"I was sent to make sure everything is good," he says before putting his beer to his lips.

"Everything is fine," Marissa's father says as he gets up and heads back into the house without another word.

"Don't worry about my dad. He's kind of a hardass on everyone *except* Marissa," Shane explains once the door closes.

"Marissa says you and your sister think she's the favorite."

"There's no 'think.' She definitely is. She can do no wrong, which means *you*, my friend, have to work twice as hard to stay in our parents' good graces." Shane is taller and larger than their father, and I remember Marissa mentioning that he played football in college.

"I'd do anything for her," I tell him and he smiles and nods but it fades just as fast as it appeared.

"Including leave your wife?" he asks and while I don't hear the judgment, I am fucking anxious because now I'm wondering if her father knows too. *Fuck.* Panic takes over because I didn't know anyone besides her sister knew about that and I'm wondering if this is all a test. *Was her father expecting me to come clean and I failed?*

"Look…" I let out a breath. "She didn't want anyone to know about that."

"My parents don't, but Autumn told her fiancé and he told me. I don't think Marissa knows that I know. I'm not trying to be in your business, but she's my baby sister and there's a very good chance my father will kill you and make it look like an accident if you hurt her, so I just want to make sure you don't have any bullshit going on."

"I don't. I'm not married. We're divorced."

"But you were married when you met her," he presses and I really wish I wasn't getting into this right now.

"Yes."

"Is that why she stayed away in Paris so long?"

I rub my forehead. "I think it was part of the reason, yes."

"Does your ex-wife know about my sister?"

"Yes."

"Jesus." He sighs. "Have they met?"

"Once."

"Were you there?"

"No. She flew to Paris and confronted her. Listen, my ex-wife and I weren't happy when I met Marissa, and I didn't tell her I was married when we met. It was a mess for a while and I take responsibility for that. But it's over and I just want to be with Marissa."

"I don't love that you made my sister the other woman, but I suppose she's just as much to blame for her involvement."

The door slides open again and Marissa finally walks out looking painfully gorgeous and immediately I want my hands on her. "Okay, enough of the inquisition please. We need to get going soon anyway." She wraps her arms around me. "Shane, go away," she says as she looks up at me like I hung the moon.

"Alright, well. Good talking to you," Shane says as he makes his way back into the house.

"Hi," she whispers as she wraps her arms around me. "Was it awful?" She runs her hand through my hair and then down my face. "My dad is in a mood for some reason. He's not usually like that. He's normally lively and more like my mom." She frowns. "What did he say to you?"

"Not to hurt you mostly and he asked about how it will be at work. He also brought up the fact that I met your mom over two years ago and I suppose he's curious about the time jump and why we weren't together while you were in Paris."

"What did you say?"

"We kind of glossed over it, but I don't think that line of questioning is over."

"I'm sorry. I didn't think it was going to be like that." She nuzzles her nose against my neck and presses her soft lips against the skin. I suddenly wish we were going back to my penthouse or somewhere we could be alone.

"It's okay," I tell her before I press a kiss to her temple. "I will tell you though, and I don't want you to panic, but..." I look towards the door and then down at her with a weak smile. "Your brother knows I was married."

She gasps and pulls out of my arms. "How?!" She pauses before she smacks her forehead. "Oh my god, I'm going to kill Autumn." She stomps her foot. "I told her not to tell him."

"Well, to be fair, she told your future brother-in-law and *he* told your brother," I explain.

"Still! She wasn't supposed to tell anyone!"

"Baby, you wouldn't tell me something like that? They're about to be married and I'm sure she told him more out of worry than anything."

"No, she told him to be a gossip!" She says and the fury all over her face is more cute than anything.

"Either way." I pull her back into my arms and run my hand gently down her back. "You're not going to share gossip with me?"

"Not if you're going to go blabbing to other people!"

"He said your parents don't know."

"Oh, I would know if my parents knew, trust me." She groans.

"I can't believe Shane knows and didn't say something to me first. I'm annoyed now. I don't even want to go." She huffs and I can see the irritation all over her face.

"Oh, we are going, but I have something we can do before that will take the edge off."

Chapter

TWENTY-THREE

Marissa

"O H FUCK, I'M COMING," I MOAN OUT JUST AS MY orgasm rolls through me. We're in Chris' car, parked in a garage around the corner from the venue working out the last bit of tension brought on by my family. His fingers continue to rub my clit as I move up and down on his dick, riding the wave of my orgasm.

We're in the backseat of his car, and I'm still in Chris' lap, his dick wedged inside of me. I feel his orgasm looming, so I press my lips to his and begin to ride him harder. "You're riding my dick so hard, baby. You want my cum?" He breathes against my lips and I nod just as he lowers his head to bite down on my nipple. I'd taken my dress completely off so as not to wrinkle it. I'm completely naked while Chris removed his pants and jacket and just unbuttoned his shirt. "You going to milk it out of me?"

"Fuck yes. I need you to come. I want to feel you," I practically beg him. His hands find my hips, pulling me down harder every time he thrusts upwards and I know that means he's getting closer.

"Fuuuuck. It gets better every time I'm inside you." His tongue darts out and draws a line up my neck before he attaches his lips to mine. "You're fucking mine, Marissa, and I'm never letting you go." His tone is low and I feel it in my sex just as his thrusts get faster and then I feel him expand inside of me. "Fuck, yes. Squeeze me, baby. Squeeze your pretty pussy around Daddy's cock." I gasp at his words and then he lets his head fall back against the seat. "Oh shit, I'm coming," he says and then he holds me hard against him at the base of his cock, while he thrusts upwards.

He eventually stops and raises his head to meet my gaze. I don't know how long we stare at each other when a smile finds his face and it's so infectious that one pulls at mine as well. I don't know if it's the sex high or the glass of wine I had at home or the smile on this gorgeous man's face, but the words fly out of my mouth. "I think I'm in love with you."

His smile grows wider and then his hands find my cheeks and he brushes his lips against mine. "I know I'm in love with you."

I've never felt this way before. I tingle all over from the top of my head to the tips of my toes and I feel like I'm experiencing a full-body high. He pulls out of me and I move to the seat next to him while he pulls on his briefs and his pants, putting his shiny dick that is still glistening with a layer of me away. He reaches into the console to pull out some wipes for me and I assume he's going to hand them to me but he pulls one out of the pack and rubs me gently between my legs, cleaning the traces of our orgasm. I let out a whimper when he ghosts the wipe over my clit and he gives me a grin when he does it again.

"Stop it." I push his hand away with a giggle as I pull on my dress and shoes. I get out of the car and spritz myself with the perfume I brought when I realized we were going to fool around before we went in. I'd curled my hair in loose waves, so thankfully my hair doesn't look much different. I touch up my makeup and check my neck for hickeys or any red marks from his beard and I'm grateful that we were more careful than usual.

"I think I look okay," I say as I close the mirror.

"Okay?" he asks as he slides into the driver's seat. "You look gorgeous."

"I just mean, not like we just had sex in your car."

He starts the car and pulls out of the garage towards the venue so we can valet the car. We were probably only ten or so minutes behind my family so I'm not surprised to see them still congregating near the front. I glare at my sister when she shoots me the largest grin and moves towards us.

"I could kill you," I whisper and she frowns at me before turning to Chris.

"Hiii!" she says as she beams up at him. "I've been waiting forever to meet you!"

"He's not a fan of you either right now!" I take a second to look her over and she looks so gorgeous in her white strapless mid-length dress. It's mostly lace with a slit up one side giving it a hint of sexy, but more than that, she looks so ridiculously happy. "Putting a pin in my annoyance for a second, I'm glad you went with this dress. You look so beautiful," I tell her as I pull her in for a hug and kiss her cheek.

"Congratulations, Autumn. It's nice to finally meet you. We're so happy for you," Chris says as he pulls her in for a hug next.

"We!" Autumn squeals and bumps my hip with hers and I roll my eyes. "Wait, why isn't he a fan?" She looks at Chris. "You're legally obligated to be a fan of me, or I'll make your life miserable." She points at him while a smile tugs at her lips.

"I didn't say that. She did." Chris nods at me and I cross my arms.

"You told your loud-mouthed fiancé some protected information who then told our equally loud-mouthed brother!" I say through gritted teeth.

Her eyes widen before she winces and shoots a glare at her

fiancé who is greeting a group of people. "Shit. I'm sorry, it slipped out."

"Is that how it's going to be now, you can't keep my secrets? I've got some of yours too, dear sister."

"No, I swear. It was just that one time," she says as she holds my hands in hers before turning to Chris. "I'm so sorry and…I know more about this situation than anyone. I should have probably given more context like the fact that you're so desperately in love with Marissa you can't see straight. That will help." She giggles before someone behind me seems to catch her attention. "Be right back." She looks at Chris. "We have so much to talk about."

Chris reaches for my hand and laces our fingers as we walk into the main room. "I like her. You two are so similar."

"Don't remind me," I groan as we make our way through the room toward a table with glasses of champagne and we both grab a flute.

"Thank you for coming." I'm already picturing a life of these types of events with him. Weddings, engagement parties, and other celebrations of love. *Maybe eventually ours.*

"No place I'd rather be," he says as he taps his glass with mine.

"Oh my god," I hear from behind Chris and when we both turn towards the voice, my heart skips a beat because we are met face to face with his ex-wife.

No. No. No.

"What are you doing here?" she asks looking at Chris and then me. "With…her," she spits out and all I care about at this moment is not making a scene in front of my entire family and everyone my sister knows.

I look at Chris with a panicked expression and it's almost as if he can read my mind. "Holly, what are *you* doing here?"

"I asked you first," she snaps as she crosses her arms in front of her chest pushing out her breasts that are very much on display in her navy strapless dress.

I want to say something smart but the last thing I want is to set her off here of all places, so I go with the truth and speak as calmly as possible in an attempt to pacify her anger.

I blink at her. "My sister is the bride."

Her eyes flash to Chris angrily. "That doesn't explain what you're doing here."

"This is not the place to have this conversation and if you can't behave civilly, I think it would be best if you left," Chris says and I internally wince because while I would love to see him put her in her place, we are clearly not on the same page about not doing that *here*.

"Excuse me? I was invited."

"Everything okay?" A man wearing an ill-fitting suit with a handlebar mustache approaches us and I'm assuming *he* was invited and she's his plus one. "Mr. Holt?" He looks at Chris confused and I look up at him with equal confusion causing Holly to look at us both with a snide smile.

"You remember my lawyer?" she says, resting a hand on the shoulder of the man she's standing with, and I feel like I'm in the midst of a car accident happening in slow motion.

If he's Holly's divorce lawyer, that means he's probably about to learn who I am. Very soon. Fuck. I do my best to control my breathing because I feel like I might have a panic attack.

"Can't say I was expecting to see you here." He laughs awkwardly before looking at me. "And Autumn's sister, correct?"

"Yes, also the woman that was screwing my husband," Holly says casually and my eyes flutter shut as I try to count to five while taking deep breaths.

"Holly, don't do this," Chris says and I can tell he's trying his best not to lose it. I can also tell his patience is wearing thin. The man with Holly turns his eyes to me and though his eyes aren't full of judgment, I can sense his disappointment.

"I didn't do anything," Holly says.

"Can I talk to you outside?" he asks and though I don't love the idea of my boyfriend getting into it with his ex-wife at my sister's shower, I don't want her around my family a minute longer. She seems like she's ready to blow up and I don't want them caught in the wreckage.

"Nope."

"Okay, well remember the divorce agreement you *signed*," he warns through gritted teeth.

"I said I wouldn't talk to any kind of press or go to your board of trustees over you sleeping with your subordinate."

"It said anything *publicly*," he corrects.

"Well, as far as I'm concerned, it's only the four of us standing here, all of whom know that you were sleeping with her while we were still married. Now if anyone were to overhear..." She trails off and I see a ghost of a smile when her eyes find something just over my shoulder. I pray it isn't anyone related to me, but when I turn around, I meet eyes that match mine. They're full of anger but not directed at me.

"Can I ask who you are?" my mother says as she takes a step next to me and then another so she's more in front of me and I already know this isn't going to end well for Holly. I'm in for an earful later, I'm sure, but Holly is about to be read for filth.

"Mom..."

She puts a hand up which is a sign I know very well that advises me not to talk anymore.

"Holly Holt. His ex-wife," she says, nodding at Chris.

She turns her gaze to the man next to her. "And you are?"

"Joseph Stanfeld. I work with Eric."

"Okay," she snaps, "I think I'm caught up. I'm going to assume you were none the wiser about this situation?" she asks as she spins her finger in a circle, indicating what just happened. "And I would remember who I'm married to before you think about lying to me."

I can see the trepidation all over his face at the idea of getting on the wrong side of Judge Collins' wife. "I was not aware."

She nods. "Well, I think it's time that your *date* goes home."

"Excuse me?" Holly sneers and in any other scenario, I'd

warn Holly that she did not want to go down this road with my mother. "I didn't do anything."

"You're disrupting my daughter's shower. That is *plenty*. Now, I would kindly ask this lovely gentleman to escort you home. You are welcome to come back, Joseph, but please I would advise you to keep better company," she says.

"I'm the bad company? *Your* daughter was sleeping with *my* husband and I'm the problem?"

"Holly, enough," Chris snaps and I feel the tears burning in my eyes over this nightmare unfolding.

"Sweetheart, what's going on?" I hear my father's voice, and *oh my god, this could not get any worse.*

"Nothing," my mother says. "Can you get me another glass of champagne though?"

"Of course." His eyes find mine and he frowns when he sees my tears. I turn my head towards Chris and then I feel his hands on my face despite still being in Holly's presence. I eventually see them move out of my periphery and I breathe a sigh of relief that she's gone.

"I'm so sorry," he whispers so quietly I don't think anyone hears him. "Please don't hate me," he says before he pulls me into his arms and against his chest. "Let's go take a walk."

When I turn my eyes back to my mom, her eyes are on us both, full of anger and judgment and sadness and disappointment and it feels like someone is taking a knife to my insides.

"Mrs. Collins—" Chris starts but she puts a finger up and shakes her head.

"I wouldn't speak."

"Mom."

"You shouldn't either." She blinks at me. "I just had to defend you because you slept with another woman's husband? To his wife? Is that really what I'm supposed to take away from this interaction?" She shakes her head when I don't respond. "We raised you better than that, Marissa."

"You don't understand—" I start but I don't even know how to make her understand. My mom wouldn't. Not over this. It doesn't matter that I didn't know at first or that she wasn't a good wife or that they didn't have a good marriage. I was the mistress and that's never a good look.

"She didn't know," Chris says and him taking the heat for all of this definitely won't help.

"Oh? Okay? But you certainly did." She blinks at him. "This is not the place to have this conversation but this is absolutely not over." She walks away without another word.

We are out on the balcony alone a few minutes later while I try to get myself together. "I'm so fucking pissed," he says, and I lean against the railing as I take a sip of my champagne.

"Is this what it's going to be like every time we see her?"

"No. It's just because this was the first time, I'm sure. She probably didn't think we'd get back together." My lip trembles and then I feel his hands again. "Hey, look at me." I look up into his blue eyes which look as sad as I feel. "I love you."

"I'm going to assume you loved your ex-wife too at one point," I hear my dad's voice and I can already see this going terribly.

Can we just get a break?

"Dad, can we not do this now?"

"He'll break her heart the same way he did mine," my dad says. "That's what your ex-wife said to me before she left."

"I would never break her heart and I didn't mean to break Holly's heart if I did at all. We had been having problems for years."

"Were you not cheating on her? With multiple women? Not even just Marissa?" Chris doesn't say anything at first and I think he's struggling with what exactly to say. "I think it's best if you leave also."

"Dad, he's not leaving. I know how bad this looks, but their marriage wasn't good. It wasn't—."

"And how would you know? Were you there? Are you just going by what he's told you? You can't be that naive."

"He wouldn't lie to me."

My father gives me a look of derision before a laugh leaves his lips. "A man cheated on his wife for years and you think he wouldn't lie to his *mistress*?" he asks. I know he didn't say it to be harsh or cruel but hearing my father of all people use that word makes me feel worse than any other time I've heard it.

"Don't call her that," Chris says and I can hear the edge in his voice while still trying to err on the side of being respectful. "I know you don't trust me, but I do love your daughter. It's been her ever since I laid eyes on her almost three years ago. Since then, I haven't been able to see anyone but her. Please don't put her in a position where she doesn't feel supported in loving me back."

My father doesn't say anything before he scrubs his hands down his face and shakes his head. "Marissa, we raised you to be honest and good and to treat people well. You've got the world at your fingertips and you're going to mess it up before you even have a chance to get started. You're only twenty-three and I can see you're already in way over your head."

"I know we didn't start in the most ideal way, but he's divorced now," I argue, but hearing his disappointment expressed so explicitly feels lower than rock bottom.

"He's your *boss*. Funny how quickly you seem to forget that."

"I love him," I say because it's the only thing I can say in this moment that my father can't refute.

"In five years, you'll wish you hadn't," he says and then he walks away.

Chapter TWENTY-FOUR

CHRIS

"You've been so quiet," Marissa says later that night as she climbs into bed next to me.

We stayed far longer at her sister's shower than either of us wanted to, but I knew she wanted to be there for her sister, and I wasn't going to leave her to deal with whatever potential fallout was brewing. Her parents didn't acknowledge me for the rest of the night and barely said more than a few words to Marissa except during pictures. From the outside, it didn't seem like anything was off, but I could feel the tension between them, and behind Marissa's smile, I could see how hurt she was.

"I'm sorry, baby. Just a lot on my mind, I guess."

She purses her lips and sits up. "Should I be concerned that I'm half naked in your bed and you haven't tried anything?"

I give her a half smile as I notice her state of undress for the first time. *Fuck, I really have been distracted if I didn't notice she's only wearing a tiny silk camisole and matching shorts.* I pull her to straddle me and rest my hands on her hips, sliding my hands underneath the soft material over her skin. "How is it going to be with your family?" I ask her.

"I don't know," she says sadly before biting down on her bottom lip. "They've never been like that with me." She lets out a sigh. "Then again, I've never done anything…that they didn't approve of."

"Will they come around?"

"Ever?" she asks. "I think so?"

"Will you be able to live with it if they don't?" I ask her the question I've been contemplating ever since her mother looked at us like Marissa was a stranger and I was the man who caused this situation. She doesn't say anything and just looks off to the side like she's considering a life that doesn't include a relationship with her parents. "Will you be okay if they never approve of me or how we came to be together?"

"I can't imagine if we continue down this road and you wanted to marry me or give them a grandchild, they'd hold onto their anger," she says. I can hear the lilt in her voice and see the nervous look in her eyes over bringing up marriage. "I don't mean tomorrow!"

"In a perfect world, I'd marry you tomorrow." I grip her thighs tighter and give them a squeeze. She giggles before shifting slightly in my lap.

I don't say what I want to say, which is that it feels like we will never live in that perfect world. First, it was my marriage and now it's her parents' reaction to said marriage, and that's not even taking into account that she works for me and I don't know how I'm going to handle HR.

"How about we let my parents get used to the idea before we spring that on them?" she says breaking me from my thoughts. I hold her steady as I try to stop her from moving against my dick but she continues to rock her hips against me. She leans over and hovers her mouth above mine. "They'll come around."

"I hate the thought that you have to wait for that. You live at home. Won't that be difficult?"

"I've actually been thinking about moving out. Not just because of this, but I do have this big fancy salary now," she jokes, "I can afford it."

"That's amazing. I'm really proud of you." I force a smile and she frowns before climbing out of my lap.

"I feel like you're shutting down on me."

"I'm not." I sit up. "This was just a lot. Your parents witnessed our first run-in with Holly and now they know and I don't want to create a divide between you and your family."

"You're not! They were just surprised and in shock," she argues.

"Maybe, but there's a good chance that the shock will never wear off, and don't tell me you don't care, because I don't believe that." I know she cares and maybe today it doesn't bother her, but at some point when the anger wears off and she misses her family, she may wish she'd done things differently.

She's about to respond when the sound of her cell phone buzzing on the nightstand stops her. When she looks at it, she shakes her head. "It's just my sister. I'll call her back. Chris…I don't know what you want me to say. I'm not suggesting we end it because my parents aren't thrilled about how we got together. It's not the end of the world. I'll talk to them." She looks down at her hands in her lap before looking up at me somberly. "Unless this is just too much for you?"

"I didn't say that. I'm thinking that this is too much for *you*. I hate that I've made things so hard for you by putting you through all my shit."

"Well, how about you let me decide what's hard for me?"

"I keep thinking about what your dad said. That you'll wake up in five years and wish you hadn't gone down this road with me."

She's silent for a moment before she speaks again. "Are you… breaking up with me?"

Her words hit me square in the chest and I hate the thought that after everything we've been through, we don't end up together. "No. I want to be with you. I've always wanted to be with you, but should it be this complicated?"

She frowns and pulls a blanket around her, to cover up her body, and I hate that she's feeling like she needs to shield herself from me. "I'm fairly certain you started this mountain of complications when you slept with me at our friend's wedding three years ago."

"I know," I tell her because I did set all of this in motion and I don't know if I had to do it all again if I would do anything differently.

"Okay, well it kind of feels like I'm having to talk you into being with me." She gets off the bed and I see her moving towards the closet. "And I'm definitely not doing that."

"You're not. I want to be with you more than fucking anything."

She comes out of the closet and she's pulled a sweatshirt over her torso. "Suddenly, it doesn't feel like it."

"It's just with work and your parents and…I kind of feel like I've fucked up your life."

Her phone begins to ring again on the nightstand and she rolls her eyes before picking it up. "Autumn, this really isn't—" She sighs. "Yes, it was kind of a mess, but can we talk about it later?" She looks at me before dropping to my couch in the corner with an exasperated sigh. "I don't see why everyone has an opinion about *my* life." She pauses and I can see the annoyance all over her face, making me wonder if Autumn, who'd previously been on our side despite our obstacles is now voicing a different opinion. "Fine, whatever. I'll be home in the morning," she says before hanging up the phone. "Well, my whole family thinks I'm making a huge mistake, and now you're acting like you have one foot out of the door of this relationship."

"That's not what this is." I shake my head at her. "The idea of not being with you…" I give her a look that I hope tells her how much I hate that idea. "I just don't want to put you in a position where being with me alienates you from everyone in your life. I know that's not what you want. You're close with your family. You're not like me who lives several states away and barely talks to them."

She doesn't say anything, and for the first time since we started this conversation, I wonder if it's setting in. "You should call your mom more," she tells me sadly and I nod in agreement because I definitely should. "And your sisters," she adds. Tears have sprung to her eyes and when she looks at me it feels like someone's standing on my chest. "So…I can't have what I want?"

"I just think you should give this some thought. This isn't just because your family doesn't like me. They don't approve of *us* together, and that might make things tense and uncomfortable. How would holidays work? Your sister's wedding? Birthdays? Things that you would want me to come to…they may not want me there and then that's just going to cause a divide."

"It already is. I'm so angry at them."

"In their own way, they think they're looking out for you," I tell her as I make my way over to the couch and sit next to her.

"So, what does this mean for you and me?"

I grab her hand and hold it in mine before dragging my lips over them. "I don't know. I want to be with you, but I don't know how it can work. We have so many things stacked against us."

"I hate this."

"So do I," I tell her. "I feel like I've waited so long to be happy. So long to be happy with *you*, and I still can't have it."

Marissa

I'm walking through my front door the next morning after a long and teary night with Chris. Neither one of us wants a breakup but even I can admit that it seems like we're no closer to seeing light at the end of the tunnel than we were two years ago. I'm upset and angry and I know exactly where to place my anger.

I find my mother who's sitting in the living room, scrolling on her iPad. She doesn't look up when I enter the room. "Where's Dad?"

"Golf." *Yep, she's pissed.*

I guess I'm going to have to start this conversation then. "So, you just have nothing to say to me?"

She puts her iPad down and looks up at me before sliding her glasses off. "What do you want me to say?"

"How about I'm sorry?"

She narrows her eyes in confusion. "For what, may I ask?"

"That was not the time for any of that last night. That was… so unlike you."

"And sleeping with a married man…that's like *you*? News to me."

I shake my head in frustration. "Mom, we didn't do anything to *you*. The way you treated us was so uncalled for."

She stands up and I can already tell I'm in for it. "Uncalled for? Your boyfriend's *wife* basically called my child a whore to her face and you think *my* behavior was uncalled for? You're lucky we didn't have the cops called! Had we been anywhere else and I had just a few more drinks, your father would have had to call in *several* favors," she says as she stomps past me.

I follow behind her into the kitchen, "I know and I get why you're angry and that you're just trying to look out for me but he loves me and I love him."

She slams the refrigerator closed as she brings out one of her sparkling waters. "Marissa, be serious; you're in love with the forbiddenness of it all. It's all of the sneaking around behind closed doors that you're in love with. Let's be honest with ourselves."

"That's not it!"

"Okay, so explain to me. He's divorced now. Fine. We'll put a pin in that for now. How does it work with you working for him? Are you going to quit your job? A job you love? A job you're doing very well at? Or are you just going to be sneaking around for the rest of your career there? That's not a life or a relationship."

I lean against the island and rest my arms on the counter. "I don't know. We haven't gotten that far, but I assume we'd have to speak with HR and I wouldn't be able to report directly to him obviously. That's currently the least of our problems. I don't want you and Dad to hate him."

"We don't hate him, but you're asking us to just be okay with how you guys got together and for us to not be skeptical about his intentions. He was married for six years and—"

"Again, there's more to that and I'll agree that no one can really know what goes on in a relationship but those two people, and there are two sides to every story, but it sounded like Dad was taking Holly's side last night by repeating her nonsense back to us."

She shrugs. "Well, I wasn't there for that."

I hesitate, not wanting to ask this question but knowing that inevitably I have to know. "Can you support me being with him?"

Her lips form a straight line. "I don't know, Marissa, and I never thought I'd ever be in the position where I'd have to be asked that by one of my children. I don't want you to get hurt."

"He won't hurt me."

"How do you know that?"

"It's just...a feeling. I know he loves me."

"Love isn't always enough. Honey, you're so young."

"Oh, here we go." I groan.

"Yes, your age definitely gives me pause. It's so easy for a young girl to get swept up in a good-looking, older, rich man and all of the promises of the world that he offers."

"He's not even that old!"

"He's thirty-five and you're twenty-three. Yes, there are bigger age gaps, but you're in very different phases of life. You just graduated college and are just starting your career; you still have student loans and live at home and he's what? A billionaire?" She scratches her head before shaking it. "Well, maybe not anymore, since his wife took half."

"That's not funny."

"Who's joking?" she asks as she walks past me again to go back into the living room. "Give it some time. If you two are really serious about each other then it shouldn't matter if you wait a few months."

"What's a few months going to do?"

"Give you some space to think about what it is *you* want?"

"I want *him*. And I waited over two years for him."

"The time he was married hardly counts." She shakes her head. "Honey, when I was twenty-three, I was dating this guy who I swore I was going to marry. I was ready to let him lock me down and I wanted to give him all the babies."

My parents met when my mother was twenty-five so I can only assume there were guys before him. My mother is beautiful now, but in her twenties, she was an absolute knockout and always had guys coming to the house asking for my grandparents' permission to take her out. I know this because my grandfather still talks about how he'd sit on the front porch with his shotgun. *It wasn't loaded but it got the message across.*

"I thought I loved him," she continues, "I thought he loved me too and maybe he did." She shrugs. "But he also loved three different other girls in neighboring towns."

"Chris isn't like that."

"Maybe not? But...do you really think it's unfathomable given how you two met?" She gives me a look that's full of uncertainty.

"He wouldn't do that to me," I whisper, but even I hear the conviction leaving my voice.

"And all I'm asking is if, you're sure?"

Chapter
TWENTY-FIVE

Marissa

Six Months Later

> **Chris: Can I see you tonight?**

I LOOK AROUND THE TABLE OF MY CO-WORKERS, MAKING sure no one happens to be looking over my shoulder. Not that they would even realize who I was texting; they're all pretty drunk. There's a handful of us here in Miami for a couple of days for a new project and a few of us decided to get a private table at a club. Chris isn't out with us, but I have a sneaking suspicion he might be showing up soon. I wouldn't say that we broke up, but we haven't been seeing each other as much as we were before. Chris has been traveling a lot these past few months and I have been trying to focus on work. Plus, I'm trying to listen to my mother's advice about giving myself some space to see what I want and he was willing to give me that space. We haven't slept together or done any of the things we usually do while we're forced to be apart.

> **Chris:** I'm over this distance between us. I want to talk.

> **Chris:** I want my girl back.

I turn to Raegan, who's seated next to me. "I'll be right back." She looks at me for a second like she's nervous and I give her leg a gentle squeeze. "Two minutes. I just have to make a call." I rub her back gently, and I want to tell Liam to leave her alone while I'm gone. *He really can't take a fucking hint that she's not interested.*

I'm like ninety-nine percent sure Beckham is in love with her and I'm pretty sure she feels something for him too, but she hasn't admitted it. Maybe I'm hoping there's something there so I can finally have someone to talk to about Chris. The fact that we've been able to keep this a secret for so long has been insane, especially after all of the times we've hooked up in his office.

I press the button to call him and he answers like always on the first ring. "I know where you guys are, so just say the word and I'm coming there." I don't immediately agree even though I know I'm going to. "I want to tell Wes about us." I'm still silent. "I miss you and nothing has changed. I'll talk to your parents, your brother, whoever. I want to be done with this space. It's been three years of knowing that I'm in love with you and I want to be with you." He pauses and I run a hand through my hair that I curled for tonight. "Am I talking to your answering machine?" He chuckles and a smile pulls at my lips. "Marissa, baby, talk to me."

"Okay, come," I whisper into the phone, "but…don't be obvious."

It doesn't take long for Chris and Mr. Beckham to show up. Chris slides in next to me while I note that Beckham sits in the closest seat to Raegan. I'm somewhat trying to keep an eye on that when I feel Chris' hand stroke my knee gently. "You look beautiful," he says as he leans forward to pour himself a drink. He's not looking directly at me but when he leans back, his blue eyes are trained on me, and it transports me back to our friend's wedding and the way he was looking at me at the bar. *He's been looking at you the same way for three years.*

"Can I come to your room later?" I whisper and his eyes light up as he pulls his drink to his lips.

"How about every night for the rest of your life?" he says behind his glass to mask what he's saying from everyone else at the table.

I narrow my eyes at him. "That's an odd way to propose," I swirl my drink around my glass with the straw before taking a sip, "but yes."

He bites down on his bottom lip, before letting out a chuckle. "I am going to ride your cunt so hard tonight."

I'm about to respond that I'm ready to go do that now when Beth, a woman from marketing returns to the table with a bottle in her hand and Liam in tow. "Who wants a shot?" I see Liam behind her and he immediately looks at Raegan and then at Mr. Beckham.

"Didn't realize you guys were coming out tonight?" Liam asks our boss quite ballsy before turning his eyes to Chris.

"This motherfucker," Chris mutters under his breath. "I'm sorry, aren't you using the company card to pay for all of this? Why wouldn't we be here? He's paying for it," he says as he points at Mr. Beckham, and I giggle. "We can't have fun too?"

Liam gives what seems like the fakest laugh before sitting down as Beth begins pouring a round of shots. "That guy needs to watch himself."

I giggle. "Why do you say that?"

"I'll tell you later," he says and I don't miss the way his hand runs down my back when he sits up to grab the shot. "So, I know you moved out recently. I'm a little hurt that I haven't been invited over to see the new place." The guy sitting on the other side of Chris turns to look at us and I can tell he's hammered.

"Holt, we were thinking of hitting a different club, you want to go?" I hear the implication loud and clear that they are probably going to a strip club. I roll my eyes before turning to talk to Raegan but am hyper-aware of the next words that come out of his mouth.

"Nah, my girl wouldn't like it."

"Your girl?" My ears perk up because to my knowledge no one in the office thinks he's dated since his divorce was finalized. "You don't mean your wife, right?"

He snorts and I turn back towards their conversation. "Definitely not my wife. I mean she might be soon…" he starts and I'm about to interrupt before he goes down a road that ends with him outing us to the entire table, when I hear Liam from across the table announce that we are out of vodka.

"I'm going to get another bottle. Rae, you want to come with me?" I can feel Raegan tense next to me, and I shoot Liam a look that I wish he would understand so he can stop embarrassing himself.

"What, you need help?" Chris snorts and I elbow him as inconspicuously as possible. He gives me a side eye with a grin.

"No, I just wanted to chat for a bit." He holds his hand out for Raegan and she gives a polite smile before she gets up and follows him out of the area. I don't miss the look that briefly crosses Mr. Beckham's face, and at this moment I am thoroughly convinced he's in love with her so I decide to help him out in case he's thinking Liam is a threat.

"I love Liam to death, but can he give it a rest?" I pick up the shot that Chris had poured for me and down it. "She's not interested," I sing, feeling the alcohol starting to warm my insides. I look at Chris who I see giving Beckham a look before his eyes turn back to me.

"What?" I ask, wondering why it seems like there's a secret that I'm not in on.

"I'll tell you later."

"Tell me now." I frown and he laughs.

"Oh, someone is feeling their drinks. Okay, but don't react—" he starts but is interrupted when I hear Mr. Beckham's voice.

"I think I'm going to head out."

When I turn around, he's standing up.

I think about the fact that Raegan may not be happy if she comes back and he's not here. "Now?" I ask. I want to tell him to hang out for a little while, just to say goodbye to her, but he's already heading towards the edge of the section. "Yeah, I have some work to do, and I want to get up early but you guys have fun."

I turn back to Chris fully prepared to unleash my hypothesis about Beckham being in love with Raegan. "Okay, you know what I think?"

"What do you think, gorgeous?" He smiles while looking down at my lips and I can't stop the giggle that leaves me. "You ready to go to my room?"

"Yes," I tell him as I grab the glass that's in front of me, wanting to finish it before I leave. "We probably shouldn't leave together though. I'll go first? I have to use the ladies' room anyway." I'm only a few feet from the table when my phone vibrates with a text from Liam.

> **Liam: Why didn't you tell me that Rae had a boyfriend?**

She does? Since when?

I'm not sure how to respond so I ignore his text for the time being and that's when I see Raegan moving through the crowd by herself. I make my way towards her before she can get back to the table and tug her into a corner away from any prying eyes or ears.

"Boyfriend?! Did you just make that up to get him to back off? Tell me fast. Or do I need to corroborate this story? I haven't answered Liam's text yet." I bring my drink to my lips and Raegan pulls it away from my mouth to smell it.

"Marissa, maybe you should slow down. You're going to be hungover tomorrow." *And fucked.* "Are you going to sleep with Chris?"

Yes.

I turn back towards the table and then to her. Chris and I haven't talked about telling anyone other than Wes, and I don't want to make this decision while I'm drunk but I do trust Raegan so I decide to go with a watered-down version of the truth. "I don't know. Maybe." I let out a sigh. "Okay, I'm going to tell you something but don't freak out."

She narrows her eyes and leans forward. "Oh god, what?"

"I've slept with him before." *Many times. In fact, I'm in love with him.*

"What?!" Her eyes widen to the size of saucers and she puts a hand over her mouth.

"Before I worked here!" I let out a guilty laugh. "And since I've worked here."

"Wow, oh my god. Wait..." She pauses. "You've worked here three years and wasn't his divorce just recently finalized?"

"I didn't know at the time." I bite my bottom lip, preparing to lie to her for now. "I met him at a wedding. His childhood best friend was marrying my college roommate and we were both in the wedding blah blah blah. I get a little slutty at weddings; I don't want to talk about it. His wife was *not* there and I don't remember seeing a ring but I was very drunk. Nevertheless, he obviously did not tell me that."

"Okay, so...how did that lead to you working here?"

"Coincidence? Karma? I don't know. I got the job before I even realized he worked here. I slept with a married man; he didn't exactly give me his credentials. It makes me cringe to think about what I did. I really am a girl's girl." And I hate that there was a period in my life when I was really anything but.

"I know." She rubs my arm and I'm grateful that it seems like she's not judging me unlike everyone else in my life when they found out.

"Please don't think less of me."

"I don't!" she says, shaking her head.

"Okay good. That's why I never told you or *anyone* that works here. I felt so ashamed after I found out. Imagine running into the guy who was the best sex of your life on your first day of work only to find out he's your married boss." I drain the rest of my glass and set it on a nearby high-top table. "Then Beckham screamed at me. Told you my day sucked." I wince. "He told me he was leaving her and then everything got so complicated and then his wife actually found out about me and it was such a mess. So, I went to Paris. I fled, because…I fell for a married man. But I ended it. I told him we were done until he was completely single. No bullshit separation either. I stayed away for a while and now…"

"Now, he's single and obviously very into you." She nods toward him and when I turn around, I meet his gaze and a smile finds his lips instantly. "You guys are definitely getting back together. He hasn't been able to take his eyes off of you all night."

I turn back towards her and shake my head. "Okay, enough about me. Boyfriend?"

"Okay. Since we are trading secrets…"

"Oh my god!!" I squeal because I knew something was going on between her and Beckham. "I knew it. I knew it, knew it, knew it!" I say, tapping her nose each time. "He's so down bad for you. I knew I wasn't crazy." I slap her arm. "How could you not tell me?! Since when?"

"Umm, the holiday party?" she answers weakly and I knew it was odd that she just disappeared out of nowhere.

I shake my head at her as a smirk plays on my lips. "I die! Of course. Oh my god. I need to know everything."

"So, when were you going to tell me about Beckham and Raegan?" I say as soon as we slide into the backseat of our Uber.

He pulls me into his lap to straddle him even though I'm in a very short dress and grips my ass. "Do we have to talk about it now?"

"Umm, yes? That's big! Does he love her?"

He closes his eyes and then opens one. "What did she say?"

"Well, she didn't explicitly use that word but something tells me you may know more about his feelings."

"He hasn't told me either but as his best friend, yeah"—he nods—"I think he's in love with her."

"Holy shit!" I smile because now thinking about all of their interactions over the past six months, they really make the cutest couple. "Well…maybe with you both being in love with subordinates, you guys can change the fraternization policy."

"Now, you see why I wanted to talk to Wes?" he asks.

"Well…he may beat you to it." I wince.

He groans and rubs a hand over his eyes. "You told Raegan?"

"I…yes?" I wince.

"Everything?"

I nod. "I mean, there's no way to squeeze three years of our relationship into the three minutes we talked, but I gave her the cliff notes."

He sighs. "Beck is going to chew my ass out for keeping this from him for so long."

"I'm sorry." I wince again. "You were staring at me like you wanted to fuck me on top of the table all night, so Raegan asked if I was going to sleep with you and then everything just kind of spilled out."

"I'm not mad." He leans forward and presses his lips to mine. "But I think the four of us are going to have a little talk tomorrow morning."

Chapter
TWENTY-SIX

CHRIS

"So, you really don't know why I called you?"

"No, and I left Raegan in bed, so this better be some sort of an emergency," Wes says as he looks at his phone before setting it down on the table.

"Well, I also reluctantly left a woman in bed and I would like to get back to her, so we can make this quick."

"I assume you slept with Marissa?" he asks.

I nod. "Not for the first time."

"You've slept with her before?" His eyes are wide. "And you didn't tell me? Also, is that why you haven't been going out as much as usual?" He takes a sip of his water before pulling a strip of bacon off of his plate. "Before you and Holly divorced? After?" he asks rattling off a series of questions.

"Before and I didn't tell you because it just got out of control so fast and there's a lot of layers to this story."

"Was this before she went to Paris?"

I nod again. "Marissa is the woman I slept with at Owen's wedding."

Wes drops the piece of bacon he's holding and his eyes widen in shock. "No fucking way." He scratches his jaw before he narrows his eyes at me. "Wait…is that why we hired her?"

I shoot him an incredulous look. "No, dick! That was a very strange coincidence that she did *not* appreciate."

"Holy fuck. So, you've…"

"Been in love with her ever since? Pretty much." I lean back in my chair and let out an exhausted sigh of relief to finally be telling Beck about this. "It's been an interesting three years."

"Did Holly ever figure it out?"

"Yeah, and that was a mess. I eventually learned that Holly had me followed which is how she initially found out about Marissa. Then, she managed to tap my apartment by slipping something into one of my bags that I took from the house when I moved out. So, Holly learned I was still talking to her and she flew to Paris and confronted her."

"Wait what? This sounds like a soap opera. What the fuck, man? So were you guys still together while she was in Paris and you were in—"

"No, she ended it and all contact and I went fucking crazy not talking to her at all, but Holly confronting her freaked her out and she told me I had to be completely divorced before we continued and I understood that even though it drove me insane. Then, when she came back, we were going to try again because I was divorced and I went to Marissa's sister's engagement party with her, and guess who showed up."

"Fuck. Are you kidding?" He lets out a laugh and shakes his head. "I'm not laughing because it's funny, I'm laughing because this is insane."

"You think? What are the chances? So, naturally, Holly exploded all over Marissa's mother. So…she doesn't exactly love me."

"Wow." He whistles. "She aired all of your business?"

"That I cheated. Cheated with Marissa. With other women. I did not come out of that party looking good." I scrub my face thinking about how I'm going to make things right with her parents.

"Oh shit. I'm sorry."

"But I don't care. I stayed away these past six months because her parents didn't believe that I'm good for her given my past, but I'm willing to do whatever it takes to win them over. They can't hate me forever. I've done shitty things for sure, but I've never done anything shitty to Marissa."

"Except bail on her the morning after Owen's wedding," he says matter of factly before taking a sip of his coffee and I give him my middle finger.

"Fuck you very much."

"Man, what are the odds? I can't believe Marissa is the girl from the wedding."

"I can't believe Raegan didn't tell you last night." I was shocked when I asked if he wanted to get breakfast so we could talk about what happened last night and he didn't know exactly what I meant. "I guess she can keep a secret." I laugh, which earns me a glare from him.

"Is she why you left Holly?"

"A big part, yes."

"So, this is…real."

"Very fucking real." I lean across the table. "Is it real with you and Raegan?"

"Yeah." He smiles. "But I told you about her months ago. This isn't new! I certainly haven't been keeping it from you for years. You guys don't have a kid somewhere, do you?" He shakes his head and the thought of having a baby with Marissa sends that familiar spark to my dick.

"I love her."

"I'm happy for you. You pining after this girl as long as you have…yeah, I bet it's real."

"Now I just have to talk to her parents." I let out a breath. "They are not a fan of me."

"You'll win them over."

A week later, I'm sitting outside of Marissa's parents' house wondering if it was the worst idea to not tell Marissa my plan. I knew she'd want to be here and I don't want her parents to think I need her to protect me. It's the middle of the workday, so Marissa is at work and she just assumes I'm out in the field. Only Wes—and maybe Raegan—knows that I'm here. I also didn't want Marissa to know I have a ring and I plan on telling her parents that. I turn off the car and get out, and just like before, Marissa's mother is standing next to my car with her hands on her hips and sunglasses over her eyes.

"Nothing ever gets by you, ma'am," I say, trying to break the tension.

She lowers her sunglasses to her nose. "Come on in," she says and I follow behind her into the house.

"Hon!" she calls.

"Yes, baby!" I hear.

"You may want to come down here! That one boy that can't seem to stay away from our daughter is here."

"Which one?" I hear.

"You mean which daughter?" She gasps. "It's not Eric!"

He appears in the living room and when his eyes meet mine, they narrow behind his round wire frames. "I was hoping it wasn't you." He crosses his arms over his chest and stares me down. "What can we help you with?

"I know I am not your favorite person and certainly not your favorite person for your daughter." I swallow nervously as they both continue to stare at me. "But...I should be. I love you daughter more than anything in the world. I've made a ton of mistakes;

I won't deny that, but I've always tried to do right by her, even when the circumstances may not have looked that way. I know I should have stayed away from her while I was married. I know that. I assume you know Alexis, her roommate from college. We met at her wedding."

Marissa's mom nods in realization and I watch as her hands fall from across her chest and she sits down on the couch. She looks at her husband and pats the space next to her. Though he's still glaring at me, I can see his hardness softening a little when he takes the seat next to her.

"Owen has been my friend since we were kids, and all I kept thinking about that entire wedding was why am I married when all I want to do is talk to the most beautiful woman I've ever laid eyes on." I slide my hand into my pocket and play with the ring box, my heart pounding at the thought of bringing it out and having her parents tell me something along the lines of *over our dead bodies*.

"I shouldn't have approached her or tried to court her but..." I pause before continuing, "I knew I was getting divorced at some point. Not an excuse," I add. "But I knew from the moment I laid eyes on her, that not only should I not be married, but I should be married to *her*. I didn't know what love at first sight felt like until I saw your daughter for the first time, and..." I trail off. "That's all I have. I'm just asking you for a chance. Now, I think at this point Marissa is ready to be with me without your blessing, but...she's going to want you around while she plans a wedding."

Marissa's mom gasps and looks at Marissa's father and then back to me. "Marriage?"

"I went into my last one with the wrong person...I know now what I want and what I need and I've never been as sure about anything as I am about Marissa and I think she feels the same way about me. I'm not planning to ask her tomorrow. We need some time as a couple with no drama, but..." I pull the box out of my pocket and set it on the coffee table in front of them. "I do have a ring."

Her mother looks down at the red velvet box and then back up at me. "Has she seen it?"

"No." I shake my head.

"Does she know it exists?"

I shake my head again. "No, I keep it in a safe at work because she's nosy."

"What about where you two work?" Her father chimes in, speaking for the first time.

"We are in the process of changing our policy. The CEO fell in love with his assistant." I chuckle. "So, Marissa won't report directly to me anymore but she can still work for the company and get promoted and thrive. I just don't have a say in her salary anymore, which is good, because I would just…give her everything."

Her mother reaches forward and picks up the ring box. She gasps when she opens it. "Oh, of course you have good taste." She shakes her head. "You really had the potential to be perfect, you know?"

I chuckle nervously because I'm not sure if they're giving me their blessing or telling me that none of this is good enough and I'm still the man who made their daughter my mistress for far too long. "I am sorry for everything. For what happened at Autumn's shower and just putting Marissa in a position like that. I was being selfish and not thinking about how everything would affect her."

Her father crosses his arms across his chest. "I had Eric pull your file so I could read some of the notes and the transcripts. I am not denying that you had a tough few years and that you got taken for *a lot* for not having a prenuptial agreement. It does seem that your ex-wife had some ulterior motives. This does *not* give you a pass, but you gave her whatever she wanted and you owned up to your mistakes. Not just with her, but in court and with your job and Marissa and now with us and I suppose I admire that, a *little*." He sighs. "And if you're really serious about marrying her… well, I guess I have to get on board with that. I'm not missing out on walking my favorite child down the aisle."

Marissa's mother gasps and smacks his arm. "Do not tell her he said that. You know Shane and Autumn already think we favor her."

"They'll be alright," he says as he stands up and puts his hand out for me to shake, and when I reach for it, he squeezes it hard. "I will have my eye on you though. All my eyes and believe me, I have eyes everywhere. If you step a toe out of line in regards to my daughter, I will have you thrown in jail," he says.

"Oh, he will not. Don't worry about that." Marissa's mom smiles as she comes to stand beside him. "He'll just kill you."

Epilogue

CHRIS

Three Months Later

"Baby, the food's here!" I hear called from the dining room. I'm at Marissa's townhouse for the third night this week. We actually spend more of our time here than my apartment and I'm hoping that she'll finally just let me buy it for us so we can live here together. I walk into the dining room to find Marissa and her sister taking the Chinese food we ordered for tonight's 'sibling dinner' out of the bags and setting the table. Shane comes in with Megan and their two kids trailing behind them.

"Did you guys figure out what game I'm spanking you all at tonight?" Shane asks and Marissa rolls her eyes.

"Because you cheat at everything!" Autumn says as she opens up the containers. "I refuse to play any more games with you."

"Sore loser." He says

"Cheater!" She shrieks.

"Okay, can we not do this here?" Marissa chimes in. "Argue at your houses. I would like peace and solitude here please."

"So, that rules out Uno," Shane jokes as he takes a sip of his wine.

"And spades," Eric says.

"And after the catastrophe caused by the last time we played Pictionary, I don't even want to do that. This is why we can't have nice things," Marissa jokes.

It didn't take long for everyone to get on board with me and Marissa after I got her parents' conditional approval. Marissa told me that her mom told her how impressed she was by me coming to talk to them, and that I'm still her most handsome future son in-law. *I'm holding onto that for if I ever need it.*

I know I am nowhere near out of the woods with them but, I am getting somewhere and I know as soon as we reveal our news, I'll be in the clear.

I follow Marissa into the kitchen and see her on a step stool reaching for glasses and I'm behind her in an instant, pulling her down gently into my arms. "None of this."

"This is going to be a long nine months if you're going to be following me around like this. I can climb on a step stool."

"No need when I'm around," I tell her as I wrap my arms around her. We haven't told anyone yet that Marissa is pregnant and I plan to have my ring on her finger when we do. For now, it's our little secret.

"You're always around and up under me!" She laughs. The one perk of us working together is that she can typically come with me whenever I have to travel and vice versa. I hate being away from her for longer than a few days, and I'm unashamed to admit that I've been known to show up in her hotel room when it's been longer than that. I cup her cheeks and press my lips to hers.

"And will continue to be for the rest of my life. I told you before, you need to get used to me being around."

She giggles. "I like the idea of that."

Marissa

One Year Later

"I'll have what the bride is having." I turn to see my husband as of two hours ago staring at me, giving me his usual devastatingly handsome smile as he leans against the bar, reminiscent of the way he did at the first wedding we were ever at together. He takes a few steps closer to me and grabs one of the shots the bartender poured and hands me the other. "You know what's going to happen tonight if we start taking shots?"

"I have a pretty good idea."

"You're probably going to get pregnant again." He raises an eyebrow and my eyes widen because we have not talked about trying for a second baby already.

"We have a three month old. How about we not put that in the universe just yet?" I blink at him as I think about our baby boy who is upstairs sleeping in a hotel room with Autumn who is pregnant with her first baby and very over any kind of party scene right now. *Even if it is her baby sister's wedding.*

"I'm just saying, pretty sure we got pregnant at your cousin's wedding." He taps his shot against mine and downs his drink. "I like that liquor makes my wife a little nasty."

"Oh, and it does nothing to you?" I say as I put a hand on my hip.

"No. That's all *you*. *You* make me a little nasty." He grabs my hand and presses his lips to my fingers. "You look so beautiful baby; I can't wait to get you out of this dress." He licks his lips as he runs his gaze down my body. I lean into him and pull his face down to kiss me. "Come dance with me."

Everyone cheers as we make our way onto the dance floor. People begin to tap their glasses with their silverware indicating that they want us to kiss, and just as the first few notes of a familiar song come on, he presses his lips to mine.

"This is the first song we danced to together," I tell him as he twirls me around the dance floor.

"I remember. I'm pretty sure I fell in love with you dancing to this song," he says just before he dips me, and I don't think I'll ever get over the things this man says or the way he makes me feel. "So, are we going to the after-party?"

"We have to make an appearance, babe."

"Really? Because I was thinking we could have our own private after-party again."

The End.

Curious about Wes and his assistant Raegan?
Check out *The Season of Secrets*!

Acknowledgements

Thank you so much for reading! As always, it takes a village to deal with my chaos, so just a few thank yous!

Tanya, Rachel and Alexandra, you guys really went through it with me with this book! I love you so big for all the support and listening to my chaotic voice memos.

Kristen Portillo, thank you for helping make this book perfect! One day I'll get my tenses and my timelines right the first time around. Until then, I'm grateful I have you to catch them. I appreciate you immensely!

Stacey Blake, thank you for always making the interiors so gorgeous and exactly what I want! Thank you for making my books so pretty!

Shaye and Lindsey, Thank you for all the things and keeping me so organized. What would I do without you? You guys are rockstars and I love you!

Ari Basulto, I would be lost without you. Thank you for all that you do to keep me organized! Thank you for running all of my teams and overall Q.B.'s life better than I could. A million thank yous.

Emily Wittig, obsessed with the cover as always! Thank you!!

Pang Thao, thank you for all of my gorgeous teasers and all of my last minute promo things and all the things I ask you to make me all the time. You're so good to me and I appreciate everything you do!

Giana, I am so thankful for you and your friendship. I love you and our chats so much! Thank you for always cheering me on.

To all of my author friends, thank you for your endless support, love, (and early copies of your books!) I love being on this ride with you all.

To the Lyric Audiobooks team, thank you so much for all of your help with bringing this to life and embracing my chaos! I appreciate you all!

To the babes on my street team and ARC team, thank you for your excitement! Thank you for your love for me and my books and that you're always willing to let me take you over a cliff. The reason I can do what I do is because of you guys in my corner. Thank you for always clapping the loudest. I love you guys so big.

To all of the bloggers and bookstagrammers and TikTokers, thank you for your edits and your reels and your videos and always sharing my books! For still talking about books I wrote two and three years ago and loving them so much. For sharing with your friends (and sometimes your family? Ha) Thank you for everything you do. (Because seriously? Videos are so hard.) Thank you for your reviews and chatting with me online. You make my days so much brighter.

And finally, and most importantly to YOU, to the readers, thank you for letting me into your minds and your hearts again with another book. I hope you enjoyed it! I love you all. We'll do this again soon. Maybe something taboo?

Also by Q.B. TYLER

STANDALONES
My Best Friend's Sister
Unconditional
Forget Me Not
Love Unexpected
Always Been You
What Was Meant to Be
Keep Her Safe

THE SECRETS UNIVERSE
The Worst Kept Secret
The Season of Secrets

BITTERSWEET UNIVERSE
Bittersweet Surrender
Bittersweet Addiction
Bittersweet Love

CAMPUS TALES SERIES
First Semester
Second Semester
Spring Semester

About
THE AUTHOR

Bestselling author and lover of forbidden romances, tacos, coffee, and wine. Q.B. Tyler gives readers sometimes angsty, sometimes emotional but always deliciously steamy romances featuring sassy heroines and the heroes that worship them. She's known for writing forbidden (and sometimes taboo) romances, so if that's your thing, you've come to the right place. When she's not writing, you can usually find her on Instagram (definitely procrastinating), shopping or at brunch.

Sign up for her newsletter to stay in touch! (https://view.flodesk.com/pages/6195b59a839edddd7aa02f8f)

Qbtyler03@gmail.com

Facebook: Q.B. Tyler
Reader Group: Q.B.'s Hive
Instagram @qbtyler.author
Bookbub: Q.B. Tyler
Twitter: @qbtyler
Goodreads: Q.B. Tyler
Tik Tok: author.qbtyler

www.Authorqbtyler.com

Printed in Great Britain
by Amazon